THE TRUEST TEST

By winter Sherrill would be off to New York, to stay with her wealthy aunt and uncle and, according to her snobbish Aunt Eloise, "be clever and make a good marriage."

Alan, too, had been called away—far away, to Egypt, to join the archaeological expedition his esteemed professor had gotten underway.

But there were more to both these tempting offers than first appeared. And, as Sherrill and Alan would soon discover, only the strength of their faith and unfailing love could bring them through the bewildering trials that lay ahead.

Bantam Books by Grace Livingston Hill
Ask your bookseller for the books you have missed

The Chance of a Lifetime
Grace Livingston Hill

BANTAM BOOKS
TORONTO · NEW YORK · LONDON

*This low-priced Bantam Book
has been completely reset in a type face
designed for easy reading, and was printed
from new plates. It contains the complete
text of the original hard-cover edition.*
NOT ONE WORD HAS BEEN OMITTED.

THE CHANCE OF A LIFETIME

*A Bantam Book | published by arrangement with
J.B. Lippincott Company*

PRINTING HISTORY
Lippincott edition originally published May 1931
Bantam edition | June 1980

ISBN 0-553-13459-0

Published simultaneously in the United States and Canada

PRINTED IN THE UNITED STATES OF AMERICA

0 9 8 7 6 5 4 3 2 1

CHAPTER I

The morning Alan MacFarlan's father broke his leg Alan got a special delivery letter from his former High School Professor, inviting him to accompany him as a sort of assistant at a small salary, on an archaelogical expedition to Egypt, which was to sail from New York in three days.

"I would have given you more notice if it had been possible," wrote Professor Hodge, "but the vacancy only just occurred through the resignation of a young man who was taken seriously ill. I have recommended you and I hope you will be able to accept. It will be the chance of your lifetime. The salary is not large nor the position notable, but the experience will be great. I am sure you will enjoy it. You are young of course, but I have great belief in your character and ability, and have told our leader that I am sure you will make good. It will be necessary for you to wire at once if you wish to hold the job, as there are three other eager applicants; but you have the precedence."

There followed a list of necessities that Alan must bring with him, and directions as to the place of meeting with the rest of the expedition.

Alan was sitting at his father's desk in the Rockland Hardware store reading this letter. He had just come from the house at his father's request to open the mail and answer one or two important letters that were expected in the mail. This letter of his own had been brought to the store by mistake instead of being delivered at the house, and therefore it happened that the great temptation of his young life was presented to him all alone, away from the watchful, loving eyes of his mother or his father.

Alan's first reaction was wonder and awe that he, Alan MacFarlan, just a graduate of the Rockland High School, had been chosen for such a marvelous honor, a place in the great expedition to Egypt! There was nothing in the whole world of honors that Alan could think of that he would more desire to do. He had always been interested in archæology, and his soul throbbed with eagerness. To go in company with Professor Hodge who had given him his first interest in ancient things, seemed the height of bliss. His eyes shone as

1

he read, and his breath came in quick gasps of wonder. He looked up at the last word of the letter with a dazed expression, and stared about him, as if to make sure that he was awake and in the land of the living, not dreaming or anything.

A chance like that to come to him! A smile broke over his face as he sat with the letter still in his hand and gazed through the iron grating that surrounded the cash desk. Across the store were shelves filled with neat boxes, green and brown and red, all labeled; gimlets and screw drivers and chisels in orderly rows, but he saw instead a wide desert under a hot orient sky, and toilers in the sand bringing forth treasures of the ancients. He saw himself with grimy, happy face, a part of the great expedition, exploring tombs and pyramids and cities of another age.

Suddenly the immediate environment snapped on his consciousness; bright gleaming tools of steel and iron—saws and hammers and nails and plows; and the desert faded. They fairly clamored at him for attention like so many helpless humans.

"What are you going to do about us?" they asked. "Your father is helpless, and we are your responsibility."

Alan's smile suddenly faded even as the desert had done.

"But this is a chance of my lifetime!" he cried out indignantly to himself. "Surely Father would want me to accept. Surely he would let nothing stand in my way."

"Yes, but are you willing to put it up to him?" winked an honest oatmeal boiler aghast. "You know what your father told you this very morning! You know how touched you were when he told you that he could bear the pain and the being laid aside, since he knew you were free to take over the store and that he could trust you to run it as well as he would have done himself."

"But there is Uncle Ned," cried out Alan's eager youth. "He has nothing in life to do now since he has retired, and surely he could look after things for a little while till Dad is on deck again!"

Then conscience spoke.

"You know what your father said this very morning about Uncle Ned. You know he told you that Uncle Ned let everything run down, and got the books all mixed up those six weeks he had charge while your father went to California last year. And you know your father said there was a crisis just now in his affairs, and that if he couldn't tide things over for the next six weeks he would lose all he had gained in his lifetime."

Alan's hand made a quick nervous movement in laying down the letter, and a heavy paper weight in the form of a small steam engine, a souvenir of the last dinner of the United Hardware Dealers the elder MacFarlan had attended fell with a clatter to the floor.

Alan stooped and picked it up, and it seemed as he did so that all the blood in his body rushed in one anguished flood to his face, and throbbed in his neck and head. Was this appalling thing true, that he was going to even *consider* whether or not it was right to accept this wonderful offer? Surely, *surely*, his father would not permit him to make such a sacrifice!

Then conscience held up before him the picture of his father as he had seen him just a few minutes before, his face white with pain, his lips set in a strong endurance, his voice weak from shock: and again he heard the trembling sentences from those strong lips that had never acknowledged failure before:

"There's a note to be met, son, the first of next week. The man is needing money badly and will foreclose if it isn't paid. I thought I had it all fixed up, but I got his letter last night, and I reckon that's what I was thinking about when I crossed the street in front of that car. You see the worst of it is he has a purchaser ready to take over the store and give him cash at once on foreclosure. I suspect it's that evil-eyed Rawley that's been hanging around asking questions the last three weeks, and there's nothing for it but to raise the money some how!—There are those city lots we've been saving for Mother.—They'll have to go, unless you can get Judge Whitely to fix up another mortgage somehow to tide us over—!"

The voice had failed with a new wave of pain, and Alan's mother had signaled him in alarm.

"That's all right, Dad," Alan's strong young voice had rung out with assurance, "I'll fix that up O.K. You don't need to worry a minute! And of course I can run the store. You needn't think anything is going wrong just because you are taking a few days' rest!"

That was how he had cheered his father one short hour before, and walked down the street with his shoulders back, and a proud feeling of responsibility upon him to take over the business and make it succeed, pull it out of a hole as it were. How his heart had responded to his father's appeal!

And here he was considering dropping the whole thing, shedding the whole responsibility like a garment that could be discarded at will and running off to play at digging up gold vases in some dead king's tomb! Calling it the chance of a lifetime, and crying out for an opportunity to fulfill his dreams and ambitions, while his father lay in pain and discouragement, and saw his own life struggles and ambitions end in utter failure, too late to mend!

Well, he couldn't do that of course! He couldn't lead his own life at the expense of all Dad had done, not now just as things were nearing a fulfillment of his dreams. And in a sense Dad was doing it all for his sake and Mother's. Who was he to presume to live his own life at the expense of his parents? And why should his life be any more important in the universe, and in the eyes of God, than his father's life and fortunes were?

He was sitting up now with the paper weight in one hand and the letter in the other staring about at the four walls of the hardware store that had always seemed so important and so friendly to him. These questions were being shouted at him by a bright chisel that caught the light of the sun through the window, by a keg of gleaming wire nails that stood behind the counter within sight at his right hand, by a bundle of ax helves that bunched together over in the corner next a great burlap bag of grass seed. All these inanimate creatures suddenly seemed to come alive and accuse him. Even a box of gay little seed packets left over from the spring seemed to reproach him. And then he seemed suddenly to have to defend himself to them all; he the son of the house who was now in command and expected to bring order out of the confusion and trouble. What made any of them *think* he was going to desert, his glance seemed to say, as his upper lip stiffened and his chin was lifted just the slightest perceptible bit?

Alan laid down the paper weight and grasping his father's pencil began to write on the back of Professor Hodge's envelope.

"Deeply grateful for your thought of me. Would like above all things to go, but impossible. Dad run over by automobile this morning. Fractured leg and other injuries. May be some time in recovering. Meantime business responsibility on me. Great r̶e̶g̶r̶e̶t̶s̶ and many thanks. Suggest Bob Lincoln. Here's wishing.
ALAN."

He counted the words carefully, and then reached out his hand for the telephone, but instead of calling Western Union as he had intended he hesitated, with his fingers on the receiver, looked about thoughtfully, firmly, as though the matter were settled of course, but stuffed the scribbled envelope down in his pocket and called his home.

"How's Dad, Mother? The doctor been there? What does he say? What? Ohhh-h! He does? Did you say he thinks it's a difficult fracture? What? He said he might be a long time in bed? What's that word? Complications? *Oh!* Worry? Why no, of course not! There's nothing whatever to worry about. Tell Dad I'm at the helm and the ship is sailing fine. I'll get all this mess straightened out in great shape, don't you be afraid. Just tell him so! Tell him—Tell him I'm having—the time of my life! Why—tell him—I'm having—" he caught his breath as if a pain had shot through him and ended in a bright voice— "Tell him I'm having the chance of a lifetime. See? And don't you worry, little Mother! Dad'll pull through beautifully. This is just his chance to rest. He's worked hard for years. It's my turn to take the helm!"

He hung up the receiver sharply and shut his lips in a fine firm line, his eyes taking on a look he wore when he had to break the enemy's luck on the football field, or win in a race, or climb a ladder to rescue someone in a village fire.

Then with a defiant glance around at the inanimate objects that had accused him he seized the telephone again and called for Western Union, firmly giving his message word for word in a clear crisp voice, feeling in his heart that he had cut his own throat, but was glad he had. Then he set to work in a mature, business-like way to open the morning mail. This sickly feeling at his stomach was not to be noticed any more than if he had got knocked out playing baseball. He had this job to do and he was going to do it. And surely he was no worse off than before he got that letter from Professor Hodge. He ought to be glad the professor thought him worthy to go on such an expedition. It maybe wasn't the only chance in the world even if good old Hodge had called it "the chance of a lifetime." Well, if it was, this store was the chance of a lifetime too. He might never have another opportunity to help Dad, and begin to repay all he had done for him. Good old Dad!

Something misty got into Alan's eyes as he opened the next envelope, and he cleared his throat and brushed his hand across his forehead. Then suddenly he forgot Egypt and

Hodge, and the expedition and the honor, and his loss and everything. For here in this letter was a challenge greater than any buried cities could give. It was even worse than Dad had hinted. The man who held the mortgage had come out in the open with sneers and threats, couched in language that was so sure of winning that it added insult to injury. What! Let that man insult his father? Not if he knew himself! If he couldn't do anything else he would thrash him. But he knew good and well he was going to do something else. He'd get that money somewhere and put Dad on the top, if he had to sell his own skin to do it. Alan's lips shut thin and hard, and his eyes took on their steely look. The desert faded, and honors held less significance. Here was another matter that called for all his nerve and powers. Other fellows could go to Egypt and do whatever was necessary to be done to unearth the secrets of the ages. But he, Alan, was the only one who could put his dad right with the world again.

All day he worked frantically, not taking time to go home for lunch, holding long telephone conversations and writing letters. Interviewing his father's lawyer, and getting in touch with the president of the bank, making an appointment with a real estate agent in the city for the next day, writing letters to two or three powerful friends of his father's whom he could not reach over the wires, sending telegrams.

It was wonderful the thrill that came to him as he realized his own responsibility, and the necessity of good judgment. If he only had someone to consult! Someone closer than just bank presidents. Of course there was Keith Washburn—and Sherrill! Sherrill had amazing good sense for a girl. But of course he could not tell either of them, good friends though they were, about his father's business. He must weather it alone. If he only could ask Dad a question or two. But his mother's various messages reporting the state of the beloved invalid, made it very plain that Dad ought not to be bothered with a thing for many a day yet.

Alan went home late to dinner that night, and tried to wear a cheerful face to cover his weariness. Now that his actual work was done, until morning, he had time to think of his own disappointment, and it cut deep into his heart and brought out the tired lines on his face more than he dreamed. Maybe he might have gone after all if he only had not been so hasty. Perhaps his plans would carry smoothly, and by to-morrow everything be straightened out, and the business safe. Surely then there could have been found somebody who would have taken over the store for a while till Dad got well. But no! He must not even think of that! Mother must never suspect, Dad must never know what he had given up. Dad would have felt even worse than he did about it. Dad was ambitious for him. Dad would have wanted him to be connected with this great matter!

His father was under opiates and in the hands of a capable nurse from the city. Alan could only tiptoe silently up to the door of the sickroom and peer anxiously into the cool dim shadows. That sleeping form with the closed eyes, the strange unnatural breathing, how it stabbed his heart! Of course he could not have gone away off to a desert and left his father like that!

Perhaps it was his need of being reassured after he had visited his father that led his footsteps out across the lawn and down the next street to the Washburn house. His mother did not need him. He had tucked her into her bed for a nice nap, kissed her, patted her, and told her not to worry. He had a strange lost feeling, like the first time he went to Kindergarten all alone. So he wandered to his friend's house.

Sherrill was at the piano playing, the lamplight falling from the tall shaded lamp on her head and shoulders, bringing out the glint of gold in her hair, the delicate curve of cheek and chin, the exquisite molding of her slim shoulders. He stood a moment and watched her wistfully. How sweet she was, and wise! What would she have advised him to do? Would she have said he must stay? But of course she would! He could not think of himself even asking her. He would not want her to think there had been any other thought in his mind for an instant than to stick by his father. And yet—She was young! She was sane! Perhaps he had been oversentimental! He longed to hear her say it. Yet he never could ask her. The only person he could feel like asking was God, and he felt that he already knew what God would have him do.

She had stopped playing now, and was wheeling a big chair up to the light. He drifted up to the open window and called her.

"Sherry, come out in the hammock and talk to me."

She came at once, in her pretty white dress, standing in the doorway poised for a second, while she called to her mother:

"Only out in the hammock, dearest. I shan't be long. Alan is here!"

They sat down in the big capacious swinging seat under the sweet smelling pines and talked.

Sherrill had had letters from two of the girls. Priscilla Maybrick was in the Catskills having a wonderful time, and Willa Barrington had gone with an aunt to Atlantic City. They talked for a while about the comparative merits of seashore and mountains, and then a silence fell between them, a pleasant silence such as brings no embarrassment between good friends.

"Had a letter from old Hodge to-day," said Alan nonchalantly, as if it were a matter of small moment. Somehow he had to let it out to someone, and Sherrill Washburn was safe and sane.

"You did!" said Sherrill interestedly. "What did he have to say? Is he still in that suburb of New York? Keith heard he had resigned."

"Why, no," said Alan, "he isn't. He did resign. Hadn't you heard? He's a high-mucky-muck in an expedition to Egypt. Archaeological, you know. Digging up some of Tut's relatives and things like that."

"You don't mean it! Really! Isn't that just wonderful? Did he say when they start?"

"Friday," said Alan grimly, and then in a tone as if he were reporting an invitation to a pink tea, he said, quite offhand:

"He asked me to go along."

"Oh, Alan!" said Sherrill clapping her hands in ecstasy; and looking at him with admiration.

"Yes," said the boy, "gave me all the dope and everything to meet him in New York, day after tomorrow."

"Day after to-morrow!" the girl gave him a quick look, and sympathy broke into her voice.

"Oh Alan! Then you can't go! Of course. But isn't that hard! Of course you wouldn't want to leave your father just now. Does he know about it?"

"No, and I don't intend he shall!" said Alan, and there was a ring of purpose in his voice. "Please don't say anything to Mother either, Sherry. It would just worry her and she's got enough to be anxious over now."

"But wouldn't they both perhaps feel you ought to have told them? It's such an important thing. Perhaps they could make other arrangements and let you go."

"There isn't a chance!" said Alan briskly, thinking of the hard work he had been doing all day. "Nobody else knows about Dad's business the way I do, and I wouldn't trust anybody to take things over. Besides, Dad may be worse hurt than we think. The doctor can't tell everything just yet. Of course, I know it's a chance of a lifetime, as old Hodge said, but it can't be helped. The way just isn't open that's all. I only mentioned it because I thought you'd like to know that Hodge had asked me. I guess it's an honor. He must know a lot of other fellows better fitted than I am."

"Of course it's an honor," said Sherill eagerly, "a great honor! But I'm not a bit surprised. I don't believe Professor Hodge knows another boy of your age that is as dependable as you. But as for being the chance of a lifetime, you can't tell. Maybe staying at home is the chance of yours. Things we want are not always the ones that are best for us. This may not be the chance of your lifetime at all."

"Evidently not!" said Alan with a little laugh that hid a twinge of bitterness. "Well it was mighty nice of him to ask me any way and I've that to remember, like saving up candy you can't eat along with your diploma and other trifling honors."

"Have you answered him yet?" asked Sherill thoughtfully.

"Sure! Wired him within an hour after the letter came."

They were silent a moment, swinging back and forth under the old pine trees, Sherrill's white dress making a patch of white in the shadows.

Footsteps were coming down the sidewalk, ringing footsteps that walked with a purpose. They paused at the rose vine arch over the gateway and hesitated, then turned in and walked more slowly up the stone flagging toward the house. About half way up they paused, and the two in the swinging seat under the trees could see that whoever it was was looking toward them. They could not quite make out his identity. It did not seem to be any of the boys who frequented their company.

"Oh, I say, Mac, is that you?" called the visitor.

Alan rose from his seat and answered, taking a step forward.

"Yes? Did you want me?"

CHAPTER II

The newcomer came swiftly forward then and held out his hand. Sherrill saw that it was Robert Lincoln, Alan's former rival on the football field.

"Hope you'll pardon me for intruding," he said, and there was something surprisingly humble in the boy's tone, "I won't keep you long. I just got a wire from Professor Hodge and I had to come and thank you. I say, Mac, you've been mighty white to recommend me after all that's past and I sure do appreciate it. I shan't forget it."

"Oh, Bob, is that you?" said Alan, much embarrassed. "You say he wired? Did you get the job? Congratulations."

"Sit down, Bob," said Sherrill rising. "I'm just going in the house for a sweater. It's a little chilly."

"Don't go," said young Lincoln, "it's nothing private. You don't mind if I tell Sherrill, do you?"

"There's nothing to tell," said Alan diffidently.

"I think there is," said Bob turning to Sherrill. "Alan's put me in for the chance of my life. I'm going with Professor Hodge to Egypt. Starting day after to-morrow. Can you beat it? And I owe it all to old Mac here. I never even heard of the job till I got the wire, and I needed something the worst way."

"Mac," he said turning back to Alan, "I owe you something more than just thanks. I owe you a lot of apologies. I guess there's plenty of humble pie coming to me. I'll own I've said mean things about you several times, and the time you thrashed me I guess I deserved it even more than you knew. But I never knew you were white like this. I thought you were a hypocrite. Now I ask your pardon. This is the whitest thing I ever knew a man to do to his enemy."

"Oh, I say, Bob, cut that out," growled Alan, "there was nothing great in what I did. Knew you were keen on such things. Happened to hear you were wanting to go away. Since I couldn't go myself I didn't see any reason why you shouldn't profit by it. I hope I'm not a dog in the manger."

"I'll say you're not!" said Bob fervently, "and I'll have to own that if the chances had been reversed I'm afraid I would

10

have been. I'd have said if I couldn't go myself you shouldn't any way."

"Aw, cut it!" said Alan. "You aren't like that, Bob, and anyhow that doesn't cut any ice. I'll own I was sore that I couldn't go myself, but I'm tickled to death you can, since I can't."

"But why can't you go, Mac? Aren't you keen about it?"

"Keen? Boy! It's like the pot of gold and the rainbow all in one to me. I'd rather go than get rich if you know what I mean. But it can't be done. My dad got run over this morning, and I've got to stay by the store and take his place. It'll be weeks, and maybe months before he's around again. Lucky if it isn't years!"

"Say! That's tough luck. I hadn't heard. Been groveling in the factory all day. But say, Mac, why couldn't I take your place? I'm a year older than you, and I could take orders. I'd have my heart in doing something like that. You go, Mac, and I'll stay!"

Alan wheeled about and faced the other boy for the first time that evening.

"Would you do that for me, Bob?" he asked, his voice all husky with feeling.

"I sure would, Mac," said Bob. "You're the first person since my sister died that's cared a straw what became of me. Look what you've done for me! Sure I'll do it gladly!"

Alan put out his hand and gripped the other's hand in a warm grasp.

"Guess I've got an apology coming, too, old man," he said still huskily. "You're great. I won't forget this. I can't accept of course, because Dad needs me, but you've taken half the sting of saying no away from me. I didn't think when I suggested your name that you would even know I was connected with it. But I'm glad now it happened. I'd—like to—feel—we are friends!"

"Suits me down to the ground," said Bob eagerly, "I haven't got many of that species. I should say you might head the list if you don't mind. And now, I wonder if you'll put me onto the ropes. I size it up that I haven't got much time. Professor Hodge said you had all directions. Do you mind letting me copy them? I know you'll want to keep the letter. It's some honor to have been asked."

"That's all right," said Alan heartily, "we're partners in this in a way, and when you get out there old man, write me a card now and then to let me know what I'm missing, see?"

"Sure thing!" said Bob. "You'll be mother, home and heaven to me, Mac. You know only too well I'm not very popular around here. Can I just step over to the door to the light and copy this?" he asked Sherrill.

"Oh, come in to the library by the desk," said Sherrill, "both of you come in. I've got a pitcher of lemonade in the refrigerator and a great big chocolate cake that needs eating."

"Oh, boy! Lead me to it!" said Bob excitedly. "I'm boarding down at the Copper Kettle and had half a chicken wing and one lettuce leaf for my supper."

Laughingly they went into the house, and Sherrill settled the boys at the library desk while she went to forage for refreshments, but Alan soon followed her to help her.

"He insists on copying it lest the paper get lost," he said, "so I'll help you rustle the grub."

Sherrill wheeled about on him with shining eyes, then went and carefully closed the dining room and pantry doors before she spoke:

"Alan MacFarlan, you blessed old hypocrite! Did you go and ask Robert Lincoln to go to Egypt in your place?"

"Oh, I just suggested his name," said Alan looking sheepish. "I thought he might as well have the chance."

"But I thought you were sworn enemies!" said Sherrill. "It isn't long since you gave him an awful thrashing!"

"Well, he needed it," said Alan thoughtfully, "but you know he almost licked me too. He's got a lot of nerve, and he's strong as wire. He's a smart kid. I think he'll make good."

"But, Alan, I thought you didn't like Bob. I thought you didn't approve of him at all."

"Well, I don't!" said Alan with a queer grin on his face, "at least I thought I didn't. But I guess I'll have to change my opinion. He certainly has showed up in great shape to-night, offering to stay in my place."

"Maybe he doesn't really want to go," suggested Sherrill.

"Yes, he does, Sherry!" protested Alan earnestly, "he told me in there just now it had been the dream of his life to do something like that, and he promised me all kinds he was going to make good. Listen, Sherry. Bob's had a rotten deal lately. His sister died last month you know and she was the only one that ever cared for him. His brother-in-law is as hard as nails. He gave Bob a job in the canning factory carrying out peelings at six dollars a week and his board. Told him if he didn't like that he could get out, it was all he would ever do for him. I think he's been kind of up against it. You know Bob. He'd never stand being humiliated by that old grouch. He'd just go to the devil pretty soon, and nobody care."

"But how do you know what he may do in Egypt? Do you trust him?"

"Sure! I think he'll make good. He used to be crazy about old Hodge. It was the only thing we ever had in common. I think maybe he'll turn out all right. He's keen on the job."

Sherrill had been buttering thin slices of bread for sandwiches and now she turned around with the knife in her hand and her eyes bright.

"Alan, I think you're just wonderful!" she said with a shining look.

"Nothing of the kind, Sherry. I've just had to grind my teeth all day to keep from boohooing because I can't go myself."

"Well, I think you're wonderful!" stated Sherrill again whirling back to her buttering. "This may be the chance of Bob's life, but I'm inclined to think you've got a bigger one yet coming to you. Now, these are ready. Get the pitcher out of the right-hand door, please. And put that plate of cake on the tray. I'll take these in."

"Say, this is some set out, Sherry!" said Alan surveying the burdened tray, "but I'm glad you did it. I believe that kid is really hungry."

Sherry flashed him a glad look and led the way with her plate of delicate sandwiches.

Bob looked up from the letter he had copied, his face flushed with eagerness, and a radiant smile that made him seem like a new person, not the boy they had disliked through the last three years of high school.

"Boy!" said Bob, "that certainly looks good! You two people are making me feel I'm leaving some real friends when I go away. I didn't think I'd ever regret leaving this little old burgh, but I certainly think I've missed a lot not having you people for friends. No, don't say anything. I know you likely wouldn't care for me any more than you ever did if I stayed, but let me go away with the illusion that you would, can't you? A fellow has to have some one to tie to!"

"You make us feel ashamed, Bob, that we have been so

unfriendly," said Sherrill. "Won't you put it this way, that we just haven't got to know the real you? We didn't mean to be horrid, really we didn't."

"You make me feel more than ashamed, Bob," said Alan, laying a friendly arm across the other's shoulder. "Let's make up for the loss from now on, shall we? What say we'll be real partners in this job across the sea. You're the representative on the field, and I'm the home correspondent or something."

"O.K. with me," said Bob heartily. "Boy, you don't know how it feels to have you say that. I can't ever thank—"

"Cut it out, Pard!" said Alan huskily. "Here, have some more lemonade!"

They had a merry time, and ate up every scrap of sandwich and every crumb of cake, drinking the lemonade to the last drop. Then suddenly Bob Lincoln sprang up.

"I must go!" he declared, looking at his watch. "It's awfully late and I've got a lot of work cut out for me to-morrow. First off I've got to hand in my resignation to the Rockland Canning Factory, which same I shall enjoy doing; and then I've got to get all the junk in that list together and pack. There's a few things in that list I don't believe I can compass, but I don't reckon it matters. I've learned pretty much to get along without things lately anyhow," and he laughed a careless little ripple, the kind he had been used to give to cover his sore feelings.

Sherrill and Alan looked at him with sudden comprehension. This was the old Bob that they had not liked. Had it been only that he had covered up his loneliness with this attitude and they had not understood him?

Then Alan spoke quickly.

"Look here, old man," he said, "you and I have got to have a good talk fest to-night. Suppose you come home with me for the night. Then we can get everything thrashed out. You know we're partners. You're taking my place, and it's sort of up to me to see that you have everything in your outfit you need. Yes, that's my part. Come on, old boy, let's get down to brass tacks!"

Bob looked at Alan with sudden wonder.

"You're great!" he said with deep feeling in his voice. "What a fool I was! I used to think all that church going you did was just a pose! I called you a hypocrite once right in the school yard! And I believed you were. But now I see—Well, I can't tell you how I feel about this. I'm not going to let you do anything more for me of course, but—It's awfully white and fine of you to talk that way."

"Come along, Pard!" said Alan laughing, "we'll settle our differences in private. Come, we haven't any time to waste."

Alan gave him a push toward the door, but he paused before Sherrill.

"Good night, Sherrill," Bob said earnestly. "You've given me an awfully nice evening, and I shall always remember it. I used to think you were high-hat, but now I see you're real. I can't thank you enough for letting me in on this pleasant evening."

Sherrill went to the door with them and called a happy good night, watching them go down the walk, Alan's arm flung across Bob's shoulders as if they had been comrades for years.

Suddenly Alan turned and sprang back toward her.

"I'm carrying off some of your property, Sherry," he laughed, handing her a handkerchief. "You dropped this under the hammock when we came into the house, and I absent-mindedly put it in my pocket."

Their fingers touched as Sherrill took her handkerchief, and she heard Alan's low whisper:

"It was great of you to do that, Sherry. He thinks you're wonderful, and I can't thank you enough."

"Oh, I was glad to have a part in it, Alan," whispered Sherrill, "and say, Alan, I've been thinking. I shouldn't wonder if, after all, this would turn out to be the chance of your lifetime. I think you've gone a long way toward saving Bob!"

He gave her fingers a squeeze and sprang back to Bob and they walked away down the street whistling together an old school song, a thing they never had done before.

"Who was that other boy, Sherrill," asked her mother looking up with pleasant curiosity in her face.

"That was Bob Lincoln, Mother."

"What! Not that Lincoln boy that Alan dislikes so much? Not the boy that made so much trouble in school and was always doing wild things? Not the one that Alan fought with?"

"Yes, Mother," laughed Sherrill, "the same boy, but you'd be surprised how nice he is, and how grateful he was for the sandwiches and cake. He hadn't had much supper. You know his sister died not long ago, and he has to get his meals almost anywhere."

"Well, but, my dear! How did he come to call on you? I'm sure he's not the kind of boy you would want to have for a friend. I hope he isn't going to start in now and bother you coming here. I'm sure your brother would not like it at all. Keith is very particular about you, you know."

"Oh, he didn't come to see me, at all, Mother; he just ran in to speak to Alan a minute—on business—and we asked him in."

"Well, but, my dear, it isn't wise to get too intimate with a boy like that. He will think he can come again. I'm surprised that Alan didn't take him away at once. It's all well enough to be kind, but I really couldn't have you asking a boy like that here regularly. Sherrill, you never stop to think about things like that—"

"Listen, Mother dear. You needn't worry about Bob. He is going to Egypt day after to-morrow to be gone three years on an archaeological expedition with Professor Hodge. So you see there's nothing to worry about at all. He came to ask Alan something, that was all, and we were just being kind to him. We found out he has been awfully lonely, and, Mother, he was so pleased to have somebody a little friendly! You ought to have heard him. I felt so ashamed I didn't know what to do."

"Is that the red-haired Lincoln boy that used to drive by here in that old rattlety bang Ford?" asked Sherrill's grandmother, looking up with sudden interest. "I always liked that boy's looks. He reminded me of a cousin of mine that ran away and joined the Navy. He came back a first rate man too. I always thought his aunt that brought him up never understood him. She fussed over him a lot."

"Now, Mother!" said Sherrill's mother with a tender smile. "You always were a romantic dear. Who would ever have thought you noticed a boy going by on the street?"

"Well, I did!" said Grandmother Sherrill, "and I'm glad you were nice to him, Sherrill. If he's going to Egypt he can't do you any harm, and anyway I'll bank on your good sense to take care of yourself anywhere."

"Now, Mother! You're spoiling Sherrill!" smiled the mother. "However did a boy like that get a chance to go on an expedition of that sort? That is a great honor. Professor Hodge must have approved of him or he never would have asked him."

It was on Sherrill's lips to tell about Alan, but remembering his request that she keep it to herself she closed her mouth and turned away smiling. By and by when it didn't matter, she would tell Mother what a wonderful boy Alan MacFarlan had been. She said good night and went singing up to her room.

"She's a good girl, Mary!" said her grandmother.

"Yes, she is, Mother, I didn't mean that about your spoiling her."

"Humph!" said Grandmother folding away her sewing and taking off her spectacles. "Yes, she's a good girl, and that Alan MacFarlan is a good boy. I'm glad they made that other boy have a good time. He never looked to me as if he was very happy."

Over at the MacFarlan house the two boys entered quietly, Bob protesting that he ought not to go in lest it might disturb the invalid. They took off their shoes and went silently up the stairs, but not so silently but that Alan's mother heard him and came out to the landing to smile at him and give him a good night kiss. She wore a pretty blue negligee and her eyes were bright and more rested looking. Bob watched her in wonder, as she reassured her son about his father.

"He's resting very well," she whispered. "The doctor thinks he may have a better day to-morrow."

Alan introduced his friend, and Mrs. MacFarlan gave him a smile of welcome, and a soft hand-clasp.

"I thought I oughtn't to come," he whispered, "but he made me."

"Alan's friends are always welcome," she said, "and you won't disturb anybody. Alan's room is over in the tower, and nobody can hear you talk."

"I wish I had a mother," said Bob, as they entered Alan's room and the light was switched on. "Gee! It must be great! I hardly remember mine."

Then he looked around Alan's room.

"Say! Boy! If I had a room like this and a mother like yours, you couldn't drag me to Egypt. I'd stay right here in my home!"

Alan looked at him and then gave a swift glance about his room, with its comfortable furnishings and its evidences on every hand that his tastes and conveniences were consulted.

"Well, there's something in that!" he grinned. "It is pretty comfortable here. I hadn't thought of it, but it would be something to leave. However, let's get down to brass tacks. Let's run over that list and see what you need to get. Here. Sit down in that big chair. You look all in. I certainly wish I'd known you before and sometimes shared my home with you."

Bob dropped into the offered chair.

"Boy!" said he. "What I've missed!"

And then the two went to work in earnest on the list.

When they finally turned in there was a good understanding and a hearty liking between them that neither would have believed possible a few hours before. It was with genuine regret that they parted next morning after eating breakfast together, and walking down town as far as the bank. Alan had insisted that he should be allowed to provide whatever of outfit Bob did not have, but finally succeeded only in getting him to accept a loan until he could repay it. They stopped at the bank and Alan cashed a check from his own private precious fund he had been saving toward a new car.

"This is coming back to you the very first bit of salary I can spare from actual expenses," said Bob as he slipped the roll of bills in his inside pocket.

"If you scrimp yourself, old boy, I'll take it unkindly. Remember you must keep in good condition, and this is the only share I can have in this affair. It really makes me feel good to have this much."

"You can't know how I appreciate it," beamed Bob with a hearty grip of the other boy's hand, "and the queer thing about it is, I wouldn't have taken a red cent from you twenty-four hours before, if I lost all the chances in the universe. That's how different I feel toward you."

"Same here!" grinned Alan sheepishly. "What fools we were, Pard! Might have had three great years to look back upon. What a team we could have made out of that High School scrub if we had just hooked up forces instead of fighting! Hope I remember this lesson always."

They parted at the street corner, Bob promising to report late that evening and spend the night again with Alan as he was leaving for New York early the next morning.

As soon as he was alone the burden of his father's responsibilities settled down upon Alan's shoulders heavily. The day looked long and hard before him. He must try to get in touch with the Judge again. Perhaps he would have to run up to the city and see those real estate people on the ten train! How hot the sun seemed, and how uninteresting his own part in life! His heart was going shopping with Bob and selecting the right sweaters and shoes for the trip. But life was not all trips to

Egypt. He had business that should engross his every ener-
gy.

In the store was a great pile of mail. Another letter of
threatening portent from the enemy, with an undertone of
assurance that made him uneasy. If he could only read just
this one letter to Dad and see what he thought ought to be
done about it. But that of course was out of the
question.

The day proved to be even harder than he had feared. The
Judge was out of town. Nobody knew just when he would
return. Meantime he would have to act as if he were not
going to return, for time was short and the crisis extreme.

He took the ten o'clock train for the city, and chased a
member of the real estate company for two hours, from place
to place, finally locating him at his office at two o'clock, only
to find that the purhaser who had been so anxious to buy the
city lots a few weeks before had gone to Europe for the
summer and the only price that could be raised on them in a
quick extremity would be so inadequate to the necessities
that it would be hardly worth the sacrifice.

The two or three other addresses of reliable mortgage and
loan companies that his father had suggested, seemed unwill-
ing to undertake negotiations outside of the city, and at five
o'clock with all offices closing, and no idea what to do next,
Alan took the train for Rockland again, weary, downhearted
and hungry, not having had time to stop for lunch. He would
like to have put his head down on the car window sill and
cried, though it was years since he had shed a tear. The
breeze that swept in at the window was hot to suffocation,
and perhaps reminded him of the desert to which he was not
going. He tried, as he closed his eyes, to send up a sort of a
prayer, but it seemed so utterly desultory that he felt as if it
had not reached beyond the car ceiling.

"Oh, God, please do something for me about this mortgage! I'm all in, and I don't know what to do. Please for
Dad's sake, don't let me wreck the business because I'm
dumb. Show me where to go and what to do! And help me
not to keep thinking about Egypt like a cry-baby!"

That was his prayer that went over and over inarticulately
till the train arrived in Rockland.

CHAPTER III

Alan looked anxiously out of the car window as he swung to his feet in the aisle, with a vague hope that perhaps he might catch a glimpse of the tall form of Judge Whiteley looming up among the people on the platform. But all he saw was Bob Lincoln with his arms full of bundles watching the people coming out of the car, an eager look on his face, a light in his eyes, that somehow brought a strange new thrill to Alan's heart as he realized that this young man who had been his enemy, was looking for him.

He felt inexplicably glad when he saw the smile that broke over Bob's face at sight of him. The other boy rushed forward and greeted him eagerly:

"I thought perhaps you'd be on this train," he said, falling alongside and fitting his stride to Alan's. "The boy you left in the store told me you'd gone to town, so I took a chance and met the train. Just thought I'd like to report progress, and show you this wire that came from the prof this morning. Didn't expect another word from him so it sort of took me off my feet. You certainly must have given him some line about me. I hadn't any reason to expect any such send off from you. I feel like two cents to think how I'd sized you up. I always thought you'd like to wipe the earth up with me, but you've certainly made me ashamed. Why, man, your recommend must have been a crackerjack! Just gaze on that!" and he handed Alan a telegram. "Glad you are going! I remember you favorably. Don't worry about qualifications. Any one MacFarlan recommends is worth getting. Shall reserve you as my personal assistant. Meet you at twelve thirty at the ship. Hodge."

Something glad broke loose in Alan's heart that lifted his spirits. It was good to have this other fellow going—good to have put him into it.

"That's great!" said he cheerily, but I didn't do a thing, really, only just suggested your name."

"H'm!" said Bob significantly, "shows how much your suggestion is worth. Look here, man! It's *you* going on this expedition, not me. See? All the time I'm gone, I'm thinking

20

that, see? I'm *you,* not myself. I've got to be what you would
be if you had gone!"

Afterwards Bob's words came back to Alan, months later,
once when he had a question as to which course of two he as
a Christian should follow, then suddenly he remembered Bob,
and his way cleared. Why, that was exactly the way it was
with a Christian. It wasn't he, Alan MacFarlan, that was
deciding whether to do this or that, it was Jesus Christ. *He*
was not living, *Christ* was living in him. Strange he had never
thought of that before! And it took Bob Lincoln, a fellow
who wasn't a Christian at all, to show him where he actually
stood in this world—if he really meant what he had pro-
fessed.

Bob declined to go home with Alan to supper, saying he
must go to see his brother-in-law, and it was the only time he
could find him at home, but he promised to come back and
spend the night, and be there as early as he could make it
after nine o'clock. He had to pack. He showed Alan the
sweater he had bought, and tore the paper from his new shoes
exhibiting them with pleasure.

"And I've saved on several things," he said, "there's ten
dollars more than I really need that I'm going to return to
you now."

"Try and do it!" said Alan, eluding Bob and striding off
toward the hardware store with a gay wave of his hand.

"Get even with you yet!" yelled Bob merrily, and went off
toward his brother-in-law's house.

A sort of a sick premonition went over Alan as he
approached the store. He wondered if there had been any
developments.

"Any phone calls?" he asked the clerk who had been
restively watching the clock, anxious to get out and play
baseball with the Twilight League, and wanting his supper
besides.

"Yep!" said the lad, "couple! Real estate man in the city,
Spur and Holden, said they'd had an offer from a man on yer
lots. He'd give you a thousand less than yer price and they
advised ya ta accept. Said it was the best you'd get this time
of year. And then a fella named Rawlins called up and said
he had a proposition ta make, but you had ta come ta terms
before eleven o'clock tamarra, ur it was all off."

"Thanks!" said Alan wearily without a change of expression, though both messages had been like broadsides. "Just

stop in the restaurant and ask 'em to send me in a cup of coffee and a ham sandwich, won't you? I haven't time to go home just now."

Then Alan climbed into his father's desk chair and attacked the mail that had arrived. All but two of the letters were bills and most of them asked for immediate payment. Why did everybody seem to be in need of money at once? The two that were not bills occupied him the rest of the evening, telephoning and telegraphing, trying to reach men who seemed to have hidden themselves beyond recall.

Alan called up his mother and found that his father was still under opiates, and the doctor felt that he would not be able to tell for several days yet just how severe the injuries were. He said he was still holding his own however. Alan thought his mother's voice sounded tired and anxious. She wanted to know how business was going and he tried to reassure her, but his voice almost broke.

It was growing dark in the store. The boy shoved the thick restaurant cup and saucer aside and flung his head down on his arms across the desk.

How hot and tired he was! How utterly he was failing in trying to take his father's place in the store! And out a few blocks away his substitute for the desert was joyously preparing for the time of his life! Only another day and he would be away into a great new world filled with wonderful experiences!

And only another day and the enemy would be upon himself and his father's business, and the judge was still away! The judge was his only hope now. He knew not where else to turn. Tomorrow morning he would have that awful Rawlins to deal with, and what would be his proposition? If he only knew! If he only had someone to consult with! There would be some humiliating terms offered of course! Oh, if he could take that infamous little Rawlins out behind the store and thrash him and so set matters right! Perhaps he would, if things got pretty bad, anyway! Perhaps he would not be able to control his anger, and would get into a fight, and then there would be a law-suit in addition to all the other trouble! Or even something worse! Then what would dad say?

He groaned softly as he thought of all the possibilities. Then suddenly the clock struck nine, and he realized that Bob had promised to meet him at the house. He must go back and look cheerful, and hear Bob talk eagerly of his plans!

Life was hard! Here was he bearing burdens he was not fit for, and missing the chance of a lifetime!

Alan reached for his hat, but as he did so the telephone rang out sharply in the empty store. With a wild hope that this might be Judge Whiteley Alan reached for the receiver.

But it was only Sherrill Washburn calling, in her capacity of president of the young people's group in the church.

"Is that you, Alan?" The tired boy thought her voice sounded like cool sweet rose petals blowing in the breeze. "Your mother said I'd find you at the store. I've been thinking, Alan. You know that fund we have for Bibles? Why shouldn't we give one to Robert Lincoln to take with him? Or do you think he would be offended? He's never been to any of our meetings, nor been with our crowd very much. But I thought—somehow—we hadn't ever tried very much. I thought—maybe—you could give it to him somehow. I wouldn't like him to feel—we were—well—trying to mission-arize him or anything! Do you think it would do, or not?"

"Sure!" said Alan heartily, albeit with the least twinge of jealousy which he knew at once was beneath him. Now, if he had been the one who was going to the desert Sherrill would be getting this Bible for him, and how wonderful it would be—whispered the tempter—to have a Bible like that to take out in the desert and read, and feel they were all praying—!

"Sure!" said Alan again recognizing the natural man cropping up, and trying to grind it beneath his heel. "Make it a *good* one. I believe it will *please* him. I sure do. Can we get it in time? He leaves early in the morning, you know."

"Yes," said Sherrill eagerly, "we got two the last time, you remember, as premiums for those who passed the examinations in the Bible course, and Cameron went away before the contest ended and we had it left over."

"Sure! I remember. Say! Those were Scofield Bibles, too, weren't they? Boy! I'm glad about that, for I don't think he knows the first thing about what the Bible means, and a Scofield Bible will be so helpful about understanding the dispensations and covenants and things like that. That was a great idea, Sherry!"

"Then you'll give it to him?"

"Sure thing, Sherry! But not as my gift, you know. I'll say it was a gift from the crowd. I'll make him understand. A reminder of us all at home or something like that. I'll give him that list of the Bible study we are all taking together. Haven't you got an extra copy?"

"Oh, yes! That's fine. Tell him to join our group in reading, and then we can send him the examination slips every month. Tell him we want to count him one of our group."

"Sure!" said Alan, "that's a great idea, Sherry! A sort of a binder to home. How about getting word around to the crowd, and having them down to the train in the morning? Just give him a little send off! Do you think they would do it?"

"I think they would, Alan! I think that's wonderful of you. May I tell them you asked it? They'll—be a little surprised, you know— They've always considered you two were enemies."

"I'd like them to know that we are not any more," said Alan gravely, setting his lips in a firm line that gave a very lovely look to his young face.

"All right, Alan!" said Sherrill with a lilt to her voice, "I'll send the Bible right over to your house. Keith is going past there and he can leave it at the door without troubling anybody, can't he? And I'll begin calling up the bunch right away. Is it the eight thirty train? All right. And we'll have the farewell hymn ready too. How's that?"

"O.K. The very thing!" said Alan feeling a lump in his throat at the thought. Oh, why hadn't he known Bob before? How wrong, how sinful it was to get angry at any one—to judge any one—to pick out any human soul and make powerless one's influence toward him! Why had he never thought of that before?

Sherrill's voice sang gayly over the wire:

"That's *great* of you, Alan! Simply *great!*"

"Nothing of the kind!" said the boy huskily with a thrill of pleasure at her tone, nevertheless.

The musty old office looked almost glorified to his eyes as he hung up the receiver and looked about him. Well, at least if he could not go to the desert he could have a part in preparing his substitute. Now, wasn't that great of Sherrill to remember that Bible!

He reached for his hat again and then caught sight of the open safe. He must lock that up of course before he left. How careless he had almost been. It showed he was not fit to take charge of the business. He must buck up and get his mind in working order.

He stooped to swing the big safe door shut, and then remembered something else. What was it his father had said about papers in the safe? He ought to have looked them over earlier in the evening. How careless of him to have gone to the city and left the safe unlocked. But then Joe who had stayed behind was of course perfectly trustworthy. Dad always trusted Joe utterly. But it was careless nevertheless.

Papers? Yes, now he remembered. The deed to the lots in the city! Well, he should have taken those with him of course. If there had been a chance of selling he would have needed them. Yes, and the Westbrook Securities. And the Insurance Papers! Of course! And what were these?

He drew forth an envelope, and opened out one of the crisp crackling documents, drawing his brows in a frown. The other papers lay beside him on the floor.

Suddenly a noise just behind him startled him and he glanced up.

There was a window behind the desk that furnished light in the daytime, and its shade was stretched high, for Joe had been reading a novel late in the afternoon and wanted all the light he could get. Instinctively Alan looked toward the window whence the sound had come. Was that a face he had seen vanishing as he looked up or were his nerves getting on edge? Nerves, of course. Who would want to look in at a back window of the hardware store at this time of night? It opened on a back alley. Nevertheless it was careless to work at the safe so near to an open window. He reached up and drew the shade down with a snap, and then turned back to his papers lying in a heap on the floor in a little pool of bright light from the drop lamp, their titles standing out clearly. Anyone looking in the window could easily have read them. But of course there had been no one looking in. Should he take those papers home with him now and get acquainted with them? Perhaps that would be a good idea. Or would they be safer here behind a time lock? Safer? Why they were safe enough anywhere, weren't they? What were they anyway? Of course he ought to know what was under his care. Or would it be time enough for that to-morrow? It was late now for his tryst with Bob. He must go at once.

When he had turned out the lights and locked the door he glanced back uneasily, as an inexperienced nurse might look anxiously at the sleeping infant placed in her care, and wondered if he had done everything that was usually done at night in leaving the store.

Then his mind switched ahead to Bob and the Bible, and

Sherrill. Great girl Sherrill. She was not just an ordinary girl. Not just Girl! She was as good as a fellow in some ways. A real comrade.

Bob met him at the corner.

"I thought I'd wait for you here," he said, "and not disturb the house for two incomings."

"That was thoughtful of you, Kid!" said Alan. "I say, old man, I've been thinking all day how tough it's going to be to lose you, now, just as I've found you."

"Same here!" said Bob. "I've been kicking myself all over the place all day that I've been such a fool as not to know what a prince of a fellow you are."

Arm in arm they walked up the street, cementing a friendship quickly ripened over the ashes of a dead hatred.

As they swung into the street where Alan lived a car drew up at the MacFarlan house, and some one leaned out and signaled.

"That you, Mac?" called Keith Washburn. "Here's a package Sherrill sent over. Evening, Bob."

"Thanks awfully, Keith. Won't you come in?" said Alan, taking the package.

"Wish I could, Mac, but I'm on my way over to West Grove. Just got a wire from a man I've been wanting to see for some time, and he's taking the midnight train, so I'm hot foot to get there in time to ask him a few questions before he leaves. How about going with me, both of you? I'd be awfully glad of company."

"Sorry, Keith, but Bob is leaving in the morning, and we've got some things to do before he goes."

"Oh, yes, Sherrill told me about it. Great chance, Bob. Wouldn't mind being in your boots. Dig up a few kings and buried cities for me, won't you? Hope you have a wonderful time. We'll think about you. Let us know how you're coming on now and then. Well, sorry you can't go with me. So long!"

Bob looked after the car wistfully. Somehow the home town and the home folks had suddenly taken on a friendly look they had never shown before.

"I like him," he said suddenly, as if he were thinking aloud.

"He certainly is a prince of a fellow!" said Alan, as he got out his latch key.

The boys went quietly upstairs to Alan's room, and sat

down to talk. As they turned on the light they saw a big pitcher of milk and a plate of sandwiches and cake.

"Draw up and let's have a bite," said Alan. "My mother thinks I haven't had any supper evidently."

"Is that the kind of thing mothers do?" said Bob wistfully. "Good night! And you wanted to go to the desert! Well, if I had a mother like that I don't know but I'd have turned the job over to some other fellow too."

"Say," said Alan thoughtfully, "you begin to make me think I haven't been half appreciative of my lot."

When they had cleared the plates, and finished the milk Alan reached for the package and untied it.

"This," he said, as he opened the box, "is for you, Bob. It's from the bunch. They want you to take it with you. Think you've got room to carry it?"

He felt just the least bit embarrassed now that he had begun. He was not quite sure how Bob would take the gift of a Bible. Perhaps after all, as Sherrill had suggested, he might resent it. He had the name of not caring much for religion or churches.

"For me?" said Bob with pleased surprise. "From *the bunch?* Say, what have you been saying to *them?* The bunch never cared a red cent for me."

"That's all you know about it, Bob," said Alan. "And I haven't said a word to them. It was all cooked up by the bunch. Sherrill Washburn is president, you know, this year, and she called me up awhile ago and asked if I thought you would mind their giving it to you."

"Mind?" said Bob. "Indeed I do mind. I mind so much that I'll carry it all the way in my hands if there isn't any other place for it. What is it?"

"That's it, Bob. I guess maybe they thought it wasn't quite in your line. They didn't know but you might like something else better. You see, it's—*a Bible!"*

Alan stripped off the confining paper, and handed over the beautifully bound Scofield Bible.

The other boy took it with a look of awe and reverence that astonished MacFarlan. He held it in his hand a moment and felt of its covers, opened it and noted its suppleness, its gold edges, its fine paper, its clear print, and then looked down for an instant almost as if he were going to cry.

"I've never had a Bible," he said huskily at last, "but I'll see to it hereafter that it's in my line. I sure am grateful."

"I think they've written something in the front," said Alan to cover his own deep feeling. He reached over and turned the pages back to the fly-leaf where it was inscribed "To Robert Fulton Lincoln with the best wishes of his friends of the West Avenue Young People's Group." There followed a long string of autographs, most of them belonging to Robert Lincoln's former schoolmates, and at the bottom in small script, "2 Timothy 2:15."

"Here, I've got to get my name in that space they left there," said Alan, getting out his fountain pen. "You see, I happen to be vice president of that bunch and hence the space."

Bob watched him write his name, and a strange half embarrassed silence filled the room till it was written.

"Thanks a lot," he said deeply affected, studying the names one by one. "Do you know— I never thought— I wouldn't have expected— That is— Well, you see I've always thought nobody over there liked me. I've always felt awfully alone in this town. I guess that's what made me act so rotten to you all. I thought you were a— Well, I may as well confess it. I thought you were a lot of high-hat hypocrites!"

A strange, shamed look passed over Alan's face as if he had suddenly looked in the glass and found his face all dirt.

"Say, Bob," he began with a voice of deep contrition, "I'm mighty sorry. I can't ever forgive myself. But, old man, I'm beginning to think that perhaps your estimate of us was true. But Bob, we didn't have an idea of it. Honest, we didn't! Why, Kid, we prayed for you the time you got hit by the automobile. We prayed in our Sunday night meeting for you."

"I know you did," said Bob with a thoughtful faraway look, "and I *hated* it. One of the little kids told me, and I thought you did it for show off. But—say, Mac, I wish you'd pray for me again. I need it! It's mighty kind of stark living in this little old world all alone, even if I have got the chance of my lifetime."

A great wave of love and joy thrilled up from Alan's heart.

"I sure will!" he said with a ring in his voice, "let's do it now. And I wish you'd pray for me. If ever a Christian felt mean and self-centered, and all kinds of a rotten fool, I do. Come on."

They knelt beside the big leather couch at the foot of the bed, Robert shyly, awkwardly, wondering just what he had brought upon himself by his impulsive words, but Alan in young eagerness, his arm flung across his companion's shoulders.

"Oh, God," he prayed, "I've been all kinds of a fool, but I thank you that you've shown me before it was too late. I thank you that you've given me this friend, and may we be friends always. And now won't you just bless him, and show him what the Lord Jesus has done for him. We thank you together that the blood of Christ is sufficient to cover all our sins and mistakes, the sins and mistakes of both of us, and that even such carelessness as I have been guilty of, such lack of true witnessing for Christ, cannot keep either of us from wearing the robe of righteousness, because it is Christ's righteousness that we may wear and not our own. Help Bob to make a surrender of himself to you before he goes, and when he goes may he take you with him, and feel that he is never alone. We ask it in the name of Jesus."

There was silence in the room for a moment as they continued to kneel, and then Alan said softly:

"You pray too, Kid, it'll be good to remember. Kind of bind us together, you know, till you come back."

Bob caught his breath softly, and then after a pause, he spoke huskily, hesitantly:

"Oh God—I'm pretty much of a sinner, I guess. I—don't think—I'd be much good—to you— But I need somebody—mighty bad! If you'll take me—I'm yours."

He caught his breath again in a little quick gasp and added:

"Thanks for sending Mac into my life—and for this great chance to go in his place."

They talked a long time after the light was out and they were in bed, Alan explaining what it meant to be born again, what he had meant by "robe of righteousness," showing his new friend how Christ had taken his sins entirely upon himself and nailed them to the cross when he died, and that if he was willing to accept that freedom from the law that had been purchased on the cross, he had a right to stand clear and clean before God, not in his own righteousness, but in the righteousness of Christ.

Bob asked a lot of questions. The whole subject was utterly new to him. The clock struck two before the boys turned over and decided to get a little sleep. Alan had forgotten all about his own worries in the joy of leading another soul into the light. Both boys were just drifting off into unconsciousness when they were vaguely aware of a car stopping before the door of the house. A moment later a pebble sharply struck the glass of the window, and a low whistle followed this signal.

They were alert and upright at once, and Alan sprang out of bed and went to the window.

"Who's there?" Alan called softly, sharply from the window.

"That you, Mac?" whispered Keith Washburn softly. "Say, Mac, did you leave a light down in the store?"

"Why, no!" said Alan, "of course not."

"Are you sure?"

"*Absotive*ly!" said Alan. "I know because I stumbled over a box of tin things Joe had left in the way."

"Well, there's one down there now," said Keith impressively, "just saw it as I went by. And what's more it's moving around like a flash light, in the back of the store."

"Wait a second. I'll be down!" said Alan, flying into his clothes.

CHAPTER IV

"Don't get up, Bob," said Alan struggling into a sweater, "Remember you've got a journey to go tomorrow. It's likely nothing. Go on asleep. I'll be back in three jerks of a lamb's tail."

"Cut it!" said Bob jerking on his shoes. "Whaddaya think I am anyway, Mac?"

Keith was waiting for them downstairs, the engine running softly, and he started the car before they were fairly in.

"Sure you weren't dreaming, Wash?" asked Alan, wondering why his teeth had a tendency to chatter, and trying to remember whether he had finally brought those papers home with him or left them in the safe. He had a ghastly feeling that he had left them in the safe. Oh, if Dad were only well!

"Dreaming!" said Keith contemptuously, "Well, I might have been of course. I saw the light when I first rounded the corner of the post office and I thought it was queer. Thought you must have forgotten to turn it out, or else you decided to leave it burning, but when I got around in front of the store it was all dark so I concluded I had been mistaken. Thought it was just a reflection or something. But when I got down to your corner I looked back and it flashed up again, and moved around. Then I decided you had gone down to the store after something, but somehow I wasn't easy and thought I better see if I could get in touch with you. Thought maybe you could explain it."

They were rounding the corner into the main street now, and suddenly Bob laid a detaining hand on the wheel.

"Better stop here, Washburn," he suggested. "If you go nearer the engine can be heard."

"That's right, Lincoln. I ought to have thought of that. I'll park here in the shadow, and we'll sneak up. Probably it's only some trick of the street lights reflecting somewhere, and I'll feel like two cents. Probably I've only got a case of nerves riding half the night. If it is I'll feel cheap as dirt to think I waked you up, but it's always just as well to be on the safe side."

"Sure thing!" said Alan with set lips as he swung to the ground softly, and wondered for the fortieth time whether he had taken those papers home or left them in the safe.

"There sure is a light there!" whispered Bob as they stole along, walking on the grass at the edge of the pavement so that their feet made no sound. "There! See there! It's moving around! Now, it's gone! No, there it is again!"

"I'll slide around to the alley!" whispered Alan. "It might be I can look in the back window. They're operating down by the safe, whoever it is. You two watch this side and the front, will you?"

"Don't do anything rash, Mac! Perhaps we better call the officer. He ought to be in the region about now."

"No, wait! I want to get a line on things first," said Alan as he slid off into the darkness, plunging swiftly down the alleyway that separated his father's store from the millinery store just beyond, and passed the window behind his father's desk.

Softly Washburn and Lincoln stepped up to the front of the store and tried to look through the front windows, but the window decorations prevented their seeing more than an indefinite dancing light that went here and there, and sometimes disappeared entirely.

Keith stepped to the door and peered through the glass, but a stand full of brooms stood right in his line of vision, and he could not be sure, though once he thought he saw a dark form move across the dim distance, and then the light appeared from a new angle.

How did the man get into the store, if man it was?

Softly he slid his hand down to the door latch and tried it, taking great care, but the creaking old latch suddenly gave forth a grating sound and simultaneously the light inside the store went out. There followed a dull thud, as of heavy books falling, and then a crash of metal, a lot of heavy metal articles falling against one another, a sort of scuffling sound, and then silence. Ominous silence.

Frantically Keith put his shoulder to the door and tried to push it open, but the old door was held by heavy bolts at top and bottom, and was made of strong oak planks. Keith could not do anything but rattle it.

"We'd better call Mac and break this door open," said Keith. "This looks queer!" But Bob had already disappeared down the alley, and Keith tiptoed to the corner of the store, with a sharp eye out, however, toward the front that there should be no possibility of anyone escaping in that direction.

Meanwhile Alan, as he ran down the alley, had been still trying to solve the problem about those papers. Had he taken them home or left them in the safe? And what were they worth anyway? Deeds and securities! Insurance papers! If they were lost or stolen did that spell calamity, or was everything so recorded that they would lose nothing? And why would anybody want to get any of those papers? It must have something to do with the people who were trying to foreclose the mortgage—unless perhaps this was just a common thief looking for money in the safe. What was that paper his father had spoken about? The "agreement" he had called it, something about not foreclosing under certain conditions! It was queer how his father's words came back now in the stress of panic. Oh, how careless he had been not to attend to this matter right away!

But there was no more time to think about it now. He had arrived at the end of the alley, just under the window back of the safe, and he saw to his horror that the window was wide open, and the light was dancing about just inside.

Cautiously he approached. If he only had an old box or something to stand on so that he could see the situation and know just what to do. There might be more than one person inside, in which case he would need help. He ought to have brought his little revolver along perhaps, but he had not taken time to think when he left home, and besides, he hadn't considered any serious danger.

While he paused, watching the window, he heard the thud of the ledger falling, knew just what it was, saw the light go out, distinctly heard a hurried step, and then the crash of the metal. That would be that stack of children's hoes and shovels and rakes clattering together. He could almost visualize the intruder now, and knew just which way he was moving.

Almost instantly there appeared a dark form at the window. He could see the gleam of a white hand laid on the window sill, as the light from the next street showed it up. The man was coming out!

He crouched close to the wall. There was no time to signal his friends. It did not even occur to him. He was no coward. He crouched and held his breath as the intruder climbed out on the window sill, hung an instant and then dropped.

But he dropped into Alan MacFarland's arms, and they grappled together and fell, rolling over in the alley.

Not for an instant did Alan let go his hold, though his prisoner kicked and struggled, and applied even his teeth to the attack.

Silently they rolled about in the alley, Alan finally getting the upper hand, and administering the good thrashing he well knew how to give, but not yet having been able to get a good glimpse of the man's features. Suddenly the victim in desperation wrenched his right arm loose and swift as lightning gave him a smashing blow on his nose, that made all the stars in the firmament flash out in bright splinters before his stunned gaze, and sent him crashing down into awful darkness in the alley, in a black obliteration.

It was Bob Lincoln who dislodged the enemy from his throat, and lifted him tenderly in his arms. The enemy melted away in the darkness but not before Keith had sighted him running and come hard on his tracks sending forth a sharp warning whistle which brought the officers of the law in short order. But the burglar was gone! Keith had followed at a wild speed, but when he came to the end of the alley there was no one there, and no trace anywhere of anyone in the peaceful silent darkness. He ran up and down the street in either direction but finding nothing more returned to the place where Alan was lying.

Bob had succeeded in bringing him back to consciousness, and was wiping the blood away from his face. One of the officers had a big flash turned on, and they were talking in low voices. Alan, his voice a little shaky, was telling how it all had happened.

Alan presently insisted on getting upon his feet. He was all right of course. What did they think he was? A baby? Just a little punch in the nose, what was that? All he was sorry about was that the man got away.

They went inside the store, and saw the safe. It had been blown open with noiseless powder. There were papers strewn wildly about on the floor, and the little stack of children's garden tools was lying across them. There were the day book and ledger too, on the floor where they had fallen when the man fled. Alan shut his lips in a tight line! Who could have done it? What would his father say when he heard of this new disaster? And how much had the man been able to get away with? Was it his fault in any way? Yes, at least in part, for he never should have opened the safe with the shade up and a light inside. Besides, he now remembered he had left the iron shutters of that window, that were always closed at sundown, wide open! He hadn't even remembered to fasten the window. It might even have been left wide open for all he remembered. He certainly hadn't done anything to it except to draw down the shade.

They went home at last, back to bed, leaving the police in charge. They could find no trace of the robber anywhere.

Alan felt a little shaky, and found that he had a black eye as well as a bloody face, and many minor bruises.

"Bob, you saved my life, you know," he remarked as they went up the walk to the MacFarlan house.

"Aw, cut it! Nothing of the kind!" said Bob. "I just helped out a little. You'd have been up in a second more."

"No," said Alan seriously, "I was gone. He had me by the throat. I was choking to death. I remember thinking it was all over with me. You came just in time. Say, Kid, this binds us close. I shan't ever forget."

Bob threw an impulsive arm across Alan's shoulder.

"That's great of you, Mac," he said; "then we've got something on both sides to bind us. I'll never forget either."

Back in the room while Alan washed his bruises, Bob stood handling his new Bible again, admiring it, turning the pages, reading again the inscription and the names. As he came to the little reference at the bottom of the page he studied it thoughtfully.

"Say, Mac, what's this down at the bottom? What does it mean? Two Timothy two fifteen?"

"Oh, that reference?" said Alan emerging from the towel, "that's the group's text for the year, Second Timothy, two fifteen. You know the verse. 'Study to show thyself approved unto God, a workman that needeth not to be ashamed, rightly dividing the word of truth.' You'll find the verse marked in the Bible likely. Trust Sherrill Washburn for that. Here, I'll show you."

Alan fluttered the leaves over, and handed the Bible back open to the chapter, and there sure enough the fifteenth verse stood out marked clearly in black lines.

Robert read the verse over slowly, thoughtfully, and then looked up with a smile:

"So, it seems I have a higher boss than old Hodge, haven't I?" he said thoughtfully. "One that comes first. Well, if I can show myself approved unto God, I guess old Hodge oughtta be satisfied. How about it?"

"Sure thing, Bob," said Alan pulling his sweater off and flinging it across a chair.

"But say! What does this last line mean? 'Rightly dividing the word of truth'?"

"Oh that means understanding how to take the Bible, which thing was written to the Jews, which to the Gentiles, and which to the church. Dispensations, and covenants and all that. It makes it a lot clearer what it all means, you know. We have Scofield's little book to read, you know. There's an extra copy around here somewhere. Yes, here it is. You can take it with you and that'll explain. It's only a pamphlet so it won't take much room, and it clears things a lot. And by the way, here's our course of study. I promised Sherry I'd give it to you. Stick it in the book. We want you to keep up with us, and we'll send you the exams when they come in and then we can all be getting a line on the same things, see?"

Bob accepted the book and papers eagerly and would have sat down to examine them then and there, but Alan reminded him that it was almost four o'clock and he had less than four hours to sleep before his journey.

"That's all right, Mac," said the boy, "I'll have plenty of time on ship board. However, you need your sleep too. I'll turn in now."

Morning came all too soon for the two young sleepers, but nevertheless they were alert early.

"Say, Kid, you're some beaut!" announced Bob rubbing the sleep out of his eyes and gazing at the other boy. "Boy! You look as if you'd been in a fight for sure."

"Well, I don't want any worse one," laughed Alan. Then suddenly sobering he sprang out of bed wildly.

"Great Cats!" he exclaimed, "I never looked to see if I brought home those papers last night."

He dashed wildly toward his coat which hung in the closet, and fumbled in first one pocket then another, finally bringing out a bundle of official looking documents fastened together with rubber bands.

"Well, I'll be jiggered! Here they are!" he exclaimed, his face breaking into joy, "now whaddaya think of that? Brought 'em home after all, and didn't remember a thing about it. Boy! I'm glad! Now the next thing is, is that Agreement among 'em or did that poor fish get away with it?"

"What are you talking about?" asked Bob looking over his shoulder at the sheaf of papers. "Was there something in that safe somebody wanted? Have you any idea who that burglar was?"

"Well, not exactly, but there is a man trying to put something over on Dad, and I just reckoned he might be hunting some papers or something. I don't know for sure, because I can't ask Dad till he gets better. I've got to figure it out for myself. But I'd give two cents right now if I could have got a good look into that fellow's face before he cleared out. I don't suppose we'll ever get a line on him."

"H'm!" said Bob thoughtfully. "Wish I was staying a day or two. I'd like to help you search it out."

"Here's an agreement," said Alan thoughtfully. "Might be it." He opened it and read, and then folded the papers away in his coat pocket again. "Guess I'll put these in the safety deposit box in the bank this morning. Come, Bob, we've got to get a hustle on. You don't want to miss that train, and we've several things to do before train time. We'll just get down and eat a bite and then we can take it easy. What have you left to do yet? Anything but gather up your baggage?"

"Oh, just one or two little things," said Bob. "It won't take me long."

Alan's mother had ordered breakfast served at once when they came down, honey dew melon, chops, fried potatoes, waffles and amber coffee. She came smiling in as the boys sat down.

"Why this is a banquet, Mrs. MacFarland," said Bob rising and pulling back her chair. "You oughtn't to have done it. All this! And I'm sure you don't have breakfast at this hour every morning."

"You're going on a journey," said the smiling mother. "You'll need a good breakfast. And besides, we're so happy this morning we want to celebrate. Alan, your father is really better, the doctor says. It will be a long time before he pulls back to things, but he has passed the worst, he hopes."

It was a happy meal, and Bob's heart warmed with the feeling that he belonged and might help rejoice in the happiness and relief of these new friends. All too quickly the minutes passed, and the boys started out together, but just as they went out the door the telephone rang and Alan was called to answer.

"I'll start on," called Bob. "Meet you at the post office. How's that? Got to leave my address or my brother-in-law will examine any letters that might come."

But Bob did not go at once to the post office. Instead he sprinted down the back street and entered the alley, the scene of the fracas the night before. He walked over the ground pretty thoroughly examining everything, and then followed the path down among the weeds into the fields where the fugitive had disappeared. Yes, there were tracks in the grass, tall weeds lying flat as if a heavy hasty foot had crushed them, but they ended in a group of elderberry bushes down near the railroad, no sign of any footsteps beyond the bushes. He stood looking at the vague path thoughtfully a moment and then retraced his steps. He did not notice a frail young girl with big troubled eyes watching him from behind the back fence on the other side of the alley, until he was opposite her, and then he saw that it was Lancey Kennedy, the niece of Mrs. Corwin who kept the millinery store on the other side of the alley, and lived in a small apartment over the store. Bob didn't know her very well. She was shy and retiring, and had been in town only about a year. She had come to live in Rockland with her aunt after the death of her parents. But she had been in his class in high school, and of course he recognized her. She was one of the best students in the class.

He would have passed her with a brief nod of good morning, but he saw that she was waiting to speak to him, and it suddenly struck him how lovely her eyes were, great deep brown wells. What was the matter with him this morning?

He paused as she spoke:

"I was waiting to speak to you. There's something I think you ought to know," she said in a voice that seemed almost frightened. "Weren't you here last night? I thought I heard them call you 'Bob' and it seemed like your voice that answered."

"Sure, I was here," he answered, stepping a little closer. "Did they wake you up?"

"Why, I hadn't been asleep," she said, "I was worried. You see my room is in the third story back, and just as I turned my light out I heard a noise out here in the alley and I looked out and I was sure I saw a man's feet disappearing into the window of the store."

"The dickens! You did?" said Bob with a whistle of astonishment.

"But I wasn't sure at all," said Lancey. "It is awfully dark in the alley. But I waited and pretty soon I saw a light in the store. Sometimes I wasn't sure but it was just the reflection of the street light over there on the glass. I thought it was my imagination. Then I got so excited I didn't know what to do. It seemed as if I ought to tell somebody, but I couldn't get down without waking my aunt, and I knew she wouldn't hear to my calling anybody. She would have said I was a romantic little fool. So I waited, but I guess I ought to have gone anyway. But before I got my courage up I saw someone else come down the alley, and a man jumped out of the window, and then it all happened. I wanted to scream out, but I was so frightened I couldn't make a sound, and when I got control of myself I saw two other people come running, and I heard Mr. Washburn call out, 'Get him, Bob?' and you answered, and then I knew there was no need. But I saw the man run down in those bushes, and then it was so dark beyond I couldn't see him any longer. I knew you all were onto him, so I needn't do anything more, and I wasn't sure but the police had got him, for they were all in a bunch when they came back. But after they had all gone I sat there awhile just watching that group of elderberry bushes till it seemed to move and walk up across the grass, and pretty soon I saw it really was a man moving in the darkest places across the end of our back fence. He had come right out of the bushes, or behind the bushes. He must have hid till you all went away. And he kept so close to the fence I could only see the top of his head sometimes. He would move a few steps and then stop a long time."

Bob was listening in fascination, watching the girl's sweet face, thinking with his subconscious mind how strange it was he had never noticed what pretty delicate features she had, and that lovely oval of her pale cheeks that just now was tinged the least bit with the pink of excitement.

"When I saw he was turning in between our store and the bakery," went on Lancey, "I slipped out of my room and went down in the store to watch and see if he came out into the street, and just as I got in the store he went by the window. I saw he was limping, and he had no hat on. He went very slowly, watching the street each way, and finally crossed the street, and went into Mrs. Brower's boarding house. He had a latch key and he seemed a long time getting the door open, and very nervous looking each way, and once he dropped the key. I heard it ring on the door stone."

"Was there any light at Mrs. Brower's?" asked Bob quickly.

"No, not for a long time," answered Lancey, "I watched. But just when I thought there was no use watching any more there came a light in the third-story back room. It has a side window that looks down on the road to their garage, and a hand pulled down the shade quick. I could only see a hand and an arm. And then I wondered what I ought to do. I felt somebody ought to know, but wasn't sure who. So I've slipped out here every time I could get away, to see if some of them wouldn't come back, so I could tell them without being noticed. I knew my aunt would be furious if her name got tangled up in it. And I wasn't at all sure I ought to let it get known anyway, only to the people to whom it mattered. After the light went out I was so cold that I went back to my room, but I couldn't sleep all night. Do you think it is important? Do you think I should tell the police?"

"You poor Kid!" said Bob his voice full of tenderness. "Don't worry any more about it. Sure I think it's important, but you needn't do anything about it. I'll tell MacFarlan, and then if he wants to know more he can ask you. I'll tell him to keep your name out of it, see? He'll understand. He's a prince."

"Oh, thank you!" said Lancey with a sigh of relief. "I was afraid my aunt would have to know about it, and she isn't—well—it's not easy to make her understand. She would have thought I ought not to have been watching. She would have thought I was to blame somehow."

"You poor Kid!" said Bob again, his voice bringing the rosy color into her cheeks. "Leave it to me! I'll try to get another chance to speak to you about it without calling the attention of the town. Could I call you up?"

"Oh, no," said Lancey shrinking. "My aunt would be sure to answer, or question, and be most unpleasant."

"All right! You just trust me. I'll get word to you somehow. Write you a note or something. Don't you worry. If anybody questions you, I'll see they do it most discreetly. Thanks for giving me the dope. You sure are some detective, Kid. There comes Mac's car. See you later if I can. So long!"

He was gone up the alley appearing quite casually beside the car as Alan drew up at the drug store, and the girl stood in the back garden among the hollyhocks, her bright hair blowing in little rings around her sweet face, watching the boy depart, and hearing over again his comforting voice, "Leave it to me, Kid!"

Then suddenly, into the sunshine burst a sharp voice:

"Lancey Kennedy. What on earth are you doing mooning out there in the garden at this hour. The coffee pot has boiled over and the toast has burned to a crisp. I declare! The Kennedy in you comes out stronger every day. Whatever do you think you're worth in life, anyway?"

"You sure are some detective, Kid," rang softly Bob Lincoln's voice in her heart as she turned in dismay to go into the house.

"And he thought it would be important, too," she told herself as she entered the kitchen, and came under the dark purple frown of her relative.

CHAPTER V

Quietly Lancey stood under the drenching downpour of words that followed, until there came a piercing question at the end:

"Who was that man that went out of the alley? Didn't I see you talking to him? If you're going to turn out to be *that* kind of a girl you can go! Do you hear? You can *go!* I'll harbor no huzzies in my home, running after every man that comes along!"

Lancey's cheeks burned crimson, and then drained white as a sheet, and her eyes fairly blazed as she faced her angry aunt.

"He was just one of the boys from high school, Aunt Theresa. I scarcely know him at all, but there was nothing unusual in his stopping to say good morning was there? We have been in the same classes every day all last winter."

"My experience is that when that once begins it never stops at good morning. But I just want you to understand that you're not to have hangers-on. I won't stand it."

Lancey's cheeks were very red but she kept her voice steady, and her chin up as she answered:

"Well, you won't be troubled with *him*, Aunt Theresa, I understand he's leaving to-day for Egypt."

"Thank goodness!" said the loving aunt, "and now, eat your breakfast in a hurry. You'll have to take what you can find since you've burned up the toast, for you can't take time to make any more now. You've got to finish putting up that package that has to be returned to New York and hurry it to the station in time for the train. I've told them in the letter that it starts on this same train with the letter, so be quick about it. And while you are there you might as well wait for the local train to come out and bring back those things I ordered sent by baggage master's stamp last night. Can't do a thing till I get that velvet, and Mrs. Treadwell wants her hat this afternoon. Now for mercy's sake don't get to mooning any more. I'm sure I don't know what you'll eat. The bread hasn't come yet and those were the last two slices you burned up."

"I'm sorry," said Lancey cheerfully, a great light of joy coming into her eyes which she could ill restrain, "I'll just take a cracker and hurry. I think this clock is a little slow."

The thing that Lancey desired above all others just now was to go to the station and see Robert Lincoln off to Egypt. Sherrill Washburn had come in yesterday while Aunt Theresa was out for a few minutes and told her all about it, but she had not entertained the possibility of getting off so early in the morning, and she would sooner have bitten her tongue out than explain and ask permission to go. But now the way was free. There would be fifteen whole minutes between those trains and the express would pass the other way just after the local on which her package was due. Nobody knew how much she wanted to be on the platform among the farewell party to see her classmate off, and help in the farewell song. And now the way was most miraculously opened.

She fairly flew up the stairs to get her hat. She tied the package firmly, and addressed it carefully, with hands that trembled with their eagerness and haste, and was soon on her way to the station. The morning seemed to have suddenly become golden.

The bunch were all there on the platform chattering like so many blackbirds when Alan and Bob arrived at the station, and Lancey Kennedy shyly among the rest. No sooner had they sighted Bob than they set up a cheer, led by Phil Mattison,

> "Lincoln! Lincoln! Link! Link! Lincoln!
> Lincoln! Lincoln! Robert of Lincoln!
> Bob O'Link! Bob O'Link!
> Spinck! Spank! Spinck!"

Then Riggs Rathbone, the lad who owned what the others were pleased to call a "whiskey tenor" sprang upon the baggage truck and signing for attention broke forth into a ballad to the tune of "Old Grimes is Dead."

> "Wake up, good Rockland citizens,
> Wake up from your long nap!
> Bob Lincoln's sailing Egypt way
> To put us on the map!
> To put us on the map, my friends,
> Put Rockland on the map!
> Bob Lincoln's sailing Egypt way
> To put us on the map!"

Mid laughter and cheers he began another verse in stentorian tones and everybody hushed to listen, all on a broad grin:

> "Look out King Tutt, your poor old mutt!
> Warn all your mummy friends!
> Bob Lincoln's sailing down their way!
> All secrecy now ends—"

There were eleven verses, each funnier than the last, dealing with phrases such as "buried cities," and "a thousand pities," and ending finally with "he'll broadcast every one."

Every one was in a gale of laughter when the song was done, and then a quiet seemed to fall upon them and they gathered in smaller groups and began to talk. Several came up to Bob and said nice things to him, wished him well, congratulated him on the honor he had won, to be going on such a notable expedition and in such distinguished company.

Robert Lincoln's face was white with astonishment and humble surprise. He was almost embarrassed by everybody's friendliness. It needed only a distant glimpse of his disagreeable brother-in-law driving by on the street just as the crowd set up another cheer, to be fairly overwhelming. He turned his face in embarrassment as the brother looked on in amazement.

> "Lincoln! Lincoln! Rah! rah rah!
> Bob Lincoln! Bob Lincoln!
> *Egypt! Egypt! Egypt!*"

Looking around to find his own confidence, he saw Lancey Kennedy, standing shyly just behind him, with shining eyes and a glow on her face that reminded him of the pink hollyhock near which she had stood an hour ago. He stepped quickly back and stood beside her, stooping to speak to her in a low tone.

"I told Mac," he said guardedly. "He's awfully glad to know about it. He says it makes things a lot plainer. They won't bring your name in. He seemed terribly grateful to you."

Lancey's heart warmed with joy, and her smile gave all the answer that was needed, even without the murmured "I'm glad" that she managed to voice.

Then suddenly there was a stir among the crowd. The train was coming. Far down the track it showed a speck of unfolding black with a plume of gray.

Riggs Rathbone jumped upon the baggage truck again and began to sing, and as every one around took up the words Robert Lincoln stooped over with a sudden impulse, and whispered into Lancey's ear: "Would you mind if I wrote to you sometimes?"

"Oh, that would be wonderful!" murmured Lancey softly.

"Thanks awfully!" said Robert, "that'll mean a lot to me, to have a girl back home!" and he caught her hand in a quick warm clasp and dropped it again before anyone could notice. And then the tide of song swept around them and Lancey with starry eyes joined her voice, singing from her heart:

"God be with you till we meet again—!"

The train was coming faster now. It had just stopped at Millville Junction for a second to take on a passenger at signal, and now it was approaching all too fast:

> "When life's perils thick confound you,
> Put His arms unfailing round you!"

sang Lancey and looked up at Robert with her heart in her eyes.

Then the train was upon them, and everybody tried to say a last good-by at once, and Robert was standing on the platform, a Rockland pennant in his hand that someone had given him, Alan on the step below, and everybody yelling messages in a perfect babel.

The train began to move, and Alan swung off with a quick hand clasp. Robert, waving his pennant, gave them all a swift inclusive smile, and then put his eyes upon little Lancey standing back against the brick station, waving a bit of a pink bordered handkerchief, and smiling through unmistakable tears. Her little pink frock was the last thing he could identify as the train swept him out of sight of the home town, that had never before meant much to him, but had suddenly become wondrously dear.

"I think that was the greatest thing you ever did!" said Sherrill with shining eyes, as Alan put her into his car and drove her back to the Washburn house. "You may do some things greater in your life, but I shall always feel this was the greatest."

"Great?" said Alan, "nothing great about it at all. I was having the time of my life. Sherry, he's a prince! What a fool I was! I wonder who else I'm misunderstanding and misrating. I'm going to get out the list of the people I don't like, and the people I consider my enemies, and see if I can't clean them off the slate. I shouldn't wonder if I find out I'm a pretty mean kind of a cuss, and didn't know enough to know it."

"Alan! Stop it, I say! Oh, it was great! And you did it all! Did you see how happy he looked when they cheered, and how surprised? And Alan, he told me he was going to study the Bible with us. He told me how you had been talking to him."

While they were talking it all over, Lancey in her little faded pink frock, with her heart all happy and sorry, and her face all shining and kind of teary round the lashes, was walking demurely back to the millinery store with her bundle, utterly forgetful of the scolding she would probably receive because she was a minute late from having watched the express out of sight. But for once Lancey wouldn't care.

When Alan left Sherrill at her home and drove back to the hardware store his heart grew suddenly heavy. The affairs of his father's business settled down upon his shoulders like so much lead. There were all the papers of the safe to be checked over, to make sure nothing was gone. How was he to know anyway? Was there a list somewhere? He must find out somehow.

Then there was that Rawlins coming to see him at eleven o'clock, and somehow he felt less prepared to meet him than ever. If he could only take him out and thrash him as he had done the intruder the night before. Perhaps he had already! If the tale that Lancey Kennedy had told to Bob meant anything at all it might mean that. In which case would the man come at all? And would he be able to recognize his opponent of the midnight fray? There was that to investigate of course, and perhaps he should do it at once. He might have to put the police on the matter! He must see Lancey. How the dickens was he to do that, and keep his promise to Bob not to let her aunt see him talking to Lancey? Well, it must be done somehow!

And then there was the mortgage. The real great trouble of all! What should he do next? Oh, if Judge Whiteley would only come home!

Lancey relieved him of one trouble as soon as he arrived at the store by running in for a paper of tacks, and although she seemed in a great hurry she answered all his questions quite clearly, so that when she left he felt fairly sure that Rawlins was his burglar, for Rawlins was boarding at Mrs. Brower's. But what could he have wanted from the safe? And—did he get it or not? If only his father was able to be asked a few questions! But the doctor's orders were very strict. He must not be disturbed for several days yet.

Alan spent an hour going over all the papers he could find, carefully, and only grew more and more perplexed. He tried to think of some friend of his father's that he could ask to come and help him, but he was sure that his reticent father would not have been willing to confide his troubles to anyone but Judge Whiteley, and Judge Whiteley seemed to have disappeared off the face of the earth. He groaned inwardly at the responsibility thrust upon his young shoulders.

At half past ten there came a telegram from the city:

"Was in bad automobile accident yesterday. Am in hospital. My representative will call this afternoon at five, fully empowered to act. This will be your last chance.

RAWLINS."

After Alan had read this twice he put on his hat, went over to the Brower boarding house and asked if he might see a man named Rawlins who was boarding there.

Mrs. Brower seated him in her dismal little parlor and toiled up to the third story back. It was some minutes before she returned bearing an open note in her hand.

"Why, he isn't here. He was called to the city on the early train this morning," she said glancing down at the paper in her hand as if to verify her statement.

"When will he be back?" asked Alan, trying to get a glimpse of the handwriting on the note.

"Well, I can't say fer sure," said the woman, "I guess fer supper. He generally turns up fer meals. He 'lowed he had business here fer another week yet."

Alan thanked her and departed, feeling reasonably sure that he knew his man, yet still uncertain what he ought to do next. If only Judge Whiteley were at home!

The day wore on, the store full most of the time. The story of the burglar was beginning to seep out in spite of Alan's efforts to have it kept quiet. Many people came in to ask questions which made it none the easier, and the hour of five o'clock was drawing on. Rawlin's representative would soon be there! Perhaps he ought to have told the police! He could have confided in Bill Atley. He knew how to keep his mouth shut. But Bill was chief and was on night duty this week. He would be asleep yet! And already it was five minutes after four! In despair he put his head down on the desk and began to pray. Joe had taken a customer down cellar to look over some different sizes of chicken wire, and there was no one else around for the moment. In panic and humiliation he prayed:

"Oh God! I don't know what to do! I can't do this alone! There's no one but you to ask! Won't you help me somehow quick? For Dad's sake, won't you help? For Christ's sake—! I've got to the limit!"

There were hot tears stinging into his eyes and he felt an overwhelming wave like a sob welling up uncontrollably from somewhere, just as if he had been a little kid. He must snap out of this somehow! He was a man!

But suddenly the telephone rang sharply in his ear.

He jumped and found his hand trembling as he reached for the receiver. It was probably that snake of a Rawlins, or his man, and he wasn't ready for him yet! What should he do?

"Hello!" he said weakly. His voice was almost too husky to be heard.

"Hello!" It was Judge Whiteley's voice that boomed over the wire. "Is that you, Alan? This is Whiteley. They tell me at the house you've been trying to get me several times. Is there anything important? Called the house and your mother told me about your father's accident. Anything I can do? I'm mighty sorry about it. I'm at Socker's Point. Came up yesterday to try a case and couldn't get away last night. Thought I better call you."

"Oh, yes!" said Alan eagerly. "Oh, Judge! When can I see you? I'm in an awful hole and I need your advice."

"Can't get back before eleven o'clock Monday. Case is holding over. Would three o'clock Monday suit you all right? I expect I'll have a lot of business to clean up when I get back to the court house."

"Oh—!" began Alan despairingly.

"What's the trouble, Kid, anything you can tell me now? What is it, personal, or business."

"Business!" said Alan choking over the word and wondering what he could tell, what he ought to tell over the phone.

"Business? What's the nature of it?" asked the Judge.

"Somebody's trying to skin Dad out of everything, Judge!"

"You don't say!" said the Judge in a startled tone. "We can't have that, of course. What can I do? Who is it? What is it?"

"It's—quite a story!"

"I see. Too long to tell over the phone?"

"Only a mortgage, and a man who wants his money right away and wants to sell Dad out. I've tried everything that Dad told me, but can't make any of them work, and Dad's too sick to ask now."

"What did your dad suggest?"

"Said to sell some property in the city if I could, but the only price I can get in a rush sale is a crime, and wouldn't be a drop in the bucket."

"I see! What about a new mortgage?"

"That's what Dad thought was a last resort if it could be

done, but two companies I went to in town won't handle it, and I don't know where else to try."

"H'mmm!" said a reflective voice, "well, now that oughtn't to be a hard proposition. How much time have we?"

"Only till Monday," said the boy's tired voice, "and some tough egg is coming around here at five to make some sort of a proposition. I don't know what."

"Well, you just absent yourself, see?" said the kindly voice. "Clear out and don't have a thing to say. Now you let me handle this. I'll phone Charlie Ambler right away to-night and arrange things. You take Charlie the papers—have you got the papers?"

"Oh, sure! Somebody broke into the store last night, and blew open the safe, but I'd taken the papers all home to check."

"You don't say!" said the Judge in a startled tone. "Well, don't worry. You take the papers around to Charlie at the bank the first thing Monday morning, and we'll have it all fixed up. Do you know how much it is?"

"Twelve thousand," said Alan in a worried tone.

"All right, son," said the Judge, "that's only a pint cup of trouble. Don't you worry a minute more. Just get those papers over to Charlie as soon as the bank opens and we'll have that tough egg right where he'll be helpless before he has a chance."

"Oh, thank you," said Alan in a choking voice. "I'm all kinds of grateful. I—"

"There! There! son! That's nothing!" said the cheery voice of the Judge. "Of course I'd look after things. Your father and I were always the best kind of pals. And by the way, better just put Bill Atley wise to that tough egg that's coming. It might save trouble and you can always trust Bill. All right, son! See you Monday. Call me here if you need me before."

Alan hung up the receiver in a daze of astonishment. God had answered! The telephone had rung while he was praying! "Before they call I will answer!" Why it had been made true for him! And he had never taken it as anything but a sort of a figure of speech before! He hadn't really expected an answer when he was praying.

The screen door from the street was suddenly swung open and went shut on its patent hinges with business-like precision, and Alan remembered it was nearly five o'clock. He looked up with sudden panic, and there stood Bill Atley!

Was God sending all the answers at once? A humble feeling of joy and relief filled his heart.

"Just stepped in to see if you found anything more wrong, Kid!" said Bill giving a quick glance around at the safe and desk. "Find all your papers?"

Alan sprang to his feet and drew the officer in behind the desk beginning to talk in quick low tones. He told what Lancey had seen, and of his visit to Mrs. Brower, showed the telegram and gave a brief explanation about the mortgage, and what had happened.

Bill's enigmatical face continued unchanged during the recital. Only his bright keen eyes studied the other's face, and he nodded intelligently as the story went on.

"Judge Whiteley is fixing up the mortgage all right. I'm going to pay off the other," finished Alan, finding great relief in saying the words, his voice ringing with a soft triumph, "but I thought maybe you'd like to look over this guy that's coming—if he comes!"

"I sure would!" said Bill dryly. "Suppose you just beat it out the back way, Kid, and leave me in charge. Anybody else here? Joe? All right. Let him stay. He can look after the customers. Where is he? All right! I'll give him his orders. You beat it! Don't go to your house, the guy might chase ya and try to annoy ya. I'll tell ya. Go down and see that Washburn girl ya had out riding this morning. Nothing like a lady ta make a good getaway behind. I'll call ya there if I need ya. All righty now, run along."

Something in Bill's kindly tone stung Alan. He turned with a flash of fraternity in his eyes.

"Cut it, Bill! I'm no quitter! I'll stay here and face it out. I just thought you might like to look him over for future reference if he came."

"I sure would!" said Bill fervently, "but I mean what I say! *I'll* handle this! What you don't say can't do any harm, see? I'd like to get this guy unaware. You're no quitter of course, but in this case it's better to get outta sight, see? We may need this lad's finger prints. Remember we've had a burglary last night. The fact that he didn't get away with much doesn't cut any ice. We wantta catch that bird, and keep an eye on him, and we can keep him less suspicious with you outta the way. Beat it Kid. Them's orders!"

He slapped Alan on the back with a brotherly grin, and he could make no further protest.

Alan went out the back door of the store and walked slowly across the back lots, and through the meadow till he came to Washburn's back fence which he vaulted. Sherrill was out in the garden picking red raspberries, and he joined her and began to help.

"Sherry, I've just had such a marvelous answer to prayer that it's knocked me silly!" he said as he stooped to pull off the coral globules and drop them into the china bowl she had given him.

Sherrill turned shining eyes upon him and began to laugh.

"Is that all the faith you had, Alan?" she asked. "It's knocked you silly! Then why did you pray if you didn't have any faith?"

"I don't know!" said Alan sheepishly, "I was desperate. I'd reached the limit."

"I read a little book the other day that said that God has sometimes to bring us to the limit before He can get us to come to Him at all."

"Well, I guess that's right," said the boy humbly, "I was just proud of the way I was going to handle my father's business all alone. And then when there came along something I couldn't manage, and didn't know a thing to do, I was all up a tree. I didn't think of praying till I got in a hole. I thought I could manage everything myself. I had no end of schemes for it, till they all failed flat. Then, when I prayed, the telephone rang the answer right in my ear so I jumped, and several minor answers walked right into the store afterwards. I mean it, Sherry! I'm astonished! I didn't know answers to prayer ever came right off the bat like that."

"I think," said Sherrill wisely, shaking her bowl to get more berries into it, "that God would probably give us answers like that every day if we lived close enough to Him so He could. Why, most of the time I imagine we wouldn't even hear the answers if He gave them we keep so far away and so full of ourselves. But Alan—" her voice was soft, almost shy, "I have a feeling that God is opening up big things for you. I think you are growing a lot. I think he is leading you, getting you ready for some great work for Him, some place of power and influence for the Kingdom."

"Looks like it," said Alan almost glumly, remembering suddenly, "leaving me here in this little hole of a town in a hardware store! Fat chance I've got to get ready for anything! I've got to stick here and work. I've got to keep my dad's business from going to pieces while he is laid by."

"Well," said Sherrill confidently, "I know better than that. It's reached a long way beyond that already. It's doing a lot in this town right now. What you've done for Bob Lincoln has made a lot of people see what Christ can do in a human life to change the natural man's hates and enmities. The boys all feel that. I've heard some of them talking. And then, Alan, your influence is going to reach away out to the desert in Egypt. It's traveling there now just as fast as ship can take it. I shouldn't wonder if you would find it would be even stronger for the kingdom than if you had gone yourself. I saw a look in Bob's eyes when he told me how you prayed with him, that made me sure he's going to live up to what he promised."

"Sherry!" said Alan, "you make me feel ashamed! Here I've been pitying myself because I couldn't do a thing, and you talk like that! Say, Sherry, I wish you'd pray for me. I've got some big problems to face and I'm just finding out what a fool I am."

"I have been praying," said Sherrill softly, "I've prayed all the morning."

"H'm!" said Alan thoughtfully, "so that's why that answer came so quick! I thought it couldn't be just my prayers! 'Where two of you shall agree—' But we didn't even agree! Sherry, it was wonderful! I can't get over it yet!"

"For shame, Alan! You've just the same promises to go on that I have, or anybody else, and you've just the same God—!"

The telephone was ringing wildly in the house, and Sherrill ran in to answer it, for her mother was out and her grandmother was taking a nap.

Alan picked away at the berries thoughtfully, and in a moment Sherrill called him from the door.

"It's you they want, Alan!" she called.

Alan went in and heard Bill's voice:

"It's all over, Mac," he said, "all but the shoutin'. Very obliging guy he was, Mac, tough as they make 'em, but he gave me some nice clean finger prints in a convenient place—course he wasn't aware he was doing it—and his autograph on a note to you, together with a telephone number where he said you could call the Rawlins bird.

"Course, you see, I'd had Joe tell him you wouldn't treat with nobody but Rawlins hisself, see? You'd left that word, you know. And then I give him the p'lice headquarters private wire number where he could call you, see? Told him it was a private wire if he wanted to get you direct. But when he calls, if that bird has the nerve to call, he'll talk with me, see? We've gotta sift this matter, and I guess we've got some good dope now. I'm getting a man I know in the city force, and putting him wise also, so if there's any more funny business we'll know how to act."

Alan stayed to supper at Washburn's, and helped eat some of the red raspberries with cream and angel cake, and other good things, and afterwards they sat in the hammock and talked more about prayer and how it changes things: about the young people in their church group and whom they would pray for.

"I wonder," said Alan as he took his leave finally, "if we were meant to live this way every day, praying for things and expecting them? And getting them in startling ways sometimes."

"Of course," said Sherill, "and *not* getting them sometimes when God sees it's not best. I heard a dear wonderful man from Germany who talked at our Bible Conference this spring say that God had different ways of answering prayer. He said the very lowest answer was 'Yes,' that a higher answer was 'Wait' and God gave it to those who could trust Him more. He said that sometimes to those who could trust Him most He could give the answer of 'No.' "

Alan looked down at her wonderingly, and was silent a moment.

"Sherry, that's not why He said No to me about going to the desert. I've never trusted Him like that," he said slowly. "But I'd like to. It would be a wonderful way of living."

"I think He's going to trust you that way, Alan, from now on. I'm sure He had some beautiful, wonderful reason for keeping you home from the desert."

CHAPTER VI

Sherrill Washburn turned from the door with her hands full of letters that the postman had just brought and shuffled them deftly over.

One for Grandma Sherrill with the address of her weekly religious paper in the upper left hand corner. That would be the yearly reminder that the subscription was due.

Two for Mother, the square one from Cousin Euphrasia who was a shut-in and depended on Mother for her personal touch with the outside world. The long one would be an acknowledgment of the yearly report that Mother as secretary of the Church Missionary Society had recently sent in.

A sheaf of receipted bills, a letter from a far Western investment that had practically become valueless, yet from time to time gave out gasping hope that it might revive and still be worth paying its taxes. How well each of the often recurring letters were known in the family life! How Sherrill longed for something new and exciting, just as she had longed for the last five years ever since she had begun to grow up and be impatient for real living to begin.

This time however there were two other letters at the bottom of the heap, both with a New York postmark. Sherrill hastened her step out of the darkness of the hall, back into the living room where her mother and grandmother sat sewing.

"Two real letters at last," she announced gayly to her mother, "one for you and one for me, and I believe mine is from Uncle West. What in the world do you suppose he is writing to me for? It isn't my birthday or Christmas and he never writes except to send me a check to buy my present."

"Read it and see," said Grandmother Sherrill hungrily. She had already opened her meager communication and laid it in her work basket disappointedly. There was another grandchild living out in the world who might have written to her. She was always hoping, although she had long ago begun to realize that modern youth has little time for grandmothers.

The room was very still for a minute or two while mother and daughter read their letters. There was no sound but the snip of Grandmother's scissors as she clipped off the thread from the napkins she was making out of a much worn table cloth.

Sherrill finished first and looked up watching her mother's face as she carefully turned her own letter back to the beginning and read it over.

"Well?" she asked at last as her mother completed the last page for the second time and folded the letter in her lap, looking up, "did you get one too? Of course I can't go, but what on earth do you suppose made him think of it? Who wrote yours? Not Uncle Weston, for I know his writing. You don't mean to tell me that Aunt Eloise has broken the silence of years at last?"

The mother came back as from some sudden perplexity and turned her eyes on Sherrill.

"Really, dear, you ought not to speak that way of your aunt," she reproved. "This letter is quite—well—kind, I think, and after all we may have misjudged her. You know we don't really know her at all."

"Well, what is it all about, anyway?" asked Grandmother Sherrill impatiently. "Read out your letter, Sherrill. There is little enough to break the monotony."

"Yes, read your letter," said the mother with a smile. "Is it from your uncle?"

Sherrill read her letter:

My dear Niece:

Your aunt and I want you to come and spend a few months in the city with us this winter. We think it is time that you and your cousin got acquainted, and had some good times together.

We expect to be back from the shore early in November and shall expect you as soon as you can make your arrangements to come on. Your aunt is writing your mother so I will not go into details, for she will tell you all you need to know. I am enclosing my check to cover railroad expenses, and hope that we shall be able to give you a good time.

Affectionately your Uncle,
Weston Washburn.

Sherrill crumpled the paper briskly in her fingers and looked up.

"Now read yours," she said, "or rather, let me read it. For I'm morally certain you'll leave out something or soften it down somehow, and I think I have a right to know the whole inwardness of this matter even if it does show up that aunt of mine in a bad light."

Laughingly she took possession of the other letter and began to read, while her mother, half smiling, half troubled sat back in her chair and listened.

Dear Mary:

Weston thinks we ought to do something for Sherrill so I am writing to say that she is invited to spend the winter with us and see a little of New York life. You do not need to trouble about getting her any new clothes, for Carol has plenty of things she isn't using any more that can be altered by my maid, and anyway you wouldn't know what to get.

We expect to be back in New York on the eighteenth of November at the latest and you can arrange for her to come to

us at once. I am sure a winter in New York will be a great
advantage to her and if she is clever at all she may be able to
make valuable acquaintances and a good marriage.

As ever,
ELOISE.

There was something mocking and sharp in Sherrill's voice
as she finished reading the letter and folded it elaborately,
putting it back into its envelope.

"Won't that be *nice?*" she mocked. "Mother wouldn't you
just *love* my making a good marriage? Lots of money, I
suppose, and family, and all that! Anything that would lift
this family out of obscurity and place it where it would not be
a disgrace to her highness—"

"Sherrill! Don't!" said her mother sharply. "You really
mustn't make fun of your aunt. Especially if you are going to
accept her hospitality!"

"Her hospitality! My eye! You don't for a minute suppose
that it's going to be *her* hospitality, do you? I'll wager Uncle
West had to lay down the law like a tyrant before he ever got
all that letter out of her. But what do you suppose he did it
for? Why did he want to do it?"

"My dear, he was your father's twin brother. He was very
much attached to him."

"Then why didn't he come across with something after
Daddy died? When Keith was struggling to keep the business
together, and couldn't get security why did he hedge out of
everything?"

There was an almost bitter edge to Sherrill's tone.

"I—don't know—" answered Sherrill's mother with a
clouding of her sweet serious eyes, "I have always thought
—your aunt was a great expense just then. She had to have an
operation, and she was used to everything that money could
buy—and—well I suppose he wasn't as well off at that time as
he is now, and I think he likely wants to make up for it."

"You don't mean you want me *to go!*" demanded Sherrill
almost haughtily.

"Well, of course you haven't had as many advantages as if
your father had lived," said Sherrill's mother wistfully. "I've
always wanted you to get out in the world a little. I had
expected of course that you would be able to go to college,
just as your brother did."

"Well," said Sherrill a trifle bitterly, "New York isn't
college. I'm sure I don't see just what I should get out of a

winter in New York, especially as I don't care for the clever marriage that Aunt Eloise expects me to pull off."

Grandmother broke into the silence that followed in a tone of amused soliloquy:

" 'As ever,' " she murmured with a musical little chuckle, " 'As ever Eloise.' She needn't have said that. We know she's just what she always was. Yes, she'll never change. She'll always be Eloise. Wanting to dominate everything and everybody. Wanting John Washburn's child to wear Carol's old cast offs! As if Sherrill wasn't every bit as good as her Carol. As if the Sherrill's weren't the finest old family anywhere around this neighborhood! And who was she to set up to snub them? She, the daughter of a corner groceryman."

"Oh, Mother, you mustn't put such ideas into Sherrill's head. It will be hard enough for her anyway, if she goes—"

"*If* she goes!" snorted Grandmother Sherrill. "You don't mean to say, Mary Sherrill, that you mean to let her *go?* Let her be a target for that selfish pig-eyed woman to shoot at; let her be a background for that precious little flapper of a barelegged Carol! You know what Rebecca Harlow said when she got back from the shore last week. She said she didn't wear a stocking, just sandals all around the streets, and her bathing suit was scandalous."

"Mother! Don't! I haven't said Sherrill was to go, have I? Sherrill is the one to decide. She is the one who received the invitation, and she is old enough to settle it herself. She certainly wouldn't have to go without stockings because her younger cousin does. I'm not at all sure what Sherrill ought to do. I somehow feel that perhaps her father would have wanted her to go. After all, Weston is her uncle, and she does owe something to her father's family."

"And you would let her go and wear cast off clothes and be on charity?"

"Certainly not!" said Mrs. Washburn rising, and going toward the sewing machine. "If Sherrill goes she will be able somehow to get the right clothes to wear. We have always been decently clothed."

"Humph!" sneered the grandmother with elderly wisdom, "I guess you'll find out Eloise Washburn won't care for the clothes you make. She says as much in that letter. She doesn't want you to bring anything! She says you wouldn't know what was suitable."

That was the beginning of a whole week's discussion.

When Keith Washburn came home and was told the news, and read the two letters, he said with a sensible, elder brother's far sightedness:

"Well, I think she ought to go. If for nothing else than to show her aunt and cousin—yes, and uncle too—that New York isn't the last word in decency, and culture and education. My sister can hold her own anywhere, if she wants to, and I'd like Uncle West to know it. As for Aunt Eloise and Carol, why bother about them? They're only human beings, and can't really do much. Sherrill needn't have much to do with them if she finds them unpleasant. She'll make her own place in the household and she can surely get on with anybody for six months. I'd like her to be in New York and hear some good concerts and lectures, and meet some nice people, and see the sights. It's an education, a visit like that, even if your relatives aren't all that you wish they were. Uncle Weston seems to be asking in good faith, why not accept in the same way, and try it out, at least? If things aren't pleasant you can always come home, but it is foolish to turn it down flat; and besides I don't think Dad would have liked it. He always thought a lot of his brother and wanted us to overlook Aunt Eloise's snubbing for his sake. Really, Sherry, I'm glad you got this invitation. I've been hoping to get on my feet before long so that I might send you somewhere to get a little glimpse into another kind of life. But it doesn't look as if I'd be able to do it for two or three more years yet, so I hope you see your way clear to take this, now that it has come, and get what you can out of it till I can do better for you."

Sherrill gave her brother a warm look of gratitude:

"You're not to plan to do things like that for me, Pard," she said with a caress in her voice, "I'm not a baby, and I don't need advantages. I'd rather have home and Mother and all of you, than go to a thousand New Yorks."

So day after day the discussion went on, the mother and brother always urging Sherrill to accept the invitation, Sherrill hesitant and wistful, but still holding back; and the little frail Grandmother openly against it.

At last it became necessary to make some definite reply to the invitation for they could not let it go any longer unnoticed.

In desperation, Sherrill rushed to her room one day and came down with a neatly written note: which she handed to her mother to read—

"DEAR UNCLE WESTON:" (it read,)

"I want to thank you for your kind invitation to visit you, but after thinking the matter over carefully I do not feel that I can spare the time to be away this winter. I am taking a position in the bank here and my work begins next week. It was most kind of you and Aunt Eloise to want to help me to better advantages, but I feel that I must make my own way in the world.

Again thanking you, I am

Your affectionate niece,

SHERRILL WASHBURN."

"Oh, Sherrill," said her mother disappointedly, "that won't do at all. That sounds almost rude, that about wanting to make your own way. And after all he is your uncle—"

They were interrupted at that moment by a ring of the door bell followed by the entrance, without further ceremony, of Mrs. Harriet Masters, an old school friend of Mary Washburn's who often spent part of her summers in Rockland, but who had been traveling abroad for the past two years, and had therefore not seen them for some time.

After the greetings were over and Harriet Masters had exclaimed over how Sherrill had grown, and how beautiful she was, and how much better looking she was than a lot of the girls she had seen on the continent, she asked suddenly:

"What was the discussion when I came in, Mary? You were all looking so serious I'm sure it must have been of great importance. Do tell me all about it, and let me get back into touch with the family affairs as soon as possible, for I'm terribly jealous of all that has happened since I went away."

Sherrill's face clouded over, and she half turned away with a sigh. Now it would have to be all gone over again, and she had thought it was settled! Deep down in her heart she began to wonder whether after all she didn't want to go to New York in spite of all the drawbacks. Was her hesitation born of a desire for the new experience?

"Why, it was just that Sherrill has been invited to go to New York for the winter to visit her uncle's family," began Sherrill's mother. "She has just written to decline the invitation. I feel worried lest she will be sorry some day that she did not take this chance for change and seeing the world."

"Why don't you want to go, Sherrill?" asked the visitor, searching the girl's face keenly, with the privileged eyes of a friend of long years' standing.

"Well," said Sherrill, lifting honest eyes, "I don't like my aunt and I don't like my cousin, and I don't like what I know

about her. Also I'm not sure but she is right when she says
that I wouldn't know what clothes to get if I should try to get
them. *Of course I* wouldn't wear her things, nor let them get
me anything. I could make my own if I was sure I could
make them right. The things I would need in the life they live
of course are not what I would need in Rockland. Oh I guess,
Aunt Harry, it's just pride."

"I see," said the older woman. "Well, Sherry, you're too
fine a girl to let that stand in the way of a real visit that would
surely have advantages, even though it had some unpleasantness about it. Let's see if we can't do something about those
things that stand in your way. You don't like your aunt, but
perhaps you would like her better if you knew her better. At
least give her the chance to try, and take it all in good faith.
Your cousin is only a kid, isn't she? You ought to be able to
help her, and not be bothered by her. Be fine enough yourself
so that nothing unpleasant they can do will touch you. You
know I have heard of a little white flower that grows down on
the edge of coal mines, and is so white and fine like velvet
that it stands out in terrible contrast to the sooty blackness all
about it. You'd think it would get soiled and spoiled by the
soot, but they say it is protected by some substance that will
not hold the soil. The dirt rolls off, and does not stick. And
you, little girl, have always seemed to me to be somehow
surrounded by your mother's religion and your mother's love
in just such a way. What harm can any snobbishness do you
if you live above it?"

"Yes, I know," said Sherrill, "I've tried to think that
way—but—that doesn't solve the clothes problem."

"Oh, well," said the guest, "I can help you to solve that.
I've a whole trunk full of clothes that I just bought in Paris,
and you're welcome to copy every one of them with varia-
tions suitable to your age. Come over tomorrow morning with
your tape measure and your thimble and let's begin. It will
give me a new interest in life. And by the way, I brought you
a present of an evening dress. I wasn't sure whether you
would have much use for it in this quiet little place, but it just
looked like what I thought you would be by this time, and I
had to buy it. Don't look troubled, Mary, it isn't extreme in
its style, it's modest and simple and will just suit Sherrill. It's
quite conservative and has little puffs of sleeves even, the very
latest thing in evening gowns and the back is not low-cut
either, but not even an unliked Aunt could disapprove of it
for I bought it at one of the great exclusive places in Paris

noted for its lovely lines and styles and there is a little duck of an evening wrap goes with it. Wait till you see it. Now, that's settled, what next?"

Grandmother Sherrill gave a sigh of satisfaction. Nobody had ever suspected her of caring for grand clothes, but in her heart she had greatly coveted something really fine and lovely for the treasure of her heart, her jewel of a grandchild. Yes, and if she had one besetting sin it was pride of family, and she had cherished a secret desire for long years, that in some way the Sherrill side of the house might be able to outshine unquestionably, the unpleasant aunt, daughter of a corner groceryman, who had married into the Washburn side of the house and alienated the delightful uncle from the entire family.

"Where's a pencil and paper?" said the energetic visitor, fumbling in her hand bag and bringing out a mite of a gold pencil and a little writing pad done up in blue leather. "We'd better get to work. You'll need, let me see—" and she began to scribble down items, "Sports things, evening things, informal afternoon—"

"Oh, Aunt Harry!" said Sherrill looking over her shoulder, "don't write down all that! It's perfectly appalling! I couldn't get all those things! It's silly anyway! Why if I stayed here in Rockland I'd wear the same dress all day, and maybe have an extra one to slip on evenings if there was company or a church social, or the Home and School, if I had to play—! Why should I go to spend a winter in a place where you have to pay so much attention to clothes?"

"Nonsense!" said Harriet Masters, "clothes will never do you any harm if you don't lose your proper sense of values. Everybody should be decently, and sweetly and properly clothed. Beautifully, too. No, don't misunderstand me, I don't mean expensively. I insist that people can look lovely in very cheap raiment if it is properly chosen, properly made, and a reasonable amount of attention given to putting it on to the best advantage. Of course, some occasions demand more careful dressing than others. I should say this was one of them. Your own quiet life would need only simple little frocks and perhaps a silk for best, but your aunt's standards are different, and if you are to be a guest in her house you must conform to some extent to her standards. Please notice, I only said 'to some extent.' There is no reason why you should go to extremes even to please an unliked aunt who may be disagreeable about it. I certainly would not have you

lower any of your standards for her. For instance, bare
backs! I couldn't think of you, Sherrill, in one of those
abominable ugly modern backs!"

"Oh, I'm so glad you still feel that way, Harriet," said
Sherrill's mother giving her old friend an adoring glance, "I
was so afraid that two years in Europe might have changed
your standards."

"Well, I like that, Mary! Is that all the faith you had in my
principles?"

"Oh, Harriet, you don't know how upside down the world
is getting even around here. Why Mrs. Rutherford Barnes
gave a party the other day and passed cigarettes, and they say
that even Alvira Edgars smoked. Everybody smoked except
Nettie Halloway, and she got up quickly and asked to be
excused because her baby wasn't well!"

"H'm! I always knew Nettie Halloway hadn't enough
backbone, didn't you?"

They were all laughing now, and Sherrill crinkled her nose
and laughed with the rest, then sobered quickly as her
problem settled down upon her heavily again, filling her with
a strange new excitement, mingled with a kind of moral
alarm.

"Take that somber look out of your eyes, Sherrill," demanded the guest, "you look as if you were going to the stake
instead of New York. Haven't I solved all your problems for
you?"

Sherrill smiled with a troubled wistfulness.

"You've helped a lot, Aunt Harry! It was wonderful of you
to bring me a real evening dress and wrap from Paris! I can't
believe they are going to be mine! I don't believe I had sense
enough to thank you."

"Well, wait till you see them. You may not like them. In
which case I suppose I'll have to give them to Maria Hodgkins."

Maria Hodgkins was a fat and faithful servitor of most
uncertain age, in the boarding house where Harriet Masters
always stayed, and the vision of Maria in evening dress
brought peals of laughter from them all, even Grandma
joining in.

The guest did not stay long. She had only just arrived and
her trunk had not yet been sent up, so there had been no
opportunity to unpack and settle.

"Well, I must run along back," she said arising suddenly,
"old Ephraim promised to have the trunks up inside of an

hour, and I'll have all I can do to get settled by night. But Sherrill, you run over the first thing in the morning and we'll go through my things and pick out some models for you to copy."

CHAPTER VII

"Yes, but what am I going to copy them in?" said Sherrill in a puzzled tone as she turned away from watching the guest down the walk. "It costs money, Mother, to buy materials, and I don't intend to have you and Grandmother and Keith going without things while I loaf off to the city and play millionaire."

"Oh, don't worry about that!" said Mrs. Washburn happily, "we'll manage somehow to get what you need without scrimping anybody. We always have. Now take that cloud away from your brow, Sherrill, and sing a little. I've missed your voice for a whole week, ever since your uncle's letter came. That's no way to start on a vacation. Don't you want to go? Don't you really *want* to go, child?"

"Why, yes, I suppose I do," hesitated Sherrill, "if I could go right. I'd like to see New York, and just get an idea of how our relatives live. But I can't help feeling it's not going to be congenial."

"Well, even if it isn't it will be a good experience for you. Take it as a part of your discipline of life then and make the most of it. Now, run away upstairs and get out your old things. Let's see what we've got to go on before we plan for new things. You ought to have at least one or two things that could be made over for every day. We always have bought more goods than we needed with that in mind you know. There's that green crepe with the satin back. There's a full yard and a half left of that. I'm sure that would work up into a nice little dress."

"Why yes, of course," said Sherrill looking up brightly, "I'm sure it will, and maybe the brown satin, too. I'll go and see."

"Why don't you go up attic and look in my mother's trunk?" said Grandma. "You might find some goods there. You know when your great grandmother was young they wore skirts with nine breadths in them. That ought to make one of the little skimpy makeshifts they wear now. I remember there was a real handsome brocade, gold and silver and pink rosebuds in it. It might be tarnished, I don't know. Here, I'll get the key and you go look. It's the little haircloth trunk under the eaves."

"Oh, Grandmother! You wouldn't want me to cut up great grandmother's wonderful brocade!"

"Why not?" said Grandmother Sherrill proudly, "she can't wear it any more and I'm certain I shan't! You know you'd never be seen in it the way it is now and if we wait till it comes round in fashion again we'll all be gone. I don't see making a museum of the attic. Nobody ever goes up there! If it can be of any use to you now why consider it Great Grandmother Sherrill's contribution. It goes with the name, don't you see?"

Sherrill considered this breathtaking suggestion a moment.

"But perhaps it isn't good enough!" said Grandmother Sherrill. "Perhaps they'd make fun of it in New York. Don't, for pity's sake, take it if you don't want it."

"Oh, I think it will be wonderful!" said Sherrill. "I think it is a good deal like that wonderful metal blouse Margery brought home from Chicago with her, only ten times more lovely. I'll ask Aunt Harry. She'll know."

"Yes, ask her!" said Grandmother Sherrill. "Don't get any white ancestral elephants on your hands, for pity's sake."

So Sherrill went up in the attic and came down with her arms full of quaint garments, satins, and brocades, and one fine rose pink taffeta, soft and lovely as the dew on a rose, with a big bertha of fine old lace yellowed with age. There were kerchiefs and undersleeves of old hand embroidery, sweet with lavender,—a few lovely hand wrought collars, and several yards of real valenciennes, on undergarments of an antique cut.

"They're wonderful!" said Sherrill with her eyes shining, "if you really think I ought to use them!"

"Of course you'll use them!" said Grandma Sherrill, fingering the silk, and giving the lace a firm little tug to see if it was rotten.

Then Sherrill went upstairs to the second floor and foraged out some of her own last winter's dresses, with bundles of pieces like them and brought those down. The sitting room looked as if it were ready to ride out.

Mother came to examine, unrolled the pieces, rejecting some and laying others aside for possible use.

By the time Keith came home the excitement was on.

"Well, she's going!" announced Grandmother with a twinkle.

"That's the girl! I knew she would!" said the elder brother. "What's all this, you aren't packing already!" he asked as he looked around on the laden chairs and couch.

They all tried to explain at once how much they had found that could be used and made over without purchasing new frocks, and how generous Aunt Harry had been.

Keith went around genially, looking at everything they showed him, and beaming on them all, and presently he went up to his room and came down in a few minutes with a check.

"There's a starter," he said, "I'll be able to give you more later, Kid. But that'll buy a few shoes and things. You can't make over shoes."

The check was for a hundred dollars and Sherrill knew that meant that Keith would wait that much longer for the car he was hoping to purchase soon, which he really needed in his business. She flung her arms around his neck and nearly strangled him.

"Oh, Keith," she cried, with tears in her eyes, "I feel like a pig, going away from all you dear dear people, and taking everything you've got with me! I don't need all this, really I don't, Buddy!"

"That! Why that's not much! That's only a drop in the bucket. Wait till I get rich! You'll see what I'll do for you then!"

"Well, wait till I make this clever marriage Aunt Eloise is planning for me to pull off!" laughed Sherrill, "then I'll be off your hands and you can roll in wealth!"

He caught her and gave her a great bear hug.

"If I thought you'd do that, Kid, I wouldn't let you go!" he said in mock seriousness. "I don't want any New York brother-in-laws. I want a real one from the country."

So they joked and laughed, and kidded one another, but all knew that the tears were very near the surface, because each felt that even a temporary break like this in the family was going to be a trial. They were a family closely knit together in love for one another, especially since the death of the beloved father, and kept closer than ever to one another.

Nobody felt much like eating that night when they all sat down to the evening meal, and they lingered so long over it that Alan MacFarlan came after Sherrill to go to the Young People's Church Social before she had even started to get ready to go.

"What's all the excitement?" he asked looking around on the group that next to his own family had been his closest familiars through childhood.

"Why, Sherrill's going to New York!" announced Grandma, with keen, kind, quick eyes searching the fervid young face before her. Grandma liked to tell the news and then watch the result and reaction.

"Going to New York!" echoed Alan blankly, and then Sherrill looked up and realized that here was another unknown quantity to be reckoned with. Next to Keith, Alan had been Sherrill's closest comrade and pal. "What are you going to New York for, Sherrill?"

"To make a clever marriage!" announced Sherrill wickedly, "at least that is what my unbeloved aunt is expecting me to pull off."

Alan had a stricken look.

"Why, you're only a kid, Sherrill Washburn!"

"I'm nineteen!" said Sherrill lightly. "It has been done even younger than that you know," she babbled giddily, trying to hide the pleasure in her own heart that Alan looked so miserable.

"That's all right, Alan," chimed in Keith with a twinkle, "if we don't like her choice we'll wring his neck, won't we, Kid?"

Alan tried to grin, but the stricken look remained, and he said little, though his tongue was usually glib enough with repartee and nonsense.

"No kidding. Is that straight?" he said looking at Keith.

"The straight of it is that Sherrill has had an invitation to spend the winter with her uncle in New York and we think she ought to go," answered the elder brother firmly. "It's an opportunity of course and she ought not to miss it. Don't you think that's right, Alan?"

"Sure, s'pose it is," said Alan gamely, "but meanwhile, what's to become of the young people's society and all the plans for the winter without our new president I'd like to know?"

And now the stricken look appeared on Sherrill's face, for the work they had planned to do was very dear to her heart also.

"It's probably your opportunity to take her place, Kid," said Keith. "You're first vice president, aren't you? Besides, the winter won't last forever."

"It's certain it'll never come this way again," grinned Alan, "not this one anyhow. But of course we don't want to stand in Sherry's way if she wants to go out among 'em."

"Well, she's not so keen on it, son, as she ought to be," said Keith with a warning glance at the boy, "it's up to you to encourage her, See?"

So Alan set his lips firmly.

"I see," said Alan, "make me the goat, you mean? All right, I'll think it over. All set, Sherry?"

"All set, Alan!"

"He's going to feel her going," said Grandma when they were gone.

"Nonsense! Mother! You're always so romantic. They are just good friends. They are only children yet you know."

"Well, he's a nice *child*, anyway," said Grandma with a speck of a sigh. "She won't find many in the city cleverer than he is either."

"He's been a very pleasant comrade," said her daughter firmly. "I hope Sherrill won't think of anything deeper than that for some time to come. But of course Alan is a good boy."

"Yes, Alan's all right!" said Keith rising to go back to his office for the evening, "but don't worry about him, Grand. Alan won't waste away for one winter of separation. His head is set on straight and he's the right stuff. It won't do him a bit of harm to be a little lonely for once. Well, good night, don't sit up too late thinking up frills for Sherrill. I'm glad she's going, for it's just something she needed. It isn't right for her to grow up knowing just Rockland."

Out in the moonlight Alan and Sherrill were walking along together talking about the committee they were both on, and the plans for the evening.

Suddenly a silence fell upon them, and then Alan broke it with a queer, troubled sound to his voice.

"Say, Sherry, what's all this swell marriage you're talking about? What's the idea?"

Sherrill laughed.

"Oh, that's a joke. Didn't Keith tell you?"

"You heard all he told me," said Alan gravely.

"For pity's sake, don't take it seriously, Alan," chided Sherrill, "it's only fun. It was that aunt of mine, the one I don't like, Aunt Eloise. She is always saying something disagreeable. She wrote that if I was clever I might make a good marriage while I was up there. Get me off the family hands, you know, and all that." Sherrill laughed, "Imagine me!"

But Alan did not laugh.

"Well," he said glumly, "it's what's to be expected, of course, when you go away like that for a whole winter."

"Alan MacFarlan!" said Sherrill stopping short on the sidewalk, "if you talk like that I'm going straight back home! I never expected *you* to speak *that way!* I thought you were my friend and understood me. I thought you had a sense of humor!"

There were almost tears in Sherrill's eyes.

Alan put out a hand gravely and just touched the tip of Sherrill's elbow protectingly, as if he were years older than she, though in fact he was but seven months older.

"There's usually some kind of truth behind all jokes," he said seriously. "I just didn't like the idea, that's all. It means—well—sort of the end—you know."

"The end of what?" Sherrill asked sharply.

"Well, the end of this. Sherrill, you know we've been friends for a long time."

Sherrill stopped again and whirled toward him, half indignant, half amused.

"Now, look here, Alan! You've simply got to stop this ridiculous nonsense," she said earnestly. "I never saw you act so foolish in all my life. I thought you had more sense. Why, Alan MacFarlan, I'm just a kid yet. You said so yourself only a few minutes ago. I haven't an idea of getting married for ages yet."

"Corinne Arliss was only sixteen when she was married."

"Well, I like that! If you want to class me with Corinne Arliss I'm done. Do you think my mother brought me up to run away just out of the cradle with a lazy sporty boy like Sam Howe?"

"Well, you needn't get angry with me, Sherry," said the boy disconsolately, "it's only that it sort of seems like the end of things to have you go away like this for a whole winter, and just when we'd planned all these things—! And then to have you talk about making a clever match—it seems as if you'd suddenly grown up—that's all!"

"You make me very cross!" said Sherrill. "For just one word more I'll stay at home! Do you think I *want* to go away?

I've been holding off for a week saying I wouldn't go, till the family made such a fuss I had to give in. Keith was the worst. He thinks my father would have wanted me to go. My uncle is his only brother you know and they were very close to one another. Besides, Keith thinks I owe it to Father to go."

"I suppose you do," said Alan gloomily. "Forget it, Sherry! I'm an old grouch. Of course you must go, only it's going to be tough sledding without you."

"Oh, well," said Sherrill cheerfully, "a winter won't take long to pass. It will be like the time you went to Canada with your father. It didn't last forever you know, although it did seem pretty long while it was going on, I'll admit."

"All right!" said Alan with a deep breath, trying to put on a cheery atmosphere, "here goes! I'm game. But what are we going to do for a president for our society?"

"Not anything!" said Sherrill, "I'm not moving away. I expect to return before the year is up. A winter is over in the spring you remember, and if you ask me I'll tell you it'll be a remarkably early spring this year if I have anything to say about it."

"But what do you mean? We can't get along all winter without some head, can we?"

"Well, aren't you vice president? Isn't that what a vice president is for, to take the place of president? You are dumb, Alan, my dear! Come to think of it that is just one more reason why I should go, to give you your rightful place in this society. You wouldn't take the office of president though it has been offered you three times to my certain knowledge, so now you are having it thrust upon you."

She flung a triumphant smile at him through the darkness, and Alan grinned back.

"I only said no because I wanted you to be president," he growled.

"Didn't I know it, Alan MacFarlan! Serves you right then. You're a peach, of course, but you're like an open book to me. And, of course, you know that the only reason I consented was because I could make you tell me how to run things right, so your everlasting modesty wouldn't seal your mouth and keep the society from having the benefit of your wisdom."

"Bologny!" said Alan in a more light-hearted tone.

"No bologny about it!" said Sherrill. "Those are facts. Just wait till I tell the society what they are to do and expect."

"Say, look here, Sherrill, don't you go to putting anything

over on me now. I won't stand for being pushed to the front."

"I don't see that you can help it," said Sherrill triumphantly. "You are vice president, aren't you? By no act of your own. And your duty is to take the president's place when she can't serve. That pushes you into the place automatically, don't you see? That's what you are there for."

"Oh, well," said Alan, "if you put it that way of course I'll do my best. But on one condition. You've got to write to me and tell me every week what you want done, and I'll report to you—"

"Why, of course, Alan MacFarlan. That goes without saying. Did you suppose I was going to be mum as an oyster all winter? Don't you know I hate to go worse than you hate to have me? You poor fish! I'll bore you to death with directions, and watch every mail for your reports— Just as I did when you went to Canada—and got nothing for my eagerness but half a dozen skimpy little post cards inscribed 'O.K.A.M.' or something to that effect."

"Oh, well," said Alan, "I was only a kid then! I was too much interested in that new country."

"You're only a kid now, Alan, and don't go to thinking you're grown up, please, for you'll spoil everything if you do. We've always grown up together you know, and it isn't fair for you to get ahead of me while I'm gone."

"You don't think New York, and all those clever marriages your Aunt is going to try to thrust upon you are going to age you any!" parried Alan.

"Certainly not," said Sherrill cheerily. "Now take off that grouch and don't let everybody know we've been having a fight."

She gave his arm a friendly little pat and they went up the steps of the house where they were to spend the evening together.

The door was flung wide, and happy voices, and brightness greeted them eagerly. Sherrill felt a pang at the thought of leaving it all that threatened to overwhelm her. How hard it was going to be to drop out of all this dear circle where all her interests had been since childhood.

She went in with her own bright smile, however, feeling that for Alan's sake at least she must not let anything seem different.

They rushed upon her eagerly.

"You're late, Sherrill! You two have been making such a fuss about everybody being on time and here you are ten whole minutes behind time yourselves."

It was Alan who answered with a grave smile:

"It couldn't be helped this time, Willa, Keith had something important to tell me. We got away just as soon as possible!"

Sherrill gave him a quick glanee and noticed the quiet gravity on his usually merry face. So then her going was really cutting deep with Alan! She wondered why that should give her a pleasant sort of satisfaction, and somehow make it easier for her to go through the evening just as usual!

CHAPTER VIII

The social committee had outdone itself. The house in which this festivity was being held was a big plain roomy old affair that would have been the better of several coats of paint both outside and inside. The furniture was, some of it, rare because very old, but the rest was plain and cheap. Yet it was a home where they all loved to go, the home of the beloved physician of Rockland, Dr. Barrington. Willa Barrington and her brother Fred were among the most active in the younger set. Since they all could remember, the Barrington home had been the center of some of their most delightful good times.

The doctor's office was housed in a neat little building down on the corner of the lot, facing on both streets, and quite separate from the house, so that the clamor of joyous laughter and many young voices would not be disturbing. The Barrington lot was deep and they had all helped to make the excellent tennis court at the back, and contributed to the substantial back stops and other paraphernalia of the game. They had even planted the row of cosmos across the side fence that gave the tennis court a lovely setting in the fall; they had kept the lawn about the edge carefully cut, dividing the labor with the son of the house, so they all felt that they part owned the place. As indeed they felt about several other homes in which their activities were welcome at any time they chose to come.

But to-night the social committee had simply smothered the wide plain old rooms with bowers of lovely autumn colors. Great branches of autumn leaves framed all the pictures, and hid the mantels, and embowered the stair rail and newel post. Masses of outdoor pompon chrysanthemums filled the room with their spicy fragrance. White and pink in the old parlors, in vases and bowls, and lovely old pitchers, standing on tables, and peering from between the curtains in the wide old window seats; flame color and gold in the dining room banked on the fine old sideboard—the sideboard that had been in the family for nearly two hundred years with two tall white candles in queer brass candlesticks at either side.

The dining-room ceiling had been curiously decorated. Lines of fine invisible wires had been strung across the room at intervals, and from it hung single flowers of bright chrysanthemums, on silver wires, interspersed with especially lovely autumn leaves, either singly or in tall sprays, giving an effect of a fall garden.

From the chandelier above the long dining table, which was spread to its full length and surrounded by a heterogeneous collection of chairs, came many small ribbons, in shades of crimson and green and brown and gold, coming from a common center and spreading each to a place card at the table, cunningly fashioned from a folded card and cut and painted in the shape of an autumn leaf.

Beside each place card stood a tiny toy candlestick each containing a small yellow candle, and beside each candle lay half a cake of paraffin. Those guests who had penetrated to the dining-room before they were expected to do so exclaimed and wondered, and a few who were wise exulted in the fun that lay before them.

The entertainment committee were consulting around the old square piano in the parlor, and a collection of instruments, running from cello and violin down to guitar, ukulele and banjo made it plain that an orchestra had a part in the program.

The girls were in pretty light dresses, varying from a few flowered chiffons, to printed dimities and organdies. The boys made no attempt at evening dress. Some of them even came in knickers and sweaters. They were a democratic informal crowd, all knowing one another well, and not met together for a display of raiment; just a jolly crowd who had grown up together, and were not judging one another by worldly standards.

"They're all here now, Prissy!" called Willa, as Sherrill came downstairs after having taken off her wraps, and become enveloped as it were in the smiles and welcoming glances of her companions.

Priscilla Maybrick bustled her orchestra into position and they struck into a gay little medley of familiar songs that ended, each one in just the right place to make a laughable sentence with the words of the next melody, and kept the company in a series of out-breaking laughter, as they listened and followed the words.

"Now," called Priscilla swinging around on the piano stool as the last note of the orchestra died away, "Phil Mattison will read an original poem of greeting from the new social committee, one verse written by each member of the committee."

The poem was received with enthusiasm, being cunningly devised and each verse rhyming with the name of its writer which finished its last line.

At its close Priscilla Maybrick announced that as this was to be an original evening, the next item on the program would be an original song written and sung by Rose Mattison and Riggs Rathbone in collaboration.

The song was indeed original, containing a verse about almost every member of the group, a rollicking laugh-provoking bit of humor only to be appreciated by a local listener.

Sherrill, standing on the lower step of the stairway, just opposite the wide arched parlor doorway, looked across the bright laughing company and suddenly felt tears stinging into her eyes. How dear they all were! How could she go away and leave them for a whole winter? What was New York to this dear throng?

Then her eyes were drawn irresistibly across the room to where Alan stood with grave earnest eyes upon her. Alan, who seemed suddenly to be older, more thoughtful than he had been that morning when she had met him racketing around in his old Ford, collecting cakes for the evening. She sent him a bright flash of a smile, and his came instantly back, only somehow it seemed to have a depth of gravity in it that Alan's smile had never held before, and she found herself wishing she could just put her head down on the newel post and sob out:

"I don't want to go to New York! I *won't* go to New York!"

But Priscilla Maybrick was calling them all to order after the last verse of the solo was over. She was rapping on the back of a chair with a little wooden nut cracker mall that

Willa had produced and they were having fun about that even. How every little trick of the occasion was being photographed on Sherrill's brain to remember hungrily when she was gone from it all!

Pang after pang! It beat upon her soul, and made her feel that she could not go away. Yet she knew her letter of acceptance had already been mailed to her uncle, and she was bound to go now, at least for a time.

"When the orchestra begins to play you are all to form in line, and march out into the dining room where you will find your seats by the place cards," announced Priscilla Maybrick.

As Sherrill turned to swing into line she found Alan suddenly by her side, and felt a comforting sense of strength about her. His fingers just touched hers with a quick furtive clasp as they stood together for the instant and he said in a low tone:

"You're a good old sport, Sherry!"

She felt the warm color spring into her cheeks, and a glow about her heart, as she walked along beside him. It had always been so. Alan had seemed to have some uncanny way of knowing when she felt sad. And suddenly it began to seem as if she must not go away and leave Alan. Yet of course that was absurd. She must go now. And Alan would be here when she came back. It would be good to go soon and get it over and get back to all the dear people.

When they entered the dining room all the little candles had been lighted, and the little cakes of paraffin lay white and mysterious before them.

With many exclamations and much laughter they all found their seats. Alan and Sherrill were placed next one another. Willa always favored friends if she could and put them together. She knew how to make everyone have a good time. Besides, were not these two the chief officers of the group?

When they were all seated they were told that the next item on the program was for each person to mold, out of the block of paraffin before them, any object they pleased. The only implements they were allowed to work with were their own two hands and the warmth of the little candle before them. They might make people or animals, whichever they chose, and might choose whether they should model the whole figure in miniature or use all their material in head and shoulders, or a figure on a bust.

Most of the company exclaimed in dismay as they took up the paraffin and felt its hardness.

"Why, we never can do that!" they said. "It is too hard. Give us knives."

The social committee had some ado to convince them that it was possible to work that cold hard substance into malleability. But upon being assured that it was possible, they finally all set to work, holding the wax high over the candle flame, and working away with eager hands.

It was Sherrill who first voiced the discovery that the hard wax was yielding.

"This certainly is a good example for the Lookout Committee," she said earnestly. "If that wax will yield to a tiny candle like that we ought not to be discouraged when we try to bring new members, even from down on the Flats."

"There's one thing you forget, Sherry," announced Alan gravely, "the warm human hand has a lot to do with molding the thing. It isn't that it just brings the wax in contact with the flame either, but it molds it and works over it, and keeps close to it to know how near it needs to get. It gets a lot of heat from the hand too. I guess there must be a lesson in that somehow, isn't there?"

He looked up with his old grin gleaming, and they all laughed.

"Listen to Alan!" said Willa, "he's caught the preaching habit from Sherrill. Pretty soon he'll be studying to be a preacher!"

"I guess that's right," said Sherrill following out Alan's thought, "it's no good to go down after those Flats boys and girls unless we keep a warm human interest in them every minute, and follow it up continually. But we must not forget that it is the candle after all that makes the wax soft. The hand alone could not do it. I notice this wax gets cool mighty quick if I don't keep it near that flame. I expect the prayer meeting committee might get some idea out of that. Wouldn't prayer have something to do with keeping close to the Flame?"

"That's all right, Sherry," called out Priscilla Maybrick from across the table where she was working away with her chunk of wax, "I'll go. I hate those old Flats like everything. It smells of oil cloth in the making down there, and chokes me, but I'll go. I don't like that Mary Ross you sent me after, either. She needs to wash her hair, and she is coarse and loud and hard if there ever was one, but I'll go and I'll pray for her too. Only Sherry! Don't rub it in on me to-night. Have a heart. This is a social, and I'm molding a saint out of my paraffin! Yes, I am, see his halo?"

They all laughed at Priscilla and stretched their necks to catch a look of saintlikeness in the uncertain lump that she held in her hand.

"I shall make a Rolls-Royce out of mine!" announced Phil Mattison. "It's the only way I shall probably ever get one."

"Mine begins to look like an Indian papoose," said Rose Hawthorn studying her wax with a troubled perplexity. "I think I'll just wait and see what it turns out to be and then name it afterwards."

Amid the laughter and chatter the various lumps of wax were beginning to take shape. There was a soldier, and a sailor, a dog and an elephant, a dresden shepherdess, and a bust of George Washington. There were several attempts at presidents, past and present, and other noted characters, but in the end it was Sherrill's head of an Indian chief that took the first prize, with a model of Spike, the Barrington collie as a near second, and Rose Hawthorn's papoose took the booby prize. There were boxes of candy for the first and second prizes and a rag doll for the booby prize. Everybody was full of laughter and talk as they rose from the table and went into the parlor for the music that came next on the program, and the charades which were to follow.

"But I'm sure," said Sherrill as she shoved back her chair and picked up her Indian chief, "that the Lookout Committee must have had a hand in this amusement. I can't help feeling that we've all had a wonderful lesson as to what can be made out of the most unpromising material."

"She would!" said Rose Hawthorn picking up her papoose, and tucking her leggy rag doll under her arm, "Sherrill would! She always does! Now I shall never be able to enjoy my new doll without thinking of some little worthless infant down on the Flats that needs going after and working into an angel."

Sherrill smiled understandingly at Rose. Dear Rose! Did she mean anything beneath all that whimsical banter? What a helper she would be down on the Flats if she ever got near enough to the flame of the Spirit to get warmed into working for others. Dear, helpless, pretty Rose, who nevertheless had a warm, true heart.

The two charades which had been carefully worked out beforehand were rushed through in great shape, and found most difficult to guess, although when they finally were solved they were voted the best charades that anyone had ever witnessed in Rockland.

Hard upon their finish came the refreshments, an innovation, apple tarts served with a generous trimming of Mother Barrington's homemade ice cream atop and hot chocolate in the thin old Barrington china cups with whipped cream atop.

"Myum! Myum!" said everybody audibly as the trays arrived with their delectable burdens.

The chatter that went on while all were eating was broken when Priscilla Maybrick rose with her gavel. When at last silence was restored she said:

"Next month's social is in the hands of our president, Sherrill Washburn. Sherrill have you any announcement to make about it?"

Sherrill, with a quick catch of her breath, arose with her plate in her hand, though Alan swiftly and silently relieved her of it. She had a sudden remembrance that the social she was about to announce would probably be her last for the winter, if her plans carried out for going to New York, and her voice had a queer little catch in it as she spoke which no one but Alan understood.

"It's our Thanksgiving Social," she announced bravely. "We all are to bring a slip of paper on which are written the special things we are most thankful for during the past year. They will be read at the close of the evening, but without the names. Make them true, of course."

"There will be a Thanksgiving dinner," went on Sherrill gaining control of her voice as she spoke, "but it will not be at the usual noon hour when we have our home dinners. We mustn't break in on home plans. This dinner will be held at half past seven in the evening at Howard Evans'!"

Everybody drew a quick breath and looked at Howard Evans who was a newcomer among them, his father having recently bought a rundown farm on the edge of town. The old farm house was small and unpretentious, and everybody immediately wondered where there would be room for a dinner table big enough to hold the whole crowd. The question stood in their eyes as they looked at him. Howard turned red as his red hair, under the battery of eyes, and wished he had never suggested having the crowd at his place, but Sherrill's voice went quietly on, with a twinkle of mischief in her eyes.

"You don't need to know many of the plans, only I'll tell you a secret. Howard's father is building a perfectly princely fireplace in his big new barn, and it's all to be lighted with pumpkin lanterns. We've borrowed the long tables from the church basement for the occasion. Two big gas ranges have been loaned and Mr. Evans is connecting them in a couple of stalls to take care of the cooking, and we're going to have a wonderful time. Your part is to bring the guests."

"Guests?" the question was popping all over the room.

"Yes, guests!" said Sherrill smiling. "This isn't going to be just ourselves. Every one of us has to bring a guest. The men have to bring men, and the girls have to bring girls. And now, listen. Perhaps you won't all like this plan, but we are asking you to try it in good faith and with all your hearts for this once any way. The guests are to be from *the Flats!*"

There was a sudden dead silence in the room like something flung down that could be heard.

Then back by the hallway came Rose's soft speculative voice in a plaintive little meditation as if she were thinking aloud.

"She would!" she said, "Sherrill would just wish something like that on us all! And she knows we won't any of us wear halos but her!"

The whole room burst into laughter, though some of it seemed almost touched with tears, and then Sherrill, smiling herself, lifted her hand.

"Listen—you—*dears!*" There was something very tender in her voice. "I don't want to wish something disagreeable on you all, but I do think we've got to look after those people down there and bear witness to them somehow. Alan"—with a sudden inspiration she looked toward him—"Won't you— would you be willing to pray that God will make us willing, and then show us how?"

Without an instant's hesitation Alan's voice came clear and steady, Alan who always shirked out of leading a meeting or being called on to pray or speak anywhere. Alan who always did his work quietly, and would never take the lead:

"Dear Father in heaven, make us ashamed that we haven't been after these whom you love, long ago. Help us to forget ourselves and be at your service wholeheartedly. Show us how to work wisely, and be with us. We ask it in Christ's name."

The room was hushed when he was finished. Very quietly they all said good night. A few of the girls slipped up to

Sherrill and whispered: "Oh, Sherrill, I think it was wonderful of you to think of that. I'm afraid I'm not as good as you are—"

"Oh, don't!" said Sherrill, "it was not my thought. It was God's. He's been making me think of it a long time, only I hated to propose it because I knew it would be awfully unpopular, and terribly hard work. In fact I'm not terribly keen on it myself, but I got to the place where I had to do it. And girls, the girl *I've* got to invite myself is one that made faces at me when I was in the first grade in school."

"Sherrill! Not *Maria Morse*! You don't mean you would invite Maria Morse?"

"I'm going to try," said Sherrill. "I think God wants me to. She's lost her mother, and she's taking care of her eight little brothers and sisters, and working in the mill besides, and I think we girls ought to give her our friendship."

"Do you believe she wants it, Sherrill?" asked Rose Hawthorn thoughtfully.

"Probably not," said Sherrill, "but I guess it's up to us to make her want it, isn't it? After all, it depends a lot on how we go about it, and I guess the only way to do that is to pray a lot about it. I feel all shaky when I think of going to invite her. But girls, when I do, you've got to be awfully nice to her afterward!"

Out in the starlight Alan and Sherrill walked along silently for a whole block after they had parted from the others. Finally Alan spoke:

"You didn't tell them you were going, Sherry," he said gravely with a question in his voice.

"Oh!" said Sherrill, "I know, I forgot it until just as we were leaving, and then somehow I just couldn't. I thought, perhaps—well, perhaps I won't tell anybody until the Thanksgiving dinner is over. Will you help me keep my secret? I can be getting ready you know—but—well, who knows but something will turn up that I wouldn't have to go after all?"

Alan turned to her with a happy light in his eyes.

"Sherrill, I believe you don't really *want* to go after all," he said, his voice vibrant with something she did not understand.

"No, I don't, Alan! It just seems as if I couldn't!" said Sherrill with a little catch in her voice.

"That makes it a whole lot better," said the grave young voice, and Alan gave Sherrill's hand a friendly little squeeze in the darkness.

CHAPTER IX

Sherrill put it to the family next morning at the breakfast table just before Keith left for business.

"Say, folks, I'm going all right," she declared seriously, "but I want you to do one thing for me. Please don't tell anybody yet—not a soul, until I give you permission."

Keith wheeled around from the door, his hat in his hand.

"What's all this, little sister, you're not trying to slide out of it again?" he asked, studying her face keenly.

"No, Keith, truly," she answered, meeting his eyes steadily, "I just would rather get used to the idea myself first, and besides, I don't want to have the crowd all know it till after we get our plans all made for that Thanksgiving dinner. I'm not going till after Thanksgiving anyway! I couldn't stand that!"

"Of course not!" said Keith crisply. "We couldn't be thankful without you, I'm afraid."

"Of course not!" said Grandma radiantly.

"Of course not!" echoed Sherrill's mother with a relieved sigh. It wasn't going to be at all easy for her family to get along without Sherrill.

"But what Thanksgiving dinner is this, little sister?" questioned Keith turning back after he had opened the hall door. "You're not planning to eat dinner with the crowd on that day? We can't stand for that you know."

"Oh, it's not to take the place of the home dinner. It's in the evening in Evans' barn, and we're inviting guests from the Flats!" announced Sherrill gravely. "I'm afraid if the crowd thinks I'm going away so soon they won't think it necessary to carry out all the plans."

"I see!" said Keith with a curious tender light in his eyes as he watched his sweet-faced sister. "Well, you can count on me, Kid. Anything I can do for that dinner? Suppose I furnish the ice cream? I've heard of a place up in the city where you can order it made in the shape of different flowers, or fruit—something appropriate for Thanksgiving. How about that? Like that? Well, count on me for the ice cream. Let me know how many accept. Double your own crowd I suppose? All right. Give me a few days' notice."

"Such a brother!" said Sherrill with her eyes shining. "Ought I to let him, Mother? And after he's given me that big check too. I just know he won't get himself a new overcoat this winter, and he ought to have one. His old one isn't near heavy enough for cold weather. Ought I, Mother?"

"Yes," said the mother, "he likes to help out, and it won't hurt him. He's proud of you, Sherrill. You're doing some of the things he would like to be doing if he only had the time."

"It makes a lump in my throat," said Sherrill as she brushed a tear from her eye. "Why should I want to go away even for a week from such a dear, wonderful family and hometown as I have?"

"There, there, Sherrill!" said her mother crisply taking a deep breath to keep away a certain tendency to tears that arose in her own throat. "Don't get us all to weeping. This is something that you ought to do and you're going to do it right! Come, let's get these dishes out of the way and then get to ripping. We ought to do that the first thing, and get the old things out of the way. Then we can tell rightly what new things we have to buy. You've got a good month now to work in and we ought to be able to get a pretty good wardrobe up in that length of time. What time did you tell Aunt Harry you were coming?"

"Half past ten," said Sherrill, "but I can rip up the brown and the green before that and perhaps get them sponged off so we can see how much good material we have to work with."

"I'll help rip," said Grandma, getting out her best glasses and beginning to hunt in her table drawer for the razor blade she kept for ripping.

"You better rip up those lace things and I'll wash them while you're gone," said Mary Washburn. "Some of the yellowest ones we'll just dip in coffee and call them ecru-lace."

"Why, of course!" laughed Sherrill, "I read in the fashion magazine that was all the style now!"

So they hurried through the dishes talking happily and then sat down with Grandma who had already ripped up a good part of the green dress.

"They'll want you to learn to dance!" said Grandma after a silence during which nothing had been heard but the snip, snip snip of scissors and parting stitches.

Sherrill jerked her thoughts back from her plans about the

Flats young people and gave attention to her grandmother amusedly.

"Well," said Sherrill disinterestedly, "let them want. I'll just tell them I *don't* want."

"You'll have to learn to be very courteous in your declining, Sherrill," warned her mother, "you'll have to learn to say no so pleasantly that they'll be just as pleased as if you had said yes. Wasn't it Longfellow that tried to do that when he had to decline an invitation to speak at some school commencement? Or was it Bryant?"

"Oh, I don't remember, Mother. But of course I'll try to be polite."

"It won't be so easy!" said Grandma grimly. She had been lying awake half the night thinking of things that might happen to Sherrill. "You'll be in their house. Besides, you have never been tried. You don't know how much you'll want to do what they ask you to do."

"Grandmother!" said Sherrill, dropping her hands with their burden of lace and scissors in her lap in dismay, "you don't have much faith in me, do you?"

"Well, yes, I have faith in—well, in the way you were brought up. And I know you are a sweet good girl. But you put a good sound apple among a lot of rotten ones and leave it there long enough and you know what'll happen."

"Well, Grandmother, I'm not going to stay there long enough for that. And anyway, if I see myself getting specked I'll send for Keith to come and drag me home! Besides, isn't God supposed to keep His children?"

"I'm not so sure He's going to keep you when you go amongst the world. You remember what a peck of trouble the Israelites got into when they went down into Egypt, and Lot when he went to live in Sodom."

"Mother!" said Mary Washburn, "you ought not to talk that way to the child. She's almost on the edge of backing out even now."

"Well, perhaps not," said Grandma, "but I wouldn't like to see Sherrill spoiled."

"Grandmother!" said Sherrill earnestly, "there's a difference you don't take into account. I'm not going into Sodom to live, nor because I want to go. If this isn't an up and down duty I won't stir a step! Aren't we told to be in the world and not of it? Can't God help me through a place like that?"

"Yes," said Grandma a bit doubtfully, "I suppose He can—if you let Him."

"Well, I'm letting Him!" said Sherrill. "Now, Mother, I've got these laces all ripped, hadn't I better wash them before I go? I think there is time."

"No, you run along. Harriet likes to do things when she plans. I'll wash the lace and have it all ready for you when you get back. She'll likely want you to stay to lunch, so don't worry about anything here. Grandma and I'll just have that little bit of soup that was left over, and we won't make a bit of fuss."

But Sherrill was back inside of half an hour, two great boxes in her arms and her eyes shining like two stars. Behind her came the beloved friend of the family, her face almost as pleased as Sherrill's.

"I couldn't wait, Mother!" called Sherrill from the walk as she came through the garden, "I want you and Grandmother to see what wonderful things I've got!"

"She's going to put them on over here and let you see them the first time," announced the satisfied donor as she entered behind Sherrill, carrying two more boxes.

"For the land sakes!" exclaimed Grandma, laying her ripping razor blade carefully away in the drawer and preparing to enjoy the show. "If it takes all those boxes to hold what you've bought her I don't think there's much need of our ripping up any more old clothes."

"Oh, there isn't much," said Harriet Masters, "remember I haven't any daughter to spend on and I just enjoyed picking out pretty things for Sherrill. Mary always said she might be half mine sometimes."

"Of course!" said Mary Washburn quickly, remembering Mary's little daughter who had lived but three short months and whose death was followed by the tragic death of the baby's father. If it gave this dear friend pleasure to take a motherly interest in her child, why they must not let a false idea of independence spoil that pleasure. She sent Sherrill a warning glance and wreathed her own face in smiles of eagerness. After all, of course any mother wanted to see her dear girl dressed in beautiful garments, even if she could not afford to buy them for her herself.

So Sherrill put on the lovely white velvet first, whose frosty sheen and simplicity of cut made Sherrill look like a young seraph just dropped down from some heavenly sphere.

It was fashioned cunningly, so plain, so simple, so modest, and becoming that a little child might have worn it, yet with a trick of line, and fold and fulness here and there, a sweep of delicate edge, and curve, that gave it a classic look. Silver girdled and silver clasped, it had an air that marked it with distinction, while yet being so severely simple that even to the unsophisticated eyes of Grandma it did not look or seem out of place, or overdressed for Sherrill.

"She'll need a pair of silver slippers of course," said the family adviser, "but they will go with other evening things too. Silver stockings and slippers."

"I'd like to see her dressed in that going around with other pretty girls," said Sherrill's mother wistfully.

"You wouldn't like what a good many of the other girls wore," said her friend. "How the girls of to-day can go around showing so much of their ugly bony spines I can't understand, and their long skinny arms. If it isn't legs its arms, and if it isn't knees its spines. Just somehow to look naked, that's all they care!"

Sherrill's mother looked troubled.

"Perhaps I ought not to make her go," said she in a worried tone. "I know the dressing of to-day is not what I approve, and I have reason to suspect that my sister-in-law does not think as I do about these things."

The visitor gave her a curious thoughtful look and wondered if she had any realization just what a far cry it was between the world's standards and those of the guarded group where Sherrill had grown up, but she gave a little encouraging laugh.

"Oh, well," she said gayly, "Sherrill has got to learn to hold her own among those who don't see as she does. Here's hoping your sister-in-law will strike a happy medium between Rockland and the ultraextremists."

"Mother, New York isn't the only place where they have bare backs. Helen Clancy has one. I saw it at the dressmaker's when I went with Rose Hawthorn to her fitting."

"Well, of course," said Mrs. Washburn, "Helen has no mother. What could you expect of the niece of Mrs. Rutherford Barnes?"

"What I'm worried about," said Grandma, "is that Sherrill will get all her ideas changed when she gets used to seeing people wear these outlandish things, and doing the things she's always been taught to feel are wrong."

"But, dearie," said Mrs. Masters, "don't you give Sherrill the credit of having something more than ideas? I think they go deeper than that. Somewhere behind it all there is a principle, and it's the principle that Sherrill will be true to, no matter what, or I'm very much mistaken in Sherrill."

Sherrill gave her friend a grateful glance, and went on admiring the lovely folds of the velvet.

"It's wonderful, Harriet," said Mary Washburn, "we never can thank you enough."

"Well, don't try," said Harriet Masters shortly. "If Sherrill gets half as much pleasure out of it as I did in buying it for her I'll be more than paid. Now Sherrill, get out the other things!"

"It looks like the heavenly garment of righteousness," said Grandma wistfully as Sherrill walked across the room, and the graceful folds of the velvet clung about her like a lily sheath.

But Mary said nothing more as she watched her girl. She was thinking what Sherrill's father would have said at the sweet vision she made in the lovely frock. Wishing he were where she might tell him about it at least.

The wrap was a gay little affair of satin and embroidery. Grandma and Mother looked at their girl in the strange soft garments as if she had suddenly become a tableau. The grand clothes seemed to set her apart in another world from them.

Then there was a charming turquoise taffeta, full and soft, with little puffed sleeves, a round neck, and a full skirt finished with bound scallops. Bunches of tiny sweetheart roses hung from the belt on slim gleaming ribbons and nestled at the corsage, and Sherrill looked like a demure doll in it.

"Oh, you oughtn't to do so much, Harriet!" reproached Mary looking at her child with tender eyes. "But that is lovely. I don't know which is prettier, the blue or the white."

"Both for different occasions. The white for very formal, the blue for gay little occasions. But it just suits her type, doesn't it? And it couldn't fit better if it had been made to order. Now, don't scold. There's just one more, and I had to get it it was so sweet. It's just one of those little knitted ensembles. They're so useful everywhere, and you have to pay so much for them over here it seemed wicked not to get it when I found just the right thing."

Harriet opened another box and brought forth a brown knitted dress of heavy silk, with coat to match. The border was of shades of rose and green and gold and blended beautifully with the woodsy shade of the brown.

"That," said Harriet practically, "will do to wear in Rockland just as well as in New York. You can use it almost anywhere and be well dressed. They are very stylish and sensible I think."

Sherrill, bright eyed and pink cheeked, arrayed herself in the knitted ensemble, and walked back and forth for their admiration, and wondered in her heart if it was altogether right to be so glad over just clothes.

Then there were some boxes of exquisite lingerie, and a charming little negligee, all butterflies on a sky blue ground that fell in lovely folds about her.

"It's just like being Cinderella," said Sherrill sitting down among her treasures excitedly, "I'm sure I never shall be able to eat or sleep again I'm so unreal."

"You precious child!" said Harriet Masters, with a tender farway look in her eyes, watching Sherrill folding her pretty things into their boxes, and thinking how her little girl would have done the same thing if she had only lived.

"I shall be completely spoiled!" declared Sherrill. "I can feel my head is turned already!" and she twisted her curly brown mop around toward her mother.

"There are some things that don't spoil," said the guest. "I think you are one of them."

"Harriet! You *will* spoil her!" said the mother with a loving, anxious glance toward her child.

"Well, if she's got to go," said Grandma, "I'm glad she's going right! I couldn't stand it to see that Eloise turn up her nose at Sherrill's outfit."

"Mother! I never suspected you of being worldly," laughed Mary, hurrying away to get some lunch on the table, and insisting that the guest should stay.

Keith came home unexpectedly for lunch and had to see the new clothes and admire everything, and join in the thanks.

"Now, I'll only have a coat to get," chanted Sherrill happily. "I can make all the rest of my outfit, I'm sure. Aunt Harry has shown me her things and there are the duckiest little dresses. So easy to copy. I'm positive I can do it. Isn't she a dear? She's letting me copy every pretty thing she's got!"

"A coat!" said Keith thoughtfully. "What kind of a coat?"

"Oh, just a coat," said Sherrill contentedly. "I can perfectly well get it and all the little things I need out of that wonderful check you gave me."

"Mmm!" said Keith, "well, don't get it right away. I may have an idea!"

"Now, Keith!" said Sherrill in instant alarm. "You're not to do another thing for me. If you do I'll go and spend this whole check on a new suit and an overcoat for you! So there!"

It was a happy lunch time, and the guest enjoyed it as much as anyone, entering into the plans for Sherrill's journey as if she were her own mother. They ate the excellent fried potatoes and cold ham and apple sauce and raised biscuits with a relish, and talked so long that Keith suddenly looked at his watch and found he was going to be late at the office.

Then Sherrill gathered pins and newspapers and her pet scissors and prepared to go back with Harriet Masters and take off patterns from the imported frocks, wherewith to glorify her old clothes.

CHAPTER X

The days went by swiftly.

Willa Barrington took the position in the bank that Sherrill had given up, and Sherrill had her time free to get ready.

Every morning she spent sewing, and part of the afternoons, when she was not helping her mother in the house. Little by little the charming wardrobe grew, hanging under chintz covers in the closet of the guest room. The green satin made over after a Paquin model, with touches of old lace treated in coffee and laboriously "picked out" by Grandma's frail fingers. The brown satin became a brown crepe with Belgian embroidery on the sleeves and a quaint buckle that had come from Cairo and had an accompanying necklace of antique filigree set with queer old stones of many colors. Aunt Harriet's trunks were a never ending source of treasures to "finish off" whatever Sherrill was trying to make.

The handsome old brocade worked into a wonderful blouse and skirt with a vest of rare old lace to set off its quaintness. An old thread lace shawl of Grandma's supplied the black lace dress that Harriett Masters said was indispensable. Sherrill bought black velvet and copied a dress from Paris that looked very smart indeed when it was done. And as she hung them away, one by one, proudly, her heart ached with every new accomplishment. If only she might stay at home and wear those pretty clothes among her friends whom she loved!

Yet of course with it all there was an elation at the thought of going away and seeing things. Going away and doing things! Seeing the world, living a storybook existence for a little while in a grand mansion, and not having to lift a finger for herself. Certainly that would be fun for a while. If only she could take all the dear friends with her!

Almost every evening she saw Alan MacFarlan for a few minutes at least. But Alan was hard at work, and there was little time for the games of tennis which had made the summer so happy. Alan was working day and night, trying to pull his father's business back into shape. With Judge Whiteley's assistance things were bidding fair to be on a more prosperous basis than ever before, but Alan was pale and thin and wore his lips in a determined line that made him seem suddenly older. Sometimes Sherrill felt just a little hurt that he had to stay away so much, couldn't even go down to the Flats with her as he used to do to call on some of their protégés in the early evening. She had to get Keith to take her once or twice.

But one day in the third week of November Alan came early in the evening and brought a little box with him, and when he gave it to Sherrill he sat and watched her open it like a child with a new doll.

Sherrill was astonished. Alan had never given her presents, except now and then a book at Christmas, or a box of candy for her birthday, and this was neither. She opened the box, and lifted out a necklace of pearl beads, holding them up with delight.

"Oh, Alan!" she said, "how lovely! How wonderful for you to give them to me! But you shouldn't have spent so much money on me—"

"Now don't begin that, Sherry!" protested the boy. "I've had the time of my life earning the money for those. I wanted you to have something to take with you to remind you of me. I only wish they were real pearls. Some day maybe I can buy pearls. But these are good imitations. Your Mrs. Masters picked them out for me in the city. She said they were what everybody was wearing and were good enough to go with your Paris dresses."

"Oh, Alan, they are lovely!" said Sherrill ecstatically, "I wouldn't want real pearls. I'd be afraid they would be stolen. And these are beautiful! They look real to me. Why, Alan, Alan!" and her voice drew near to tears, "I'll—have to give you a kiss for those!"

Then right before her grandmother who was sitting in her rocker darning some old lace for Sherrill's dress, and before her mother who was setting the table for breakfast, and before Keith who had looked up from reading the evening paper, she rushed over and dropped a tiny little kiss on the very top of Alan's handsome brown head. Then she slipped back to her chair and began to put the beads around her neck.

Alan's face turned purple, but his eyes took on a happy light and Grandma had a satisfied look around her lips.

"Now you know why I couldn't come over and help you with the place cards for the Thanksgiving dinner," said the boy to cover his embarrassment. "Mrs. Masters was going in town the next day to get the necklace and I had to see her about it."

"Oh, Alan! And I scolded you for not coming to help!" said Sherrill penitently.

"Oh, that's all right!" said the boy, "does one good to be scolded. I'm glad you like it if it *is* only beads. Just put it on when your aunt brings around that other guy she expects you to land, and perhaps you won't forget old friends entirely."

He finished with a laugh, but there was a huskiness in his voice, and Sherrill's eyes were misty with feeling as she gave him a look that comforted him.

After they had gone into the parlor to try over some of the songs that were to be sung at the Thanksgiving dinner, and Keith had gone out to see a man on business, Grandma looked up with a gleam in her old eye.

"That was a nice pretty thing for that boy to do," she said with a keen look at her daugher.

"Yes, wasn't it," said Mary quickly. "He's a dear boy."

"In my day we wouldn't have thought we could accept anything valuable like that unless we were engaged."

"Nonsense, Mother! They're only beads!" said Mary Washburn sharply, "and he's only a boy! Don't, for pity's sake, put anything like that into Sherrill's head!"

"Well, I'm not quite a fool, Mary, though you seem to think I am sometimes," replied the old lady smartly, "but I don't see that that's any worse than talking about Sherrill's going to New York to make a clever marriage."

"Oh, Mother!" said Mary and her voice had a note of anguish in it, "that wasn't serious. We were only joking about what Eloise had said. Sherrill doesn't take anything but fun out of that."

"Well, I can tell you who did," said Grandma wisely, nodding toward the parlor door, "that boy in there did!"

"Oh, Mother, no he didn't," said Mary. "He knew we were just joking."

"He's a nice boy, Mary, and Sherrill oughtn't to hurt him."

"Mother, please don't talk that way. Sherrill isn't going to hurt anybody. They will hear you. I wouldn't have any notions put in their heads just now for anything. They are just children I tell you."

"Well, Mary, I can tell you one thing," said her mother after a pause, "they won't be children when Sherrill gets back. They'll have grown up! If you want to keep Sherrill a child a little longer you better keep her at home."

"I wish I could!" said Mary fervently, with a sudden pang that her child was to go away, "but I guess it's right that she should go."

Sherrill was in the parlor singing Thanksgiving songs with Alan, and their voices blended sweetly, the soprano and the tenor.

"We worship Thee, we bless Thee—" they sang, and their earnest faces bent over the book together, heads almost touching. Mary peered into the dusk of the room lighted only by the piano lamp, saw the good sweet wholesome look on both faces, and took heart of hope. Yes, they were still children. Her mother might be right about their soon growing up, but it hadn't come yet, thanks be! She felt a panic at the thought of the untried way that lay ahead of her girl. Oh, if she only dared hold her back and guard her! Yet Sherrill had good blood, a strong foundation of character, and an abiding faith in Jesus Christ. Was not that enough to keep her through the perils of city life for a few short months? Oh, was she right in sending her out when she did not have to do so?

The day before Thanksgiving Keith came home with a great brown shiny box, long and narrow and very distinctive looking.

"What's that, Keith?" asked Grandma looking as excited as a girl.

"It's something for Sherrill," said Keith, eagerly. "Where is she?"

"She went upstairs to get my apron," said Mary Washburn. "She'll be down in a minute."

"Call her!" said Grandma impatiently, two pink spots blooming out on her old cheeks.

"I'm coming, Grand, what is it?" asked Sherrill hearing the discussion as she came down the stairs.

"Keith has got something for you, Sherrill, I want to see what it is. Hurry and open it, child!"

"For me?" said Sherrill, eagerness flashing into her eyes at once, followed by a troubled look. "Keith! You know I told you you mustn't get me anything else," she said in quite a determined tone. "I have everything, just everything I need. Since I got that new fur collar for my coat I'm just fixed fine now in every particular."

"This isn't from me," said Keith triumphantly, "it's from Father and Mother."

Mary Washburn gave a startled look at her son, and then a light broke into her face, and she instantly flashed her joy in a signal to Keith that whatever it was he had done, he had given it in that beautiful way. "From Father!—and Mother!"

Sherrill turned from her brother to her mother with startled eyes, and then said, "Oh! How *lovely!*" in a little sound like a sob of pleasure.

"Yes," went on Keith, "I knew Father would have done it if he were here. He would have wanted his daughter to have everything she ought to have for such a visit to his brother's family. So, when there came in a check to-day for the sale of that old land that we all have thought worthless so long, and Father left in my care to do what I thought best about, I just turned some of it into this for you, Sister. Mother gets the rest for something equally nice that she needs."

Keith lifted the shiny big brown cover and picked back a corner of the tissue paper wrappings awkwardly.

"Lift it out, Sherry, and see if it fits," he commanded.

Sherrill, breathless, too filled with emotion to speak, bent forward with awed face, and plunged in her hand.

"Oh!" she cried, "oh, Keith! Not a real fur coat! Not for *me*? Oh, Keith, a squirrel coat! And I've always wanted one!" She dropped the sleeve she had touched and turning flung her arms about her mother's neck and buried her face in her shoulder, weeping.

"Mother, I can't go away! Not from you all when you have done all these wonderful things for me!"

Mary Washburn held her child close and kissed the top of her head. That was the only place she could reach.

"But, Sherrill, it's Keith you should thank, dear. He says the present is from your father and me, but he never told me anything about it. It all came out of his own thought. He's right, dear, Father would have done it if he had been here, but it was really Keith who did it, because Father gave that land to him!"

And then Sherrill wept upon her brother's neck, and clung there.

"But I can't take it at all. I can't even try it on, Keith," she managed to murmur at last, "not unless you promise up and down to get yourself that new suit and overcoat you need."

"Oh, sure, little sister, I'll get some clothes. Sure, I'll get them right away. Have them all ready to meet you at the train when you get back. Dress up so fine and fancy you won't know this old hecker when you come riding in from New York town expecting to be ashamed of your old country family! Come, Kid, cut this sob stuff and try on that coat! If it doesn't fit I'll have to exchange it before to-morrow morning for my man leaves on the early train and I want you to have the coat for your journey."

So Sherrill was prevailed upon at last to open the papers and try on the coat.

Like a young princess she looked enveloped in the rich fur, of dyed brown squirrel. Its ample proportions and lovely lines showed at once that Keith had not taken up with some poor bargain coat. Keith had found a little gem of a coat, and Mary Washburn's heart was happy about her girl. With a coat like that she would be warm and comfortable, and look right wherever she went.

But Sherrill stood before the long glass in the parlor and looked at herself in dismay.

"Mother, it isn't right for me to have a coat like this. You never had a fur coat in your life, and you ought to have one first. I can't take it, really I can't. Not when you never had one," she said coming back to her mother's side and looking first at her mother and then at her brother.

"Well, she's going to have one now, Kid, so you don't have

to be a little martyr. I've been planning for it ever since last winter. I knew she was cold in that old black coat every time she went to church. And when this money came I knew it was an answer to my prayers. So stop trying to refuse it, and see if it fits. You see I got it from a buyer of one of the big New York houses. He happened to be here visiting his sister, Glen Howard's wife, and Glen introduced me and mentioned about his being a buyer of furs in New York and we got to talking. I suppose Glen must have said something pretty nice about you, for he offered to get me a bargain, and cut his commission, and it just arrived to-night. I've been in hot water for a week lest it wouldn't come in time. And I've been dead afraid it wouldn't turn out to be the right thing and would have to be sent back after all. Hurry up, Kid, and look at it carefully. Are you sure it fits? It seems to be a good quality of fur, doesn't it? I had Hastings Moore look at it and he said it was wonderful. You know he bought a squirrel coat up in Canada for his wife last winter and he knows about furs. He says I only paid three quarters the amount he paid for hers and he thinks it's better value than hers. Look at the lining, Kid, do you like that, or would you rather have had some kind of bright flowers on it? They had flowered linings. But I picked this, it seemed more like you."

He talked as eagerly as any of them, and so fast they couldn't answer his questions.

When Alan dropped in to see if Sherrill wanted him to go on any more errands, there they all were in the middle of the floor, smiles and tears, half finished sentences and answers all jumbled up together.

Even Grandma had hobbled up from her chair in spite of rheumatism and come over to lay reverent hands on the lovely fur garment.

And then Alan had to see the coat, inside and out, to notice the pretty scalloped cuffs on the sleeves, the trick of a pocket, the beauty of the skins, the shimmer of the lining, and above all how Sherrill looked as she walked across the room with it buttoned up about her chin, and completely eclipsing her ears and most of her hair.

"And this is the way I shall wear it when I go out in the evening to a symphony concert," said Sherrill suddenly, unfastening the coat, flinging the great scalloped cape-collar back over her shoulders, and gathering the garment close about her waist. She held her head high and swung across the room haughtily. "That is the way they wear them for evening.

I've seen them in the fur catalogues that come in the mail, and in the fashion magazines."

"Yes," said Alan gravely, "I see now how you'll go about making that clever marriage you talked about. But won't you remember always to keep my pearls about your neck when you walk like that?"

Sherrill laughed, putting her hand to her throat where the pearls were, and the pretty color flushed into her cheeks.

"Why, of course," she said, "pearls and fur like this always go together, don't they?"

Then she went and sat down and looked so serious that Keith asked her anxiously:

"Don't you like it, Kid? Tell me the truth. I suppose I was a fool to think I could pick out a thing like this for you, but I'd much rather know if there is something else you would rather have! It isn't too late to change, really, little sister."

"Oh, Keith," said Sherrill lifting shining eyes, "there is nothing in this world I would rather have than this beautiful coat. But I was just thinking how almost dreadful it is for me, just little me, to have a grand thing like this. I don't deserve it. And there are so many people haven't even got warm things. I don't believe it's right for me to have all this."

"Nonsense, Sherrill," said her mother quickly, "that's not for you to consider. You didn't ask for it, did you? You didn't even buy it for yourself. It was a gift. You've nothing to do with that. Besides, it is a sensible warm thing that will last for years if you take reasonable care of it, and save buying other coats, and it is just the thing for you to wear on your trip. It is cold up in New York. You would need a fur coat with those thin evening dresses It will last a lifetime almost."

"No," said Keith quickly, "it won't last a lifetime, but by the time it gets shabby I shall be in shape to get her another one—"

"Or someone else will—" put in Alan in a low tone, so that only Grandma heard him.

Sherrill settled down at last to enjoy her lovely coat and they had a beautiful evening all together, talking about it, and enjoying one another. It was the last night they were to spend together before Sherrill went to New York, for the next day was Thanksgiving and the barn dinner was to come off then.

Every little while they made Sherrill get up and put on her coat and walk around the room, and once she went upstairs and got one of her new hats that Harriet Masters had helped her buy, and paraded around like a lady of Fashion.

"Grandma has been afraid I would come back utterly spoiled," said Sherrill when she had taken off her hat and coat for the fifth time and folded the coat away in its shiny brown box, "but she miscalculated the time. I'm *going away spoiled!* I couldn't be worse spoiled than I am, so why bother? Pearls and furs and velvets! My cousin Carol won't be in it at all with me. Really, Mother, I'm ashamed. A quiet Christian girl like me looking like a fashion plate! What would those girls from the Flats say to me if they knew I could dress like this? What would Mary Morse say? You know I've had a terrible time to make her promise to come to-morrow night, and I had to tell her I would wear this old blue dress before she would say yes, because she said she hadn't a new dress to wear."

"Well, dearie," said her mother with a tender look, "you're wearing the old blue dress for Mary Morse's sake to-morrow, and next week you'll wear the blue taffeta for cousin Carol's sake. Life after all is a comparative thing, and clothes suit certain places. Clothes are a means to an end, not an end in themselves. If God hadn't sent these lovely things for you to wear, without any attempt on your part to bring it about, why then my girl would have gone happily off in the next best thing she could have got. I know you, Sherrill. But the pretty things have come and you may just be thankful for them. There have often been times when you couldn't have them, couldn't even have a lot of things you needed, and you have always been sweet and cheerful about it, so we all like to have you have this beautiful surprise."

It seemed that the little group who loved her could scarcely bear to break up that night, so sweet it was to sit and look at the dear girl, and be happy in her happiness, so hard it was going to be to have her gone, even for a short time.

But at last Alan got up with a sigh and declared he must go home.

And the next day was Thanksgiving.

CHAPTER XI

Sherrill spent the early morning putting last things in her trunk. Her mother insisted that she was to have no part in the preparation of the dinner, for she would have enough else to do.

So the turkey had been stuffed the day before, and went into the oven in ample time to be ready to eat at one o'clock. It was to be watched over by Grandma who was too lame to go to the Thanksgiving service. She said that no one else quite knew how to baste a turkey to the right brown anyway, and she rather enjoyed being left with the responsibility.

Keith took his mother and sister in his car to the church and they three sat in the old pew together each of them thinking how it would be a long time before they sat there together again, and praying quietly for one another.

Sherrill wore her new coat for the first time. Keith had asked her to. He said he wanted to see how his sister looked in her "glad rags." So Sherrill wore one of her new hats and her coat, and sat quite conscious of her raiment for a while, as the eyes of her friends sent glances of admiration her way.

Alan MacFarlan across the aisle watched her furtively, and was glad that she was also wearing his string of pearls. He was thinking how much he would like to be up in New York this winter and take Sherrill to symphony concerts and church, and all sorts of nice interesting places. How proud he would be to take her somewhere in that coat. Perhaps he would in the spring, if spring ever came. She wouldn't wear that coat to the barn dinner that evening he was sure, if it were only just on account of Mary Morse.

He watched Keith take his mother and sister away home, and followed them with a wistful glance. Then he went dutifully home to his own family Thanksgiving dinner. For he had a family that was just as anxious to have him all to themselves as Sherrill's family were to have her. But he consoled himself with the thought that anyhow, he was to drive Sherrill up to the Evans barn late that afternoon to set the tables, and that later, when it grew dark he would drive her down to the Flats after Mary Morse. Then he would sit beside her at the barn dinner, with Mary at her other side, and his dinner guest, Sam O'Reilly, on his other side. Later he would drive them all home, and perhaps stay a few minutes with Sherrill to say good-bye, for she was leaving early in the morning. Oh, it was to be a large evening. Sherrill wasn't gone yet!

The turkey was wonderful! Grandma knew how to cook

turkey. She had stuffed it too with the old family recipe that
nobody could quite imitate. Yet Sherrill somehow could not
eat. It seemed to her that there were tears in her throat where
the food should go down, that hindered her from swallowing.
She wanted to laugh and she wanted to cry, and she wished,
Oh, how she wished, that she were going to stay at home and
enjoy all her lovely things with the people who loved her
instead of having to go off among strangers and try to satisfy
people who would be always criticising her and judging her
by her clothes.

But then, Mother and Keith and Grandmother all felt the
same way of course, and everyone tried to be jolly and
tender and make the time go pleasantly. By the time the
pumpkin pie came Sherrill was laughing with them, and telling
all the funny things she meant to say to her New York
relatives when she arrived, although they all knew she would
rather cut out her tongue than say any of them.

She even put on her new fur coat and stuck up her chin and
stuck out a spineless little hand indifferently to a supposed
Aunt Eloise, saying quite loftily:

"Pleased ta meet ya, Awntie!" and sent them all off in peals
of laughter!

Suddenly they looked up and Alan stood among them.

Oh! The time had gone! The Thanksgiving dinner was
over. There would be no more family all together now until
Sherrill got back from New York!

With a pang she jumped up and rushed around, helping her
mother put away things and carry out dishes in spite of
protest.

They all went to work and scrambled the dishes into the
kitchen, the boys carrying out the things for the refrigerator,
and piling dishes in treacherous towers, helping to scrape up,
and put away, everybody laughing and talking. It was as if
they were hanging on to the very last minutes when they
could all be together! Her dear family—and Alan! How
precious they all seemed to her as she looked up from the
pantry drawer where she had been looking out clean dish
towels. Her eyes blurred with sudden tears and a great
longing to throw up her journey even now at the last minute.
Only of course she knew she could not do that now.

And then in the midst of it all came Harriet Masters, who
had declined to eat the Thanksgiving dinner with them
because a very old lady at the boarding house who had been
taken suddenly ill had begged her to stay with her. But now

the old lady was better, and asleep, and Hannah Maria the second girl, for a consideration, was sitting in the hall to listen if she called, and Harriet had slipped away for a few minutes.

They got her a plate with some of Grandma's pie and while she ate they washed the dishes. At least, Sherrill washed them and Keith and Alan wiped them, while Mary Washburn put them away.

Alan watched Sherrill's hands working swiftly, skillfully among the soap bubbles in the great dish pan, plunging the dishes in and out again, into the rinsing water and out on the drain board, another and another, how quickly she did it! How pretty her hands looked with the sparkle of the suds on the back!

They talked and laughed and kept as gay as could be, yet all of them were feeling the coming separation as if Sherrill were going around the world for an indefinite stay instead of just running up to New York for perhaps only three months. How they all loved her! Ridiculous of course to feel it so, but it was the first break in the family since the father had gone away when Sherrill was a very little girl.

The dishes were all in shining rows on the shelf in a very short space of time, and Alan and Sherrill started out on their rounds.

"And haven't you even told Willa and Rose that you are going away?" asked the boy when Sherrill was seated in his car on the way to the Evans barn.

"No, I haven't," said Sherrill, suddenly appalled at the task before her. "I somehow couldn't before this came off. It would look to them like deserting after the first gun was shot. I don't know but it is, only—well I can't help it now. But I'd so much rather stay."

"Well, you better not tell them till the end, then," advised Alan. "It would just spoil the evening, and we want it to succeed you know."

"Of course," said Sherrill, "and it's going to, I know. I prayed all during church service this morning for it."

"Here too," said Alan shyly.

Two other cars were standing before the Evans barn door when they arrived, and a bevy of young people poured out to greet them, all talking at once.

"The ice cream hasn't come yet, Sherrill," called Willa Barrington, "what time did your brother say it would be here? Hadn't I better send my brother down to ask him about it?

You know you can't always depend on things on holidays and it wouldn't do to have to run after it at the last minute."

"It doesn't come till the five o'clock train, Willa! It's a special, and Holly Beach is bringing it up as soon as the train comes in. You needn't worry a minute about it. Keith okayed it last night."

"Sherrill, I can't find the place cards. I thought you said you gave them to Willa but she hasn't seen them," called Rose.

"Sherrill, can't Alan go down and get Harvey to open up the store and give us some more candles? We lack eight more, since those other Flatters have accepted."

"Sherrill, didn't you say Mrs. Foster said we could have some of her chrysanthemums? She didn't send them!"

"Sherrill, do you know how to work this oven regulator? Mrs. Marker thinks the turkey is cooking too fast."

"Sherrill, are you going to seat the girl guests on our right or our left?"

"Sherrill, how soon do you want the fire lit? Not more than a half hour before they arrive, do you? Say, can't you get Keith to come up and help the men get that electric light wire fixed over the tables?"

"Sherrill, Mrs. Marker wants to know who promised celery? She says she knows where we can get some more if you'll ask."

"Sherrill, did you intend to put electric bulbs in those pumpkin lanterns or real candles?"

"Sherrill, is the piano in the place you wanted it?"

"Sherrill, where are the forks? And can't we use the same forks for pie?"

"Sherrill, how many cakes were promised? Didn't you say twelve? Well, there are only eleven."

It was a perfect bedlam. But Sherrill walked in as calm as a summer morning and had them all straightened out in no time.

"The place cards are in that white box over the first stall. Alan has a whole gross of candles in the car, he'll get them. Can't Dickie run down to Mrs. Foster's and cut the chrysanthemums? He knows how, and she said she would be away and couldn't. Here, I'll set that regulator. Yes, the girls on the right. No, Sam, don't light the fire yet. Yes, Rose, Keith is sending up a man from the Company. He'll be here in half an hour to fix the lights. The celery is wrapped in a wet towel over there in the corner on a beam. Candles in the pumpkins, of course. It wouldn't seem real without them. No, the piano must go over there by the speaker's table so everybody can see the singers. I've brought the forks and the other cake! Of course we'll use the same forks."

Alan stood back and watched her in admiration for an instant, then he set to work helping her with all his wits. How was he ever to fill her place while she was gone?

They had thought that everything was ready for the dinner, the day before, except just setting the tables and cooking the food, but now it seemed as if everything was left until the last minute, and it took every second of hard work before they felt that all was as it should be, and the various members could take time to rush after their invited guests.

Alan and Sherrill were the last to leave the barn. Only the two women who had been hired to do the cooking were in the far stalls busy over the two gas ranges that had been temporarily installed, and they were discussing in loud cheerful tones the various ways of making turkey gravy.

Alan stood in front of the fireplace watching Sherrill as she flitted from table to table putting last touches to the flowers, scattering a few late roses that someone had sent over on the table cloth in front of the invited guests, a rose to a plate, changing the position of the butter plates, and sugar bowls, setting on the dishes of celery, making sure that the guests were placed exactly according to the chart that had been so carefully made out by the committee.

Then she stood back and looked, her head on one side, and turning with a smile came over to where Alan stood.

"It's lovely, isn't it, Alan?" she said with satisfaction.

"Why, I guess so," said Alan taking a quick inclusive glance, "yes, yes it is. I hadn't been noticing."

"You—hadn't been noticing! Why, Alan! Aren't you interested? Don't you think it's wonderful?"

"Sure I do," said the boy heartily, "but I was looking at you. Say, that dress you have on is just the color of your eyes. Is that one of your new togs?"

"Oh, Alan! You're hopeless!" laughed Sherrill. "This is the old blue dress I've worn two winters. I'm wearing it to-night because I promised Mary Morse I would. She felt uncomfortable about coming where she thought everybody would wear evening dress, so I just told her I would wear what I had on."

"Like you," said Alan studying her intently. "But it's not

the clothes you wear, it's *you*. You look dressed up in anything."

"Alan, I believe you've been kissing the blarney stone. I never knew you to be so flattering before," said Sherrill looking at him in astonishment. "Come on. It's time to go after our guests. But I hate to leave here it looks so pretty."

"It certainly does," said Alan with late enthusiasm, "looks nice enough to live in, doesn't it?"

"It does, doesn't it? Wouldn't it be fun to make over a barn into a perfectly beautiful house."

He studied her face thoughtfully.

"Would you like to live in it?"

"Of course I would. You could do wonderful things with some of these old barns. Take that one on the field next to our house now. Can't you just think what wonderful porches, and nooks and crannies, and rooms on different levels could be made, with a great wide staircase in the center, and a skylight in the top story letting the sunlight in?"

"H'm!" said Alan thoughtfully, "I hadn't thought about it, but maybe it would. You ought to study architecture."

"I'd like to. Come, we must go. We're supposed to be back here in half an hour, and we don't want to be late twice in one afternoon. The others have all gone after their guests, and we mustn't let them arrive ahead of the officers."

Alan was still thoughtful as he climbed into the car beside her and stepped on the gas. Sherrill turned her head and looked back.

"It's going to be lovely. See, Dick Hazelton has come on his bicycle and he's going to light all the lanterns and touch off the fire just as he sees the cars coming up the hill. It certainly will be cheerful when we get back."

"It certainly will," said Alan, looking down at her, "and you did it all. I'm afraid it's bad policy however, beginning the season with such a success. Just look what a flunk the rest are going to be with you gone."

"Indeed they are not. You are going to make each one better than the last. Aunt Harriet has promised to help you with the next one, and she's a wonder. She knows more new things to do to get people talking and acquainted. Wait till you see what she has to suggest. She's been telling me, and you are to go over there to-morrow night and get the whole thing planned out so you can get your committees to work at once."

"Oh, am I?" said Alan unenthusiastically. "Well, if you say so I suppose I am, but it looks mighty dumb to me without you around to stir us up."

"But Alan! You mustn't be a crape hanger. I thought you believed in being cheerful! Come now, don't spoil my last night!"

"All right, I won't!" said the boy setting his mouth in one of his old grins, "I'll be as cheerful as a little red lantern. Is this the street that Morse woman lives in? Now, which house in that row do you guess it is?"

"The third from the last," said Sherrill quickly, "I went to see her yesterday so I'm sure."

They drew up at the curb and Sherrill watched her escort as he went to the dingy unpainted door and knocked. Noticed how courteously he lifted his hat to the slatternly neighbor who opened the door, and who was expecting to care for the baby while Mary Morse was away.

Mary came out presently, looking half frightened, and drawing her shabby coat on over an attempt at holiday garb as she came. A little three year old toddled after her and embarrassed her more deeply by insisting on having a kiss on her dirty little face. Mary administered a slap furtively, and sent the child in crying, and then looked after her with distress in her eyes.

"Go comfort her, Mary," called Sherrill, "don't leave her feeling unhappy. We've plenty of time to wait for you."

Mary gave a grateful glance toward the car, vanishing precipitately into the gloomy house, whence presently the sobs ceased, and Mary reappeared with an air of excitement upon her.

"She's awful spoiled," said Mary as she climbed excitedly into the car. "I've had her and the baby mostly since they was born, and they don't know what to make of me going off."

"Poor little kid," said Sherrill. "Alan, didn't we have a bag of peppermints somewhere about this car? Here it is, in this pocket. They won't need them up at the supper. I noticed the dishes were all filled. Take them back to her."

"Oh, don't trouble," said Mary embarrassedly, "she's gotta learn I ain't on tap all the time."

But Alan found the peppermints, and took them back to the door where five children were crowded with open mouths, staring at the car, the weeping baby in the foreground.

But when Alan popped a peppermint into her mouth, and

handed her the whole bag, she looked up in the midst of a howl and bestowed first a wondering stare and then a ravishing smile, that showed beauty even through the dirt.

"Poor little beggar," said Alan afterward, "she thought I was an angel from heaven. I'll remember that and take peppermints next time I go."

(But that was on the way home much later in the evening).

Sherrill welcomed Mary with her best smile, and chattered pleasantly all the way without making it necessary for Mary to answer once, and they drove around to get Alan's guest, Sam O'Reilly.

Sam jumped into the front seat with Alan with scant courtesy and a bravado to cover his embarrassment. His hair was very wet and very slick, so wet from recent combing that a drop or two kept dripping down his red neck, and down one cheek. His collar was too tight, and he kept easing it up and out, and his flaring necktie matched his red hair. He acknowledged the greetings from Sherrill with downcast eyes and a "fresh" remark which under other circumstances might have annoyed her, but her mind was intent on making a success of this party, and it gave her a keen understanding that passed over little trifles. She realized that was Sam's way of carrying off what was to him a terribly trying ordeal.

The sun had set leaving a deep crimson streak in the west, and above in a clear emerald field a single star shone like a jewel as they drove up to the barn.

CHAPTER XII

The great doors were open wide and the fire flamed up around the big logs in the wide fireplace, playing over the new boards of the floor, and the gleaming tables with their white cloths, and shining glass and silver, flickering over the big beams overhead, and throwing furtive shadows in the distant corners where sheaves of corn and wheat were stacked and strange pumpkin faces gleamed out unexpectedly from every shadow.

"Oh, my Land! Ain't that wonderful!" said Mary Morse with a choking sound in her voice as if she wanted to cry, "it looks just like heaven might be, don't it?"

"Gee, that's great!" said Sam O'Reilly, his volubility suddenly hushed into silence after that one exclamation.

"It does look cheery, doesn't it?" said Alan eagerly, realizing all at once how great and far-reaching had been this scheme of Sherrill's to get together with the young people of the Flats; thinking that only Sherrill, of all their merry bunch, could have conceived and carried out such an occasion.

They alighted and joined the other merry arrivals who were thronging strangely, almost awedly, into the wide barn door. The hosts and hostesses escorted their guests to the dressing rooms in the extreme far corners of the barn, girls to the right, boys to the left, where were pegs for hanging their hats and coats, and dressing tables with mirrors and pumpkin-hooded lights. Great screens stretched across in front gave privacy.

In the soft weird light of the big open fire, with the quaint little pumpkin faces grinning from the dark corners, it seemed a strange enchanted land into which the company had arrived. The strangers shrank back and stared, then entered hesitating, shyly, and giggling over the newness of everything.

The hosts and hostesses had unbent royally. They companioned, with the girls and boys from the Flats merrily. They led their guests in, and helped them hang their wraps on the wooden pegs, and introduced them to those who were standing around, just as if they were all strangers, although many of them had gone to school together in the public school several years before, when the dividing line between social classes was not so strongly marked. But here to-night they were all ladies and gentlemen, and the guests from the Flats were on their good behavior. Indeed, they felt too strange and shy to be other than polite, though there had been one or two among the Flat boys that the other boys had been a little afraid of, lest they might get "fresh" with the girls from the Town.

Sherrill had been wise in anticipating any such possibility by putting the whole thing on a somewhat formal basis. There had been written invitations, and when the company had all arrived there was a receiving line formed, the officers first, with their guests beside them, and then the committees came, chairman and members each with his or her guests, and were introduced all along the line, and took their places in the line to receive the rest.

It worked out nicely, everybody meeting quite formally

everybody else and shaking hands, stiffly, perhaps, awkwardly, but still shaking hands and acting as if they were all on an equality.

Then the orchestra slipped out of the line here and there and took their places in the corner by the piano, not far from the fireplace, and began to play, using some of the music they had practiced at the last social.

Like magic the line was formed, two men and two girls, two men and two girls.

"Who are they putting with the boy that Phil Riggs brought, the extra one he hadn't told us about?" whispered Sherrill to Alan as she stood just in front of him at the head of the line waiting for the signal to march.

"Oh, he's going with Jim Cather. You know we didn't have Jim down because he expected to have to go to Canada yesterday, but he didn't go."

"But did you tell the girls? Is the table set for two more?" asked Sherrill anxiously.

"Yes, that's all right. They take Lola Cather's two places, herself and her guest. She didn't ask any one you know."

"Why not? Isn't she coming? I hadn't heard."

"No, she took good care you shouldn't hear, I guess. But her mother told me. She said—" he lowered his voice and stepped to one side so that the two guests who stood near should not hear. "She said she didn't care to have Lola hobnobbing with the Flatters."

"Why, the idea!" said Sherrill indignantly. "I thought she wanted Lola to be a missionary some day. I heard her talking about sending her somewhere for a course of religious training."

"Yes, I asked her that," said Alan amusedly, "but she said that was different. She said she didn't care to have her mixed up socially with 'thaht clahss.' "

Alan imitated Mrs. Cather's tones so exactly that Sherrill had to giggle in spite of her indignation.

"The very idea!" she whispered. "Is she afraid Lola will elope with Buggy Whitlock?"

"I wouldn't put it past her," grinned Alan. "The poor soul. Doesn't she know this isn't a dance, nor a flirtation circle? Though of course Lola is feather-brained, and she does like to flirt awfully well. But I should think if she is going as a missionary it was about time she began to have a little discernment and self-control."

"Well, I didn't think anybody would confuse our work here with foolishness. Now isn't that dreadful! It will get out why she didn't come of course, and there will be other mothers that will get alarmed, perhaps. Although, they are all sensible except Mrs. Mason and Mrs. Sales. They are always afraid of anything unconventional. But I do hope it won't get to the Flats. It will spoil everything we could do. The idea!"

"Yes, I thought so. She let Lola go with that tough set at the Inn all summer, and I know for a fact they had petting parties and plenty of wine and cigarettes! Nice bunch they were for a prospective missionary to hobnob with!"

"Alan! Listen! We've got to pray a lot about this," said Sherrill with her brows drawn together thoughtfully, "and then just keep our gatherings strictly friendly and a rapid program, so there wouldn't be a chance for any indiscreet intimacies. Isn't it pitiful, Alan! We all went to school together, and nobody objected. We've had the same interests while we were children, and we're supposed to be going to the same heaven, if we all get there! It isn't as if we were introducing strangers in our midst either. It's just pride! It's pitiful! It's unchristian!"

"I'll say it is!" said Alan. "It's a pity they can't bring up their precious children so they have a little sense and can act like Christians, and yet not flirt with every fresh kid they meet."

"Alan, you'll look after things when I'm gone, so they won't let any unwise things go on, won't you? And you'll pray—*hard!*"

"I sure will!" said the boy vehemently.

Then the music began and the procession filed about the tables gayly, everybody intent on hunting place cards. It was Alan who asked the blessing, in the little hush that came as each stood behind a chair and wondered just what came next.

"Heavenly Father, we want to thank Thee for the good things that Thou hast given us through the year, and we ask Thy blessing on ourselves and our guests to-night, and these Thy gifts that we are to share. May everyone of us learn to know that the best gift Thou hast given us is Thyself, and yield our lives to Thee that we may grow into perfection, even as the flowers of the field, and the fruit of the earth is yielded. For Christ's sake we ask it, Amen."

Something in Sherrill's throat threatened to overwhelm her

for an instant. It seemed as if Alan had touched the very springs of her life with that little prayer. How Alan was growing into the beautiful ways of a Christian! It made Sherrill very happy.

But a soft sound from the piano was filling the room and the voices nearest the piano broke into song:

"My God, I thank Thee, who hast made the earth so
  bright,
So full of splendor and of joy, beauty and light;
So many glorious things are here, noble and right.

I thank Thee, too, that thou has made joy to abound;
So many gentle thoughts and deeds circle us round;
That in the darkest spot of earth some love is found.

I thank Thee more that all our joy is touched with pain,
That shadows fall on brightest hours, and thorns remain;
So that earth's bliss may be our guide, and not our
  chain.

For Thou, who knowest, Lord, how soon our weak
  heart clings,
Hast given us joys tender and true, yet all with wings
So that we see, gleaming on high, diviner things.

I thank Thee, Lord, that Thou hast kept the best in
  store;
We have enough, yet not too much to long for more:
A yearning for a deeper peace not known before.

I thank Thee, Lord, that here our souls, though amply
  blest,
Can never find, although they seek, a perfect rest;
Nor ever shall until they lean on Jesus' breast."

It was a double quartette, seated around the table nearest the piano who were singing, and they had practiced it so well that every word was distinct and clear, like a prayer. They sang as they stood, heads bent a little, earnestly, and before the first line was finished the great room was hushed and listening. There was something about the singing that was most impressive and in the hush that followed the last verse Sherrill thought she heard a little sniff beside her, and glancing furtively at Mary Morse she saw her rough bony hand steal up and surreptitiously flick a tear away from the side of her nose. Poor Mary was in a new world and her heart was stirred deeply already.

Sherrill felt a throb of joy.

She cast her eyes quickly about over the faces of the guests. Even Sam O'Reilly had a solemn pleased look on his freckled face. They liked it.

The hush was broken by the scraping chairs as they were shoved back for them all to be seated, and in the chatter that followed Sherrill could see that all the Flatters were smiling and settling into their places with pleased anticipation.

The table was very pretty, gay with bright pompon chrysanthemums, and the late roses. The place cards had been painted by two of the social committee, and attached to them were tiny paper baskets filled with salted nuts. Plates of bright pink and green mints stood here and there and at each place was a little glass of delicious fruit cup. Mrs. Barrington had made it, and taken as much pains with it as if it had been for a wedding. Sherrill felt a thrill at recognizing that. Dear Mrs. Barrington! She understood they wanted the Flatters to have everything just as nice as it would have been for the highest in the land!

The program committee had left only a very short space of time for the guests to have to make talk with their hosts and hostesses, recognizing that those first moments would be the most embarrassing of all the evening.

All the instruments in town that could be mustered suddenly broke forth into gay little airs, popular melodies, wildly breaking one into the other. Just three minutes of this, and when the guests were almost through their fruit cup the big overhead electric light went out leaving the room in the weird semi-darkness that the candles and pumpkin lights gave. Then a light from behind suddenly focused on a big sheet that had somehow crept above the fireplace without having been noticed—or had it been let down from above?—that was it. The guests had no time to wonder, however, for there was the main street of Rockland right before them on the screen, and there were some of the people they saw every day walking down towards them, smiling and greeting one another. Mrs. Roland with her market basket full of vegetables; and a turkey's leg sticking out behind; Mrs. Crothers with her baby in the little express wagon. They laughed and talked and nodded good-bye and passed on. Then the cashier of the bank went by and walked into the bank, and Mr. John McCormick came out and tipped his hat to the cashier. People came in and out of the postoffice next to the bank. Sherrill Washburn herself came out, waved her hand to somebody across the street, got into a car and drove away.

They all cheered when it came to that, and everybody was excited. How did they get moving pictures of the town? They twisted their necks, and watched the machine, handled by Will Rathbone, just one of those little household affairs. But Will had been sly. He had been around preparing this surprise to spring on everybody for three weeks. He had caught Willa Barrington drying her hair out on the back steps, and Rose Hawthorn powedering her nose behind a door. He had quite a piece of reel of Jimmy Dodds in overalls repairing his old Ford, crawling under it and over it, with a streak of grease and carbon down one cheek, and a wide grin on his face. He had caught almost every one of the young people's society in some funny attitude, doing something homely and common.

And then the scene shifted to the Flats, and there were the streets where some of their guests came from, not the sordid streets perhaps, but the neat ones, with little children playing mud pies. There was an adorable picture of Mary Morse's little sister, the one who had wept, with a smudge on her nose and a grin on her mouth, and a little ragged kitten upside down in her arms. There was a cute altercation between two youngsters, and then a procession of boys from the Mill, with here and there one turning and smiling straight into the camera.

Sherrill held her breath. Would the strangers be offended? But no, they were roaring with laughter at themselves, pleased as possible. And Will had been most careful what reels he had selected. There was even a picture or two of some of the girls dressed in their best, smiling and pretty, coming out and down the street. He had taken care to make the Flat people appear to advantage, and not to make fun of them any more than he had done of the other young people.

Then came a picture of their church with all the people going in, and much appreciative applause greeted this. They all wondered how he had got the picture, and he confessed that he had hidden his camera in a neighboring bush and made a long connection from the manse.

The pictures reeled on to the end amid loud applause, and a general kindly feeling, and when the light flashed up overhead again the guests found that their fruit cups had been removed and a great plate of turkey and potato and stuffing and vegetables, and all the nice things that go to make up a Thanksgiving dinner, was set before each one. Heartily they fell to eating, with good cheer and friendliness on every hand.

The program was not lacking in diversions. They introduced several solos, vocal and instrumental, one of a tune played on a saw by Harry Kelly from the Flats who brought down the house and was forced to play two encores. They staged a dialogue which introduced their society, and made plain its object and its interests, which was received with evident interest by the guests. Now and again the whole company would burst out with a song that everybody knew and even the guests would join in.

Sherrill found herself relaxing and just enjoying the evening.

But the best part of all to Sherrill was to come. She sat almost silent now, watching the happy company, her eyes alight with something sweet and far away, perhaps because her heart was praying that all might turn out as she hoped.

It was after they had finished the wonderful pumpkin pie and fancy ice cream, devoured huge pieces of the twelve beautiful layer cakes, finished the coffee and nuts and candies, and everybody was pinning a rose from the table to his neighbor's coat or dress.

The chairman of the prayer meeting committee arose and knocked on the table with a spoon for quiet:

"Friends," he said, and his voice sounded young and gay and true, "we've been having a peach of a time, but now we're going to end with the best of all, we think. Will every one bring his chair, and make a wide half circle here around the fire? We're going to move the tables back to make room. Will the work committee move those tables please, and now, will everyone come forward with his chair?"

In short order the cleared tables were out of the way, and the company gathered in a double semicircle around the fire. Someone snapped off the big overhead lights, and left a soft candle light. The candles sputtered low in the grotesque grinning pumpkin faces of the laterns, the firelight flickering up over the earnest happy faces of the young people.

Several of the committee in charge had dropped down upon cushions or just on the floor, a group at either side of the fire, and then very softly a voice started and the others took it up,

"Softly now the light of day—"

Even the boys from the Flats growled away on the bass notes, and here and there a flute-like soprano or tenor lilted in, till all the little company were singing. Just a verse of that, and then they melted into "Abide with me—Fast falls the eventide!"

"It's time for the verses now," said a second member of the Prayer-meeting committee from the shadow where he stood at the side of the fireplace, "I'm beginning, and won't you all please follow just as rapidly as possible. No compulsion of course, if you can't remember any, but we'd like you all to join. Thanksgiving verses preferably of course, but anyhow, verses! Here's mine! 'O, magnify the Lord with me, and let us exalt his name together! This poor man cried and the Lord heard him and saved him out of all his trouble!' I'm here to testify that I was in a lot of trouble last week. Lost my job and couldn't get another because of my game leg. But I made out to pray about it, and God heard me, and sent me the finest kind of a job. This is a real Thanksgiving for me to-night, I'll say!"

A voice from the other side of the circle broke in softly singing:

> "Don't stop praying, the Lord is nigh,
>   Don't stop praying, He'll hear your cry!
> God has promised, and He is true,
>   Don't stop praying! He'll answer you!"

The guests sat silent, most of them with wondering eyes, down drooping heads, hands clasped, watching the others furtively. All of a sudden they had come into an atmosphere that they did not understand, and perhaps felt themselves outsiders.

As that last verse of the impromptu chorus died away another of the group around the fire was ready with a simple little verse:

" 'I will bless the Lord at all times. His praise shall continually be in my mouth!' I'm thankful to-night that I belong to this crowd and know the Lord!" said the girl. And another took up the thread:

" 'Bless the Lord O, my soul, and forget not all His benefits!' I'm glad to-night because my mother is getting well from a serious sickness."

So the verses and the testimonies went round the room,

rapidly, from the members, now and then a hesitating word from a guest, and just at the end Mary Morse spoke out abruptly:

"I don't know any of yer verses, but I'm thankful to-night fer a smile that someone give me when I come in here. It was someone I use ta think was real proud. Thank you all fer inviting me!"

Sudden tears sprang to Sherrill's eyes as she bowed her head and began to pray, just a few words that seemed to bring them all within the circle of the throne, and left the guests with a feeling that she had just introduced them to a King.

After another song the chairman of the program committee arose:

"Well, I guess that's about all this time, but we hope you'll all come to our meeting Sunday night at seven o'clock. Make it a party call if you like and see if you like us. We want you to join us, and help in what we are trying to do for Christ. Has the president anything more to announce?"

Sherrill arose, a pretty picture in the firelight, her sweet eyes starry with feeling, her cheeks pink from the firelight:

"Just one thing," said Sherrill hurriedly, "and I don't like to have to tell you a bit. I've been putting it off till the last minute, because I love you all so much I can't bear to be left out of everything. But I've got to go away for a little while, only a few weeks I hope. If I can make it shorter I will. You've made it awfully hard to-night for me to go, we've had such a wonderful time. I mean the guests too, they've been just wonderful and I do hope they'll all come again, and join us in our Sunday meetings too. Our vice president Alan MacFarlan will carry on while I'm gone, and you all know how well he can do it, so I know my going won't make much difference, but I shall just wait and watch eagerly for every bit of news from home, and you may be sure I'll fly back just as soon as ever I can. I wouldn't go a step if it wasn't duty. I hope next month's social will be even better than this one, and that every person of you will be present. I wish I could too. Now, shall we sing a goodnight song? It's getting late and we must go home."

And quickly the chorus started to sing:

"God be with you till we meet again," till suddenly Sherrill felt that she was going to break right down and cry. Only there was Mary and she was singing too, and just then Mary turned to Sherrill and said:

"I can't ever be thankful enough you made me come to this. I may never have as good a time as this again, but I've got something to remember, anyhow!"

They took their guests home and said the good nights, and Sherrill and Alan were looking forward to the homeward ride together for last words. But the chairman of the program committee came tearing up the street just as they landed Mary at her home.

"Take me back home, will you, Al? I came down with Reds and he has to drive away out to Colterville with Alice, so I took the chance of catching you."

Of course they took him in, and they had a pleasant chat about how well everything had passed off, but there was no chance for any quiet good-bys for which they had both hoped. Alan did walk up the path to the door with Sherrill, but it was only a step away from the car, and Tom was watching them. They could not linger.

"Goodnight, Sherry!" said Alan with a choke in his voice. "It was all wonderful, and just as great as you wanted it to be, wasn't it? You have been simply great!"

"Don't, Alan, please," said Sherrill, her own voice vibrant with feeling, "you've worked just as hard, and been— wonderful!"

Her hand was on the door latch, her other hand in his. He crushed her fingers softly, impulsively and then flung away from her,

"I'm not going to say good-by, Sherry," he said almost gruffly, "I'll just say goodnight," and he was off through the moonlight whistling hard as he drove down the street. Sherrill watched him out of sight and then went into the house, her eyes full of tears.

How dear he was, and this was the end of it. She perhaps wouldn't see him again for a long, long time. He had to go to work early in the morning she knew. Yet she understood his rushing away so hurriedly. He hadn't felt like saying good-bye—! Still, there was a little ache in her heart. The days would come, and the crowd would meet without her. They would get used to being without her. Alan would have to see some other girl home, of course. Rose Hawthorn, or Willa Barrington. Willa was dear, and had always liked Alan.—But she would not be there! But there! She was thinking about herself, and that would not do. It was all going to be hard enough in the morning without letting in new heart aches. She must rush upstairs and put the last things in her trunk, for in the morning there would be no time.

CHAPTER XIII

It was hard saying good-by to Grandma. The soft old hands moved over her face like warm rose leaves and left a touch Sherrill never would forget.

"Never forget you're a Sherrill, and a Washburn both, Sherrill," she said, her fine old eyes snapping. "You're just as good as any of them. But more than all that don't forget you're a child of the King. You belong to the royal family. Don't let them put any of the world over on you."

"I won't, Grandmother dear," said Sherrill emerging from the fragile warm embrace with Grandma's tears on her cheek, and meeting Grandma's stoic smile as she put up her lips for another kiss.

Her mother and brother went with her to the station, in Keith's old Ford, with her new sole leather suit case at her feet, almost rubbing the toe of her new shiny pump. Keith was dear, and kind, and funny, and kept them all laughing so they couldn't cry.

"Be sure to remember to say all the polite things, dear," admonished Mary Washburn, "and do be nice to your aunt, even if you don't like everything."

"But if she hands you out any of those clever marriages she spoke of," interrupted Keith, "just thank her kindly and run home to Mother, won't you, Sister? I just don't seem to care for any of those city brother-in-laws."

They picked up Harriet Masters on her way to the station. She hadn't wanted to intrude upon the family farewells by coming over to go with them.

"But you are family, you know, Aunt Harry, dear," reproached Sherrill, with her hand nestled in hers.

"You're a dear, Sherrill," said Harriet Masters, giving her hand a squeeze. "Now, don't be afraid to wear that velvet a lot, whenever there's a chance. It will clean, and you can send it to the cleaners as often as you like. The blue won't soil so easily you know, being taffeta. And by the way, I don't know as I told you, I think that little pink taffeta you made out of great grandmother's is just as pretty as the blue. You look like a rose in it."

So they chattered as they drove up to the station.

And then Sherrill had a surprise. For there were nearly all the crowd of boys and girls waiting to see her off. Those that worked had got off for an hour, and those that didn't had got together in a hurry and bought her a lovely hand bag from them all, exquisitely fitted, the finest thing that was to be found in Rockland. A sample bag from the one jeweler's window.

"If you had only told us sooner we might have done something really fine," said Rose Hawthorn who would rather the bag had come from the city, "but I thought you'd like to know that it was Mary Morse who suggested it, last night. She whispered to me as she was going out the door that if we were going to get something for you please count her in for a dollar, and she would bring it to me in the morning. She brought it around at six o'clock, before I was up."

Sherrill was fairly overcome. Her smiles and her nearly-tears were so mingled that she could scarcely speak, but her eyes were searching the company wistfully, in the vain hope that Alan had come too. Of course he had said he didn't see how he could possibly get off, because a lawyer was coming out from the city with some papers that had to be signed. A whole week ago he had told her that. But still she had hoped. Well, they wouldn't have had much chance to talk of course if he had come, with all those other dear people present. Still it would have been nice to have seen him again.

There was not much time for even faint regrets however, for she had scarcely made a little hurried speech of thank you for the hand bag when the train was heard whistling at the crossing, and then there were so many people to kiss all at once, and so many last words to say that if Alan had been there she would not perhaps have been able to tell him from anybody else, for they all jumbled up together in one blur of homesickness as she smiled on them from the lower step of the parlor car, and kissed Keith who was the last, and searched out Mother's face among the crowd to throw her a last kiss.

She watched them all and kept her little new blue bordered handkerchief waving until the train swept around the curve, and Bennett's Garage hid them all from view, and then with a choking sensation in her throat and a stinging in her eyes she turned to follow the porter into the car.

She let him seat her in her chair, and place her suit case in the rack, and fix a cushion at her feet, and then she slipped a quarter in his hand and swung her chair around toward the window to look out. She did not glance at her fellow travelers. She was too aware of the swimming tears in her eyes. There! There went the coal yard and the lumber yard! How far they had come just while she was getting seated! And there was Silas Lummis' new bungalow with the baby out in the yard in a little red hood, playing with the dog! How dear even old Mrs. Cowles' little clapboard cottage looked as it whirled past! And back, on the horizon, miles away it seemed, was the dear old church steeple among the tree branches. How precious it suddenly became! There they would all meet on Sunday and she would be far away!

She dabbed at her eyes, and tried to swallow hard.

"Hello!" said a voice at her side from the next chair, "aren't you ever going to notice me!"

She swung suddenly around and there was Alan MacFarlan grinning from ear to ear!

And then, in her astonishment, two great round tears did roll out and down her cheeks, though her smiles were beaming out all over her face like a summer shower with the sun shining.

"Oh, Alan! I'm so glad you've come! I thought you said you couldn't!"

She was struggling to get control of herself and seem quite casual but she could not quite manage it.

"Oh, I found I could just as well go up to the city and meet the lawyer, and it suited us both a whole lot better," he twinkled. "Wish I could go all the way up to New York with you, but I couldn't quite manage it to-day. If Dad had been on deck I would have—that is, if you didn't mind. By the way, I got a letter from Bob this morning. He's making out fine! He says he reads his Bible every day and thinks it's great! Says he never knew the Bible was like that."

Of course it was only a matter of three quarters of an hour until Alan had to get off, but it seemed to make all the difference in the world in the day, just to have had him all to herself for that little while. How they talked over the dinner and what this one said and how that one looked, and filled each other with joy, just saying the happy little things that two friends who knew each other well and have the same interests can say, and how they rejoiced together over the news from Robert Lincoln!

As they neared the city the boy grew serious.

"I say, Sherrill, don't you go to growing up much while you're gone. You won't, will you?" he spoke gravely. "You see it would be all sorts of a mess if you grew up while you were gone and I were still only a kid when you got back."

She laughingly promised she wouldn't think of it.

But after that they sat and watched the city approach, and the station where he must leave her, and couldn't think of any more last things to say, because there were so many things they would have liked to say that just stuck in their throats.

Finally Alan got up as the train drew to a standstill, and stooping deliberately over her said in a low tone:

"I'm going to pray for you every night and morning, and you're going to do the same for me, see?"

A light flashed up in Sherrill's face.

"Oh, yes!" she promised looking steadily into his eyes.

Then he stooped and kissed her lips, reverently, as if he were sealing a compact, and went quickly out of the car, and swung himself down the steps to the platform.

Their eyes met as the train moved past him on the platform. He lifted his hat as if he were doing homage to a queen, and then the train swung into motion and she could not see him any more, but her heart was very happy as she sat there for a long time with her eyes closed, just remembering all that he had said, and his good-by kiss. It somehow seemed to be a sacred thing. It was something more than just a boy and girl kiss. Something that bound them to God and prayer, and a life of the spirit. It made her feel happy and warm in her heart, and it seemed to make possible the long days that must pass before she might return to her home once more.

It was a long time before she roused herself to watch the new landscape into which she was coming, before she even noticed her wonderful new fur coat that she had flung so carelessly over the back of her chair as if she were used to wearing such grandeur every day. She was going on a journey with better clothes than she had ever possessed before, and she ought to be enjoying the feel of them, and the grandeur of them, but instead she was remembering the dear faces she had left behind.

Late that afternoon the train reached New York, and Sherrill, her homesickness somewhat exorcised, roused herself to get her things together, and to be equal to the new demands that were to be made upon her. There was a new excitement upon her now. A strange city that in her mind had always held a glamor for her. New York! And she was really coming into the outskirts of the metropolis!

She sat on the edge of her chair and stared into the blankness of the tube as they were being whirled under the river. How strange to think a river was flowing over her head! She watched the people about her in the general stir of getting ready to leave the train, and tried to look as if this was not her first trip to New York. Keith had told her just what to do at every stage of the trip. So now she gathered her lovely coat about her, noted that the richly attired lady across the aisle looked at her with respect, and felt the prestige that her coat gave. Was that wrong, she wondered? No, it wasn't pride. It was just a pleasant sense that she was all right, and that no critic could find anything noticeably queer about her. Well, anyhow, the dear ones who had given her the coat wanted her to enjoy it. She would just rest in that and be happy and satisfied about her clothes. They certainly were needed just now to give her what was sometimes called "moral support," in her approaching ordeal. She found she was inwardly quaking at the thought of meeting her new relatives.

She had been told to go immediately on arrival to the telephone desk in the ladies' waiting-room and stand there until someone came for her.

The red-capped porter seized her luggage and led her up the iron stair from the train, into the amazing loftiness of the Pennsylvania Station, and although she had heard it described many times she yet was filled with awe over its vastness, and the vistas of other great spaces framed in white marble that stretched away in every direction from it.

The porter left her in the appointed place, and Sherrill stood staring around her anxiously, wondering what the aunt or the cousin who would come to meet her would be like; looking eagerly at every well dressed woman or young girl who came that way.

Back and forth, up and down, sometimes not two feet from where she stood, there paced a man in livery, watching every one who approached. Once he stopped a plain looking girl in a blue serge suit and asked her something, but she shook her head and walked on.

Sherrill watched the clock, and watched everyone who came, and her heart began to have strange misgivings. Perhaps they had forgotten her! It was a quarter to five, and no one had come yet! What ought she to do? Would her uncle

discover it soon and come after her? Had she perhaps made
some mistake about the place she was to meet them? She
asked the telephone operator if there was more than one
telephone desk in the ladies' waiting room, and was coldly told
no. Finally she decided to telephone to her uncle's house and
find out what to do. Of course she might take a taxi, but
perhaps they would come for her just after she had left.
Perhaps they would not like that. She must not make a
mistake right at the start. She would telephone. Surely that
could do no harm. She would say she was not sure she had
found the spot where they had told her to meet them. "Some
one will meet you," was what the letter said.

So she looked up the telephone number and finally approached the operator and asked for it.

Then just at her elbow a voice spoke most respectfully:

"Beg pardon, Miss, but I couldn't help hearing the number.
Could you happen to be waiting for Mrs. Washburn's car?"

"Oh, yes," said Sherrill whirling about with a relieved
smile, "do you know where they are? I must have missed
them."

"Right this way, Miss," said the man respectfully, stooping
to pick up her baggage, "I wasn't rightly sure whether it was
you or not," he added, and gave another respectful glance at
Sherrill's squirrel coat. He did not say that his instructions
had been to look for a very shabby looking country girl.

So Sherrill was stowed away in a handsome car, and her
checks were taken by another red-capped official, and she
rolled in state out a stone corridor into the great new city.

But there was a strange new heaviness in her heart. This
was not the way they welcomed guests in Rockland, sending a
chauffeur after them. But perhaps everybody was sick, or
something had happened. She took a long breath, sat back on
the downy cushions, and tried to prepare for whatever might
be before her.

CHAPTER XIV

It was a handsome house on Riverside Drive where they
finally arrived, but there was no welcoming door flung open,
no eager relatives waiting to greet her. Not even a costly
curtain drawn back to indicate any watcher at the window.

Instead the door was opened in answer to the chauffeur's ring by a white-capped maid who stared at her with a brief questioning glance and said, "Is this Miss Washburn?" as if she were surprised, and with another appraising glance said, "Come this way please."

Sherrill was led up a wide staircase, getting brief glimpses of stately rooms below as she passed, and down a narrow hall toward the back of the house. She had a sense of being isolated in a large boarding house, but the room when it was reached proved to be large and light, and overlooking a row of back yards.

There was a bathroom connected with the room, and a large closet, and Sherrill looked about on her new quarters with a degree of relief. It would be quite possible to feel at home in a room like that, everything else being equal, but where was the family?

"Mrs. Washburn said to say that she would be busy until seven, and Miss Washburn is out at a tea, but you would better lie down and refresh yourself, for there's a dinner and dance this evening that you're to attend. She said to say that she would see you at seven and arrange about your dress. The dinner is at half past eight."

"Oh!" said Sherrill bewildered, "oh, well, I don't think I better go anywhere to-night. I'd rather stay right here quietly and get rested."

She was beginning to feel in a panic. No one to meet her or greet her! A dance flung at her right off at the start, and no chance to get her bearings! This was even worse than she had expected! But the person in cap and apron was speaking, quite firmly, as if she had the right to order affairs.

"Oh, but I'm thinking you'll have to, Miss. Mrs. Washburn has already accepted for you. Madam would never hear to your declining. She always says a dinner engagement is a thing you *simply have* to keep. If you will just let me fix a nice hot bath for you, Miss, I'm sure you'll feel quite refreshed. I'll put some of Madam's bath salts in it. They are very helpful. And then you can lie down till it's time to go in to Madam about the dress. I believe she has had some things sent up she wants you to see."

"Oh, certainly! I don't want to upset any plans," said Sherrill doubtfully. "I'll go, of course. They promised to send my trunk up at once. I suppose it will be here soon."

"Yes, Miss, likely," said the maid, "and would you like it sent immediately to the trunk room for the night out of your way, or is there something you must have out of it first. I can unpack it for you this evening after you have gone, if you wish."

"Oh, no," said Sherrill in a new panic, "please have it brought right here. I would rather unpack it myself if you don't mind. I know just how things are, you know," and she smiled pleasantly. "But thank you just the same."

The maid looked doubtfully at her, opened her lips as if to speak, then glanced at the lovely fur coat that Sherrill was taking off, and closed her lips again. Finally she said:

"Well, Madam thought you would want your trunk to go direct to the store room. But if you prefer, of course."

"Yes, I do, please," said Sherrill firmly.

When she was alone instead of taking off her hat and following the directions for rest that she had been given, Sherrill stood looking out her window with troubled, unseeing eyes, trying to think what all this meant. How strange for her aunt not to greet her! She must not let her mother and Keith know how she had been received. Especially she must not let Grandma know. She would feel it keenly.

Then suddenly she whirled about and went and knelt down by a chair.

"Oh, my dear heavenly Father, help me not to misjudge. Help me to be strong and sweet and go through this trial which Thou hast given me, for Christ's sake."

Then she came back to the window and tried to interest herself in the small vision of the new city that she could get from these back upper windows. Were those great masts over there far beyond the buildings, or were they steeples?

A tap on the door put an end to her investigations and she opened it to find the maid with a tray containing tea and tiny sandwiches and cakes.

"Oh, you needn't have troubled to do that!" said Sherrill, and then realized that was the wrong thing to say. Probably tea was a regular meal in this house. She must take things as they came as a matter of course. That was what Harriet Masters had said, and she knew.

It was six o'clock before Sherrill's trunk came, but she had lain down for a few minutes, and felt quite rested. She had thought out the matter of clothes, comparing as much as she knew of the occasion with Harriet Master's rules, and decided that the blue taffeta was the right thing to wear tonight.

She laid out the things she would need for the evening, hung her dresses in the closet, put some of her other things away in the drawers of the bureau and her hats on the closet shelf. It did not take her long. Somehow she did not linger over the process as she had expected to do when she laid those pretty garments away in the trunk. She had in spite of her prejudices, pictured an eager cousin hovering near and admiring, and she was chagrined to find how much difference it made to her that no one was near to see what pretty things she had. Real Paris clothes and copies of them, and no one to know it. Well, it served her right for caring so much about clothes! Anyhow, she would just enjoy them and forget that they were anything different from what she might have had always.

She was just about to don her dress when the maid came to the door and tapped.

"Madam says she is ready for you now," she announced, "and you will please not put on a frock. Just wear a kimono. She is wanting you to try on something."

A flush came into Sherrill's face and she was about to rebel at the order, when she remembered her prayer to be kept sweet and do the right thing, and she closed her lips and tried to be pleasant. Well, at least she had a pretty kimono and lovely lingerie. She swept the bright folds of silk about her and rejoiced in the embroidered butterflies. They looked pretty with the silver shoes and stockings she had put on.

So she walked down the long hall, to the front of the house and waited while the maid tapped at her mistress' door. Funny, this to greet her relative first in a kimono. *Pretty kimono anyway!*

Mrs. Washburn lay in her bed, draped in a negligee of lace and orchid silk, with her face swathed in hot cloths which the attendant from time to time changed. There was no opportunity for Sherrill to give the sacrificial kiss which she had earnestly resolved upon after many soul struggles.

"So this is Sherrill, is it?" said a sharp thin voice pitched high and emanating from the steaming towels. "Well, I'm glad you came on time. I had to substitute you as a dinner guest for a friend I had visiting me who was suddenly called home by a death in the family. So annoying. But there isn't much time, so we'll have to get to work. I've got a dress here which I think ought to fit you. If it doesn't the maid knows how to take it up. Suppose you put it on right away. Where did you get that kimono? Is that something Carol has been buying again on my charge account? If it is it will simply have to go back. I can't have her doing that when she has an account of her own. Come over nearer so I can see it. What are those? Butterflies? It really is stunning! I can't say I blame her much. Perhaps I'll keep it for myself. Did she tell you you could borrow it?"

"What? This?" asked Sherrill followed the direction of the glance that came from between the hot towels. "Oh, no, this is mine. It is pretty, isn't it?"

"But it looks like an important thing," said the aunt in her superior tone. "Where on earth could you have got it?"

"Yes," said Sherrill, "it came from Paris. A friend of mother's brought it to me a few days ago."

"You don't say!" said the aunt thoughtfully. "A friend of your mother's. I didn't suppose she had friends who traveled abroad."

Sherrill's color rose, and she drew a deep breath. This was the kind of thing to expect from Aunt Eloise, of course, but it was very maddening. She must be careful.

She gathered the lovely silken folds about her and said nothing.

"Well, we'd better get to work. There isn't much time, especially if the dress has to be altered. Take off your negligee, and anything you have on under. This dress has garments that go especially with it. You can go over behind that screen. Maida will dress you."

Sherrill stood hesitantly, eyeing the maid over whose arm was slung billows of bright green silk and malines, and then looking toward the swathed face on the pillow.

"I don't think that will be necessary, Aunt Eloise," she said with a smile as sweet as if she were really grateful. "It is very kind of you, of course, but I have plenty of clothes with me."

The woman on the bed waved an impatient hand.

"Don't argue!" she said sharply, "I haven't time to discuss the matter. I want that dress tried on you at once. Afterwards we'll discuss it if there is time. Don't begin to annoy me right at the start. It's most annoying to have young people always objecting to things. Marie, this pack is getting cold. You better change it."

Sherrill was very much vexed, and her eyes had a flash of Grandmother Sherrill in them, perhaps even of Great Grandmother Sherrill, but she remembered her resolve, and after a second said gravely:

"Oh, very well," and followed the maid behind the screen. She saw at once when she threw back her kimono that her pretty lingerie commanded the respect of the woman. Nevertheless she handed forth a minute garment which she demanded should be substituted for the things Sherrill wore.

"Can't I try on the dress over these?" asked Sherrill.

"You heard Madam say that the underthings went with the dress," said the maid coldly.

So, much against her will, Sherrill put on the flimsy substitute, and when the maid flung the green dress over her head and she saw herself in the long pier glass it became immediately apparent to her why her own lingerie would not do, for her own white back gleamed at her from the looking-glass, guiltless of covering.

Sherrill surveyed herself in dismay, saying nothing at first, simply marveling at the idea that any girl would be willing to go out into company so nearly naked as she looked to herself. Also, her sense of humor which was strong, rose and battered at her self-control. She wanted to laugh at herself in such array. She could not help picturing her mother's and her grandmother's faces if they could see her now. A bare back to the waist, with a long green tail of fluffy malines and silk, and a front that was all too revealing for her sense of fineness. And what would the girls and boys in Rockland say if she should appear in a garment like this?

But while she was studying herself and trying to think what to say, and how gracefully to decline the use of this most unsuitable dress, the maid moved a leaf of the screen back, and she stood revealed before her aunt.

"It couldn't fit better if it was made for her, Madam," said the maid, "it's just her size. There'll not need to be a thing done to it."

"Well, that's a relief," said the aunt suddenly emerging from the towels, and showing a steamed complexion almost like a baby's. "Put on the wrap and let her see how it's to be worn, and then she'll be fixed."

Before Sherrill could object Maida threw about her shoulders a long black velvet wrap with a high fur collar.

"Stunning!" said the aunt, submitting to vigorous applications of ice wrapped in cheese cloth bags over her cheeks and chin and forehead and nose. "That's that! Sherrill, you better go right downstairs and sit in the library to wait for us. Your uncle hates to be kept waiting, and it's a relief to know you're ready early enough. I shan't be long now. Thank fortune you have naturally good hair, and you seem to have arranged it becomingly. Slightly ingénue but I guess it will have to do to-night because I simply can't spare Marie now, and Maida will have to go and dress Carol. Just go right down now. Those silver slippers look very well with the green. Are they the ones that came with the dress, Maida? Oh, her own? Well, they're not so bad. Maida, you show her how to find the library. I'll tell you on the way about how to behave at the dinner, Sherrill. That's all now. I haven't another minute."

"But, Aunt Eloise," began Sherrill in dismay, "I'm sorry to disappoint you, but I really would prefer to wear my own dress. I'm sure Mother would not like—"

"It makes no difference what your mother would like," cut short the aunt, "she isn't here, and she wouldn't know what was proper if she were. You are under my care and advisement now, and you are in my house. I expect you to be properly dressed when you go out with me or any of my family. Understand? Now go!"

Mrs. Washburn arose haughtily from her elegant couch and stepped into the silken garment that the maid held out for her, and Sherrill realized that she was dismissed.

In growing dismay she found herself following the maid down the hall. At the head of the stairs the maid paused coldly and said:

"You will find the library to the left of the stairs. You can't miss it. I will put Mademoiselle's garments in her room."

Sherrill hesitated at the head of the stairs looking after the woman as she disappeared into a door farther down the hall, then slowly walked down the stairs trying to think what to do.

She heard the woman come out of her room a moment later and close the door, and go on down the back stairs. Instantly she turned and fled back up to her room, the green taffeta making an alarming rustle as she tried to go silently.

Once in her room she locked the door and went to the mirror. The girl who looked back at her over the fur collar seemed an alien somehow. The wrap of course was pretty, but far too rich and ornate for her idea of the way a young girl should be dressed. But the long green freakish tails hanging below filled her with distaste. With a quick motion she flung off the wrap and laid it on the chair beside her, and took another quick survey of herself, not omitting her bare pink back, then swiftly she began to disrobe, casting aside the borrowed garments and getting into her own which Maida had left neatly folded on a chair.

Her own blue taffeta was lying on the bed where she had

left it, and she put it on, thankful that its adjustment was the work of but a moment. She unfastened the gaudy costume jewelry that had been put on her neck, and slid out of the bracelets, clasping on her own string of pearls that Alan had given her. Then she was ready, and her own eyes told her that she looked a great deal more becomingly garbed than in the borrowed clothes. But then of course, it might make her aunt very angry. Still, she could not help that. She could not go out anywhere with her back exposed that way. Her whole family would have utterly disapproved, and upheld her in her course she knew, and her own soul loathed the idea of the other dress. She had not been brought up to feel comfortable in questionable clothes. Of course, these things were worn constantly in the world she knew, and probably nobody else would even realize why she disliked them. But not even for peace and courtesy could she bring herself to go out among people dressed as her aunt had commanded.

She paused hesitantly and looked at the rich wrap lying on the bed. Should she put that on instead of her own coat so that they would not discover what she had done until it was too late to make a fuss about it? Perhaps they would insist on waiting for her to go back and change into the green after all!

Well, let them. Then she could remain at home perhaps. But even if it did make a coldness between herself and her aunt, she felt she should take a stand at once about wearing her own clothes.

So she left the velvet wrap lying on the bed where she had flung it and got her own fur coat from the closet. If her beautiful squirrel coat was not good enough to go to anything then she would stay at home. Aunt Harriet had told her that it was perfectly proper and if Harriet Masters didn't know then nobody did.

So without more ado Sherrill put on her fur coat, got out her lovely blue chiffon head scarf that came straight from Paris, and was ready. The whole performance of changing had not taken her ten minutes, and she felt sure that none of the family had gone downstairs as yet.

With her hand on the doorknob she paused, and quickly dropped to her knees:

"Dear Father, help me through this hard place, and keep me and guide me every moment this evening, for Jesus' sake," she breathed, and then went quickly downstairs to the library and sat down in a shadowed corner where she would not be much noticed if anyone came into the room, for there was only a single heavily shaded lamp burning. She was glad to sit back and close her eyes and just rest. She was more tired than she had realized, and she dreaded the evening inexpressibly. At that moment if anyone had offered her a quick transport back to Rockland she would have accepted it eagerly.

She had a full half hour to sit in the big leather chair and wait, and time to calm her heart and think over what she had done. It began to look to her as if her stay in New York was going to be a stormy one unless she was able right at the start to take her stand. Yet she found herself trembling in anticipation. Oh, why had she come?

At last she heard doors opening upstairs. A man's voice which she thought she recognized as her uncle's, her aunt's cold thin tones answering, and then another door hastily flung back, and a girl's high petulant tones. That must be her cousin!

Simultaneously Maida appeared in the doorway and peered into the elegant gloom of the room.

"Madam says you are to go right out to the car and get in, Miss Washburn," she announced. "They are late already," and turning she disappeared.

CHAPTER XV

Sherrill went into the hall and found her uncle just coming down the stairs.

"Uncle West!" she called joyously and hurried to meet him. Here at least she might be natural. Uncle West had always been nice—whenever he had had time.

He stopped and a light came into his eyes.

"Ho, ho! Little girl, so you've come! They didn't tell me! Well I'm glad to see you! I hope we're going to have a beautiful winter together. It's going to be nice to have two little girls instead of one," and he took her in his arms and kissed her warmly.

"Now, come on right out to the car," he added. "Your aunt will be down in a minute. She found a button off her slipper or something that had to be remedied I believe, but she said we were to get in. Carol? Where are you child? Carol is always the last one. Well, come on, you and I will go out and get settled."

He led her out to the car, and seated her comfortably, and Sherrill suddenly felt warm around her heart again. It wasn't going to be so bad perhaps after all if there was one friend in the family.

Mrs. Washburn came almost at once, stopping at the door to give directions to the butler, and making a great fuss about getting settled in the car. Carol came trailing behind, fretting at having to go to the dinner.

"You know I can't abide Amelia Van's dinners, Eloise," she drawled without even glancing toward her newly arrived cousin, "what you had to ring me in on this for I don't see. If your Mrs. Pearly and her stupid daughter had to go to an old funeral I don't see why that should affect me. Amelia's a pest anyway, and her dinners are never worth eating."

"Carol, that's no way to speak of your hostess," chided her father mildly. "Mrs. Van Gorton is one of your mother's friends, and that should be enough for you."

"Well, it's not enough!" retorted the girl impudently, "I don't see being a slave to anybody merely because Eloise is fool enough to accept her invitations. Here I have to go and be made a martyr when I might have been resting up a little for the dance this evening. I'll be bored to extinction. She always seats me beside that doddering old Max Pyle, just because he likes to appear young. I can't abide him, old cradle snatcher."

"Carol, you haven't spoken to your cousin yet," reproved her mother coldly as if the subject of the dinner was finally closed.

"Oh!" said Carol, turning an indifferent stare toward Sherrill, and then pausing rudely to appraise her with a startled look of surprise.

"Oh, hello!" she said indifferently. "But say, Eloise, you've certainly done her up in a stunning coat. I like that! You wouldn't get *me* a new fur coat this winter. What's the idea! I'm certainly not going to stand for that!"

"Fur coat?" said Mrs. Washburn, turning questioning eyes toward Sherrill's corner, where the light from the top of the car shone full upon her. "What do you mean?"

Then she stared.

"Where on earth did you get that coat, Sherrill?" she demanded. "That's not the wrap I gave you to wear."

"No," said Sherrill smiling and trying to speak naturally, "I thought it would be better to wear my own things, they seemed more suited to me. You see in the others I felt a little like David in Saul's armor."

"David?" questioned Mrs. Washburn with raised eyebrows and tone that implied something questionable in Sherrill's acquaintances. "Who is David? And Saul? You seem to have a great many gentlemen friends. I hope they don't live in New York."

Sherrill with difficulty controlled a wild burst of mirth. She tried to answer pleasantly with just a casual smile.

"Oh, I meant David of the Bible, you know," she explained.

"The Bible!" exclaimed her aunt caustically, "I've always considered it irreverent to bring the Bible into daily conversation in such a trivial way. I'm surprised. I always heard your family was very religious. But who was this other man you mentioned, this Saul? You must excuse me, but I feel that I should understand about all your acquaintances. I really couldn't have ordinary persons coming to see you at the house, you know, on Carol's account. And what could this person possibly have to do with your wearing my evening wrap."

Sherrill's eyes danced and she longed to make a sharp reply but she answered demurely:

"Oh, Saul was just a king," she said, "and he offered to lend David his armor in which to fight the giant. David declined because he felt he wasn't used to the armor, you know, and could do better without it."

"Well, I'm sure I think this David person was very rude!" said Aunt Eloise haughtily, "I wonder why they persist in putting such ridiculous stories in the Bible, and then expect people to read them. But I'd rather not hear any more about it. Suppose you tell me how you happen to be wearing that elegant coat. I hope you didn't borrow it for the trip."

Sherrill was suddenly so angry that she felt she would like to do something wild and primitive like scratching out her aunt's eyes, or smacking her selfish little red mouth, but she drew a deep breath and caught her quick little tongue between her teeth till the impulse passed and she managed to say steadily, although a trifle coldly:

"The coat is my own, Aunt Eloise."

"Then I suppose you got a job and spent an entire year's

wages on it!" snapped the aunt contemptuously. "It's a pity someone couldn't go around teaching poor working girls a sense of values, and the fitness of things. What is your job? Something in a bank I think your mother wrote. It certainly can't pay much. I suppose you bought it on the installment plan."

Here Uncle Weston interfered.

"Really, Eloise, don't put the child through such a catechism on the first night she is here! Let's talk of something pleasant. I'd like to know how the family are. We've scarcely had a chance to speak a word together yet. Perhaps she doesn't care to tell all her family affairs."

"Well, Weston, since she is here I feel it my duty to know all about her," said the aunt virtuously.

There was a dangerous sparkle in Sherrill's eyes as she turned to her uncle and tried to speak pleasantly:

"I have no objection to telling anything, Uncle Weston," she said. "I didn't suppose it would be of interest." Then turning back to her aunt she said steadily, "No, I have no job as yet. I am just out of school, you know, but I was to have gone into the bank this month if I had stayed at home. And no. I didn't borrow the coat from a neighbor, and I didn't buy it myself. My brother bought it for me and gave it to me as a present just before I came away."

"Your brother bought it for you? And where did he get the money?" this from the aunt in a tone as if she thought she had been deceived.

"Why, I don't *think* he stole it," smiled Sherrill, a wicked little twinkle of fun dancing in her eyes. One thing that helped her was that she could always see the funny side of everything, and often took refuge in a laugh when she felt far more like crying.

"Oh, does he steal?" asked Carol with sudden languid interest, and an impudent lift of the chin. "I never heard that he was dishonest."

"Carol! Really—you—"

"There now, Daddy, don't get tiresome! I'm sure she said she didn't *think* he stole it. What else could I think but that he was in the habit of stealing!"

"Carol, you are exceeding all bounds!" said her father angrily. But Sherrill suddenly broke into peals of laughter which cleared the atmosphere in her own heart at least.

"Don't scold her, Uncle Weston," she laughed, "she's only

kidding. Of course she didn't mean it. I'm not so touchy as all that!"

But the aunt did not join in the laughter, and the cousin only stared.

"I'm sure I've always been given to understand that your brother was very poor!" said the aunt rather indignantly. "Didn't he at one time try to borrow something from you, Weston, to pay a bill or something?"

"No," said Mr. Washburn looking down at his gloves uncomfortably. "Not a bill. He suggested that perhaps I would like to loan him some money for a year's time at a good rate of interest to help him buy a small business that he had opportunity to get. I would have been glad to do it if it had been possible, but that was just at the time when you went to the hospital for an operation, Eloise, and then were ordered abroad for a year afterward, and I couldn't see my way clear to do it. I took up the matter with him two years later, but he said he no longer needed it. By the way, Sherrill, who is he working for now? Is he getting along all right?"

"Very nicely," said Sherrill quietly. "But he isn't working for anybody. He has his own business. He bought it at the time when he wrote you. The bank gladly loaned him the money, and he has paid off the entire loan now, and is quite independent."

"You don't say!" said Uncle Weston with a light of satisfaction in his eyes. "He must be very enterprising."

"Well, but I don't understand," began Aunt Eloise fixing her husband with a glassy stare that implied she had been deceived in something, "I was quite given to understand that the family were in straitened circumstances. When you wanted me to invite—"

"Eloise!" said Uncle Weston with sternness in his voice, "we will talk of something else if you please. Remember that Sherrill is our guest."

"Oh, very well," said Mrs. Washburn and relapsed into haughty silence.

"Well, that's a peach of a coat!" said Carol grudgingly, "I'll borrow it sometimes. It will just go with my new imported brown velvet."

"You'll do nothing of the kind, Carol," said her father still sternly. "You have plenty of coats of your own, and if you haven't I'll get you what you need. But you are not to impose upon your cousin. Understand! That's a command! If I find you disobeying it I shall take back my promise about getting you a new car in the spring."

"I don't see that you need to take it out on Carol," said Carol's mother disagreeably. "The fact is, you don't understand the whole thing anyway. I told Sherrill to wear certain things which I gave her, which I felt were suitable for her to wear as our guest, and she has ignored my request."

"I'm sorry, Aunt Eloise," said Sherrill in a pleasant little voice which nevertheless had a note of firmness in it, "but I'd much rather wear my own things. Think how you would feel yourself if you came to Rockland and had to wear Mother's dresses. You wouldn't like it a bit."

"I should say not!" said the aunt with a curl of her unpleasant carmine lip. "That's hardly a parallel case."

"I want it thoroughly understood," put in Uncle Weston, "that Sherrill is to wear what she likes while she is with us. She's not to be badgered."

"Don't be silly," said his wife disagreeably, "do you want me to let her make herself a laughing stock among our friends?"

"It seems to me," said the worried uncle, "that Sherrill can be trusted not to do that. She seems to have turned herself out very well as far as I can see!"

"A lot you know about clothes, Westy!" put in his daughter impertinently. "If I were you I'd keep out of this. You won't get a rise out of Eloise no matter what you say!"

"You are impertinent, Carol!" said her father.

"I meant to be, Weston!" said his daughter imperturbably.

And then the car stopped and the chauffeur opened the door.

"There!" said Mrs. Washburn, "you've taken up all the time and I meant to tell Sherrill what she would have to do, and how to act!"

"I should think she would do very well without instructions," said her husband.

"You would!" said Carol pushing rudely past Sherrill and running up the steps of the house.

Sherrill got out and walked beside her uncle up to the door.

"You mustn't mind your aunt, Sherrill," said her uncle in a low tone as he helped her up the steps, "she doesn't really mean to sound unpleasant. She is just anxious to have everything go off all right. She is just plain spoken!"

"Of course!" said Sherrill briskly, trying to look cheerful, and feeling greatly comforted for the ordeal before her by this little word.

So they all progressed into the house, the ladies going upstairs to lay off their wraps.

Sherrill slipped out of her coat, and scarf, gave a pat to her hair before the mirror, and forgetting about her dress, stepped aside for her aunt to take the place before the dressing table. She somehow felt she had finished with the subject of clothes for the present.

But Eloise Washburn, seating herself for a last touch of lipstick got a full glimpse of her niece in her little blue French frock with its bunches of sweetheart roses, and her smile changed into an icy glare.

"Oh! And so you discarded the dress I bought for you also!" she said, as if Sherrill had broken all the laws in the Decalogue. "Well, I certainly think you have been the rudest girl that it ever was my misfortune to meet. Here I spent two days hunting for that frock, and you refused to wear it!"

"Oh," said Sherrill feeling suddenly very tired and wishing she could run away and never come back, "I'm sorry to have seemed rude and to have disappointed you, but indeed, Aunt Eloise, I couldn't wear that dress without any back. I'm not used to such things, and I should have felt—ashamed. I'm sure my mother would have been horrified at my dressing that way."

"I have told you before that your mother has nothing whatever to say about what you wear or what you do while you are with us. I am the one to judge. And you are scarcely respectable nowadays in the evening without a low cut back. I have no desire to have my hostess think I have imported a little country child to force into society. Where did you get that dress anyway? It surely wasn't bought in Rockland?"

Sherrill by this time was boiling, ready to say all the mean things she could think of, but just as she opened her lips to make a sharp retort she remembered her mother's last injunction.

"Remember, dear, the tongue is a little member. . . . Behold how great a matter a little fire kindleth." She closed her eyes with a long breath and opened them again, and spoke gravely, quietly, patiently.

"No, Aunt Eloise, it came from Paquin in Paris. Aunt Harriet Masters, a friend of Mother's brought it to me last week. She has just returned from a two years' trip abroad, and brought me some lovely things. You won't really need to worry about me——!"

Two more arrivals in the dressing room, friends of Mrs. Washburn, put an end to the conversation, and Sherrill turned away to the curtained window and gazed out on the lights of the city for an instant to steady her shaken nerves, and put up an inaudible prayer for help and strength.

She was interrupted by her cousin's voice behind her in a low tone.

"Did you say that came from Paquin? I don't believe it. Paquin wouldn't put on a back that wasn't low cut nowadays. Show me the label."

"It's in the back of the neck," said Sherrill wearily, "if you care to look. I'm sure I don't see what difference it makes."

"Well, it makes this difference," said Carol disagreeably, "that I don't see having you try to dress better than I do. If that's a Paquin I've got to have one! But I'm sure I don't see how you managed to get yourself up in all this style when you're only a hick."

"Come, girls, we're going down now! Don't keep us waiting!" came Mrs. Washburn's command, and Sherrill closed her lips on the hot words that were on the tip of her tongue, and went down to her first formal dinner in New York.

CHAPTER XVI

There was no make-up on Sherrill's face, but she needed none. Her cheeks were flaming gloriously, her eyes were sparkling with something besides pleasure, and she had bitten her lips until they were almost as red as her rude little cousin's carmine cupid's-bow that pouted from a face as artificial as a little painted mask.

When Sherrill went downstairs, walking quietly behind all the rest, keeping herself as much in the background as possible, she became aware almost at once that her French frock was a great asset. She felt inconspicuous and well dressed, and knew that the other members of the party had accepted her as all right. She knew this by that woman's intuition that can weigh the glances of her fellow women to the fraction of an atom, and know just where they have placed her. Her fingers touched the soft blue silk of her frock in quiet thankfulness that it had helped her through the first hard minutes. It was no pleasure trip to be attending her first dinner party under the displeasure of an aunt who had compelled her to be there.

But the introductions were through with more comfortably than she had hoped, and she found herself going out to dinner with an elderly gentleman of courtly presence and a humorous turn who paid her several compliments with his first sentences, told her she looked as if she had just stepped out of an old-time valentine, and called her his sweetheart in a pleasant little impersonal way that made her feel very young and put her at her ease.

She found herself seated at the table between him and a rather dumb looking young man with a tiny mustache on his upper lip that resembled a smudge of soot. But he did not seem to consider Sherrill dumb. He almost neglected the lady he had brought in to converse with her, and between the two she scarcely had opportunity to eat.

But the conversation was froth, most of it, and Sherrill, usually quick at repartee, scarcely knew how to take some of the things that were said to her. The young man conversed of plays, or pictures, and Sherrill had seen neither of them. She spoke of books that he had not read, and did not enjoy the questionable jokes and stories that he told.

On the other side, the elderly man paid open court to her in most gracious flattery that was almost embarrassing. In the few intervals that she had to herself she studied the people gathered around the table, and realized from the scraps of conversation she heard that they were nearly all talking froth.

She studied the priceless lace cloth that covered the banqueting board, the heavy silver, the glittering crystal, and monogramed china, and compared it to the Thanksgiving dinner which she had attended the night before in Howard Evans' barn with guests from the Flats, and wished she were back there again. She compared the guests at this table with those in the barn, and a startling thought came to her that they were of the same blood, made by the same Creator, living on the same earth, bound for the same ending so far as this earth was concerned. She listened to their conversation, and felt that the talk of the people from the Flats on the night before, had been infinitely preferable to what was going on about her. Doubtless the Flats could win out in blasphemy, and filth, against these people when they were off guard, but so far as last night's dinner was concerned they had been interested and courteous and well behaved. What was it about these people that made her feel as if she were in an alien land? Not just the fact that they were strangers. No, they were almost talking a strange language. Their sentences were filled with allusions to things with which she had nothing in common.

She tried to fancy any of these men and women and young people as having been present at that supper last evening. How would they have fitted? Well, she could select several of them that might have been good sports and entered into the fun, enjoyed the singing and the color and pleasantry, but would they have fitted any better than the people from the Flats into the little gathering around the fire at the close? Would they have bowed their heads in prayer and entered into that hush that brought heaven to seem so near?

"Do you know," said the young man with the smudge on his upper lip, "it really is criminal to look so serious as you are looking now."

Sherrill's face lighted with a smile.

"Oh, I didn't mean to look serious," she said, "I was just thinking."

"But you shouldn't," said the young man jauntily, "it isn't being done. People as young as you often die of thinking. And why aren't you drinking your champagne? That isn't at all wise, you know."

"I don't care for it," said Sherrill briefly.

"Oh, but you should," said the young man (his name was Elbert Girard), "it's very old and very costly. Are you really serious that you don't want it? Well, then, would you mind, since it's sitting so close to me?" and he lifted her glass and drained it as if it were his own. Presently a servant filled it again and again he drained it. So Sherrill sat and reflected that in the eyes of whoever might happen to notice she appeared to be drinking a good deal of champagne. Having been brought up with very decided opinions on the subject of drinking she felt most uncomfortable. It was therefore a great relief to her when at last the dinner was ended and they all repaired to the reception room. It seemed to her that she had been ages in this alien world, and she was beginning to feel terribly weary. She slipped into a seat in a corner behind a table and made show of examining a book that lay there. Her aunt presently discovered her and came over.

"Sherrill, you are to go with Carol now. I have made your

excuses to your hostess, and all you will have to do will be to stop beside her and say how sorry you are that it is impossible for you to remain for the evening. She understands you have a previous engagement, and only came here to fill in."

"Engagement?" echoed Sherrill blankly, the momentary relief changing to dismay. "Is Carol going somewhere else? I thought she was going home."

"Home! At this hour of the evening? Certainly not. You are going to one of the gayest little dances of the season, and you are quite lucky to have got here in time to go. It isn't everybody that is invited."

"Oh, I'm sorry to seem inappreciative, Aunt Eloise, but really I am very tired, and I'd be so glad to get to bed after my journey."

"Nonsense!" said the elder woman. "You are young! You mustn't mind being a little tired. You can sleep till noon to-morrow. You mustn't humor yourself that way."

"Well, then, would you mind if I just stayed here, please? I don't dance and I'm sure I would not be anything but a burden on my cousin."

"You don't dance! What can your mother have been thinking of? Well, you'll soon learn. No, Sherrill, I've accepted this invitation for you and it's very rude to stay away. Besides, we're all going to play bridge here, and there wouldn't be a partner for you. Come, you must hurry. Carol is waiting for you in the dressing room."

Sherrill arose precipitately. She certainly would be no more at home at a bridge party than at a dance. She hurried up to the dressing room, wondering if she could persuade Carol to leave her at the house. But when she reached the dressing room there was no sign of Carol, and the maid in attendance told her that the young ladies had all gone down to the car. Sherrill hurried after them, but found to her dismay that Carol had gone off with the first car, and left her to go in the company of strangers, most of whom she had barely met. It was of no use to ask them to take her back to her uncle's house, even if she could have made herself heard. They were all talking at once, and the young man who had sat next her at the dinner table seemed impatient to be off, so Sherrill took the place they assigned her and tried to think of some other way out. It seemed to her that she just could not go through anything more to-night. Every nerve was sore and tired. She would get hold of Carol somehow and tell her that she was almost sick she was so tired and perhaps Carol would find a way to send her home, or at least go home early herself.

But Carol was not to be interviewed. The dancing was already in full swing and she in the midst of it. When the music broke and changed she seemed to disappear utterly.

Sherrill drifted into another room finally, after having run the gauntlet of a number of invitations to dance. She felt that if anybody else asked her and she had to explain again that she did not dance she would scream or laugh or something. She was getting almost hysterical in her weariness. She felt utterly out of place and disgusted. Wine was flowing freely, and some of the young people were already silly with its effects. Carol was conspicuous for her loud voice and silly laughter, and also for the way in which she danced Sherrill's cheeks burned with shame for her. It seemed dreadful to think she belonged to her. Did her father know that she acted this way when she was out of his sight? Why didn't her mother guard her?

From her retreat in the library Sherrill could see the dancing, and every time her cousin circled the room and came within view her eyes grew more troubled. It almost seemed as if she, guest though she was, were responsible for what her cousin was doing. Finally, when she saw Carol stop dancing and sit down across the large room for the moment alone, she made her way to her side and suggested pleasantly that they might both go home now, pleading her own weariness.

But Carol only stared at her vacantly and then broke into a loud mirthless laugh of contempt, finishing with a ribald little local improvization whose chorus changed into the old drunken song, "We won't go home till morning."

With burning cheeks Sherrill retreated to the library and ensconced herself in a big chair near a light with a book. She did not notice what the book was, nor if she held it upside down or right side up, for her thoughts were burning, and her brain was seething with disgust and horror and anger that she should have allowed herself to be in such a position.

She had been sitting thus for some time wondering if the night would never end when she heard a voice at her elbow.

"Ye gods and little fishes! Why this seclusion? Am I intruding? Say, you don't look as if you belonged here with this unholy mob!"

"Oh, I *don't!*"

Sherrill got to her feet in a panic, laying the book down on the table, and lifting frightened eyes to look at a tall attractive youth with mocking laughter in his eyes. He was perhaps three or four years older than herself, and utterly sophisticated in appearance, yet he seemed to be entirely sober and respectful, and her fear died away.

"You—don't seem to belong, either!" she added with relief in her voice.

"Oh, but I do!" said the young man. "I very much belong. I'm Barney Fennimore, and this party happens to be given in my honor. Not that I care much for this sort of thing, but my aunt does so she gives it. But if you mean I'm not drunk like the rest you're entirely correct. I don't go in for it. Don't care for the bad taste next day. Besides, I'm in training."

"In training?" queried Sherrill, studying the gay handsome face of the young man.

"In training for flying. Record breaking and that sort of thing, you know. Want to keep what brains I've got steady. Say, you're something like a flower in the desert, do you know it? So unexpected."

"Well, then perhaps you're a palm tree yourself," laughed Sherrill. "You see I was looking around for an oasis, and I had begun to think there wasn't such a thing."

"Let's sit down and have a chat!" said the young man drawing up a chair. "I'd like to know how you get this way. I didn't know girls came like you any more." He was looking her over from dainty silver toe of slipper to shining golden crown of head and found her satisfying to the eye.

"I'm not so unusual in the town where I live," said Sherrill lightly, "I just come from a Christian home, that's all."

"A Christian home!" said young Fennimore, "what's that? Never saw one. Just how is that different from any other home?"

"Why—" said Sherrill looking at him thoughtfully, "it's a home where God is heard, and where the Lord Jesus has first place. It's a home where the children are taught to expect to be separated from the world. This sort of thing—" waving her hand in a slight gesture toward the other room— "has no place in it."

The young man was looking at her perplexedly.

"Do you mean you never have any good times—any happiness?"

"Oh, no!" she answered quickly, "we have lots of good times. But we wouldn't call that in there a good time. We

would call it a night-mare! But happiness? Oh, yes, wonderful
happiness. We find that in belonging to the Lord Jesus, and it
isn't dependent upon earthly things."

She looked up at him with a smile so bright on her weary
young face that he was puzzled.

"Tell me about it, please," he said wistfully. "I never heard
anything like this. It's almost uncanny. You are sure you
aren't just a spirit? Yet you seem to have a good healthy look
like any other girl, flesh and blood, blue taffeta and silver
slippers!"

Before Sherrill knew it she was deep in an explanation of
the plan of salvation. Perhaps he was only making fun of her
quietly, yet for some reason God had sent her to this party.
She had not come of her own free will. She had no part nor
lot in it. And surely if it was in God's plan for her life that
she should be here to-night then she must witness. It did seem
almost a desecration to be speaking of such holy things but a
few feet from the maudlin hilarity in the next room, but since
she was here and the opportunity had opened she would enter
and bear her witness. So she told him, in clear brief sentences,
the way to the cross for a sinner. She made it very plain that
every one, even an exemplary young moralist in training, was
a sinner. Then she showed his utter helplessness, and hope-
lessness, till Jesus took his place, and his sin, which put the
sinner on the cross too forever after if he would profit by that
costly sacrifice, and enjoy the resurrection life, and the power
of that resurrection in his own life, and the joy that came
from a full surrender to Christ.

Sherrill had been well taught and she made it very plain.
Not for nothing had she been studying her Bible and gleaning
from some of the world's greatest Bible teachers' writings.
Not for nothing had she practiced on her class of boys at
home till they knew the way of life clearly.

The young man listened in wonder. Never had he experienced the like before. And at a dance! It was a new thrill! Yet
there was also deep admiration and reverence in his eyes as
he watched her face while she talked.

"You are talking in an unknown tongue to me," he said at
last, half wistfully. "I'm not sure but I would like to learn the
alphabet though and find out what it's all about! But look
here! I'm sitting here making you talk and not doing a thing
to make you have a good time. Can't I get something for you
to eat—or to drink?" He grinned.

"Not anything, please," she said with a sudden weary look

passing over her face. "There's only one thing I want, and I don't suppose that's possible. I'd like so to go home, to my uncle's house. There wouldn't be any way I could get a taxi or anything, and just slip out and go? You see I came a long journey today and I'm really rather tired."

"There sure would!" said the young man. "I've got a car of my own in the garage and I'll like nothing better than to get away from this maudlin crowd and take you."

"Oh, but this is your party! You mustn't go away!" she said in consternation. "I wouldn't want to do anything rude—"

"Rude? To *that* bunch? You couldn't equal them if you tried in rudeness. Besides, they won't even know I'm gone. I'm simply nothing in their young lives now, except a good excuse for a carouse! Go get your wraps, and I'll be at the door with the car. I'll speak to my aunt and tell her you have to go and she'll be on the lookout for you when you come down. Don't worry! Everybody else does exactly as he likes, why shouldn't you? I'm mighty sorry to have you go of course, as far as I'm concerned, but I don't blame you at all, and I'll be glad to miss as much of this rotten stuff as possible."

So Sherrill got away at last, and drew a cool breath of the outside crisp air with relief, as she stepped into Barney Fennimore's ten-thousand-dollar car and was whirled away to her uncle's residence.

Barney would have liked to park his car in some secluded nook overlooking the Hudson and the moonlit palisades, and hold Sherrill's lovely little hand in his. Almost any other girl of his acquaintance would have expected that sort of thing. He would have enjoyed taking her in his arms, and kissing those sweet lips that were not smeared with lipstick. He felt more stirred by her than by any girl he had ever met, and there were many girls from coast to coast who would have given much for a chance to ride with him and sit in the moonlight with their heads on his shoulder, listening to his tender words.

But there was something about this girl that kept him reverently at his distance. He did not want to desecrate his thought of her by any cheap intimacies. She was of another world. She was holy. Even though he had no former acquaintances by whom to measure her, there was an innate sense of the fitness of things which put a shining wall about her.

"I can't tell you how grateful I am for this," Sherrill told him when she reached her uncle's home at last.

"When may I come and see you again?" he asked. "You're going to be here some time?"

"I'm not sure," said Sherrill, suddenly guarded.

"Meaning that you hope not if tonight is a sample of what you will have to endure?" he asked.

She laughed.

"It has been very pleasant meeting you," she said graciously.

"Then I may come again?"

"Why, I don't know why not," she smiled.

And so they said good-night.

Sherrill was suprised to find that her uncle and aunt had not yet returned, although it was long past midnight. But it was a relief not to have to explain her coming home before Carol, though that might happen too in the morning. But she was glad that she might go at once to bed.

However, sleep did not come immediately. There was much to think over, and she was too excited to get to sleep. She began to see that life in New York was not going to be a little pink dream of joy. There would be grave questions of what to her was right and wrong, constant questions involving principles for her to settle. This "chance of her lifetime," as her family had considered the visit, was going to turn out to be more of a testing, she thought, than anything else. Grandma was right. It was not going to be easy to live in the world and yet not be of it. So far as her limited experience of one evening extended, it was a practical impossibility, and she decided then and there that if she ever had a daughter she would not put her in such a position. Her very beliefs were an offense, and her presence in a worldly atmosphere was robbed of its power in witnessing just because she was there. It was all a contradiction. She should not be there. And yet she believed she had been led to come. What for, she wondered? Why had God let everybody insist on her coming? Was there something here for her to get, even in spite of the worldliness? Had He something for her here to do? If so she must look out to keep the way clear between herself and heaven that she did not miss the leading when the time came.

And so at last with a prayer on her lips she fell asleep.

The reckoning came next morning about half past eleven, which was the earliest hour that the feminine portion of the family began to stir itself. Sherrill was summoned to court in her aunt's room.

CHAPTER XVII

Aunt Eloise was sitting on a chaise longue in her room, attired in a pink chiffon negligee and almost engulfed among little lace pillows.

Carol sat sulkily in the upholstered window seat lolling against more pillows, and vouchsafed not even a glance as her cousin came in. The altercation had begun with the demand on Carol's part for a real Paquin model.

"Before you sit down," said her aunt coldly, "you may go to your room and bring that frock you wore last night. You said it was a Paquin model. I would like to see the label."

The color mounted in Sherrill's cheeks, and for an instant her eyes flashed, and she was about to refuse, but she finally turned and went for the dress without a word.

"Dear Lord, keep me! Keep me!" she prayed as she brought back the pretty silk garment. "Keep me from feeling triumphant."

Eloise Washburn looked at the label, and Carol came sulkily and looked too.

"Well, I'm glad to see you tell the truth at last. But now tell me,—" she went on as she gave a shove to the dress and sent it slithering to the floor in a little pool of blue lights, "what is this that Carol tells me about your behavior last night? I suppose I ought not to have expected it, but I did think you would know the first principles of decency without being told."

Sherrill picked up the dress, threw it over her arm, and stood waiting, but said not a word.

"Carol tells me that she was nearly mortified to death over you. She says you sat out all the dances with men, and were quite rude to everyone who asked you to dance, and then refused to accept the refreshment offered, and finally left without a word to anyone."

"Yes, and you forget the worse!" put in Carol. "She simply hogged the host! A stranger just come, and she just naturally flung herself at Barney Fennimore so that he couldn't get away to talk to any of the rest of us. I was mortified to death, and the rest of the girls were simply furious! It was pestilential! I never can lift up my head again. And they all got onto the fact that it was my cousin that was doing it. Positively, I wish I could leave home!"

Sherrill stood stern and white looking from aunt to cousin in amazement, her lips shut hard and tight.

"Well, haven't you a word to say after all that?"

"I don't know what one could say," answered Sherrill quietly, "except that there isn't a word of that true. If you feel that way about me I think I had better go home at once." There was a bit of hauteur in her voice that made the Weston-Washburns think suddenly of their husband and father, on the rare occasions when he was roused to white anger.

"Oh, now don't go and get mad!" Aunt Eloise hastened to say. "You must remember that I'm answerable to your mother for your behavior and I shall be obliged to write her what has happened if this thing isn't thoroughly understood and made right. Just explain if you can. Of course if there is any reasonable explanation—"

Mrs. Washburn realized that any precipitate flight of the guest would be most thoroughly looked into by her husband, and she had no desire to bring him into the altercation.

"I really don't see that I have anything to explain," said Sherrill steadily, "I told you that I did not dance before you made me go, but I sat out most of the dances in a room by myself, partly because I had been introduced to hardly anybody present, and I felt more embarrassed by my situation than ever before in my life. Also I have not been accustomed to attending gatherings where the young people were intoxicated, and it was most distasteful to me. I have never heard such a lot of silly talk and seen such wild actions. Perhaps it will make you angry for me to say it but I was mortified to be in a place like that. My mother would be very angry if she knew I had been taken there."

Sherrill's eyes were flashing blue fire now, and her indignation was growing.

"I certainly did decline liquor," she went on with her head up regally, "I have never been in a company where it was offered to me before, and I hope I never will be again. But my cousin is mistaken if she thinks I was rude about it. I simply said 'no thank you.'"

"And you didn't know that that was very rude indeed!" said her aunt with uplifted eyebrows. "You didn't *know* that

that is not being done? Well, of course! What can one expect of a girl brought up in the country, and by a fanatical mother!"

Sherrill was growing angrier every minute. This mention of her mother made her coldly furious.

"If you had been there last night, Aunt Eloise, and seen the condition of my cousin Carol, you would have wished that you were a fanatical mother too! I heard one of the young men say she was 'silly drunk.' "

She said this and then realized that she was saying the very things she had so resolved and prayed not to say.

"Indeed!" said her aunt frozenly. "Of course it is to be expected that you will retaliate by trying to get something on Carol. Fortunately I have sense enough to realize that you are wildly exaggerating, and are speaking out of your ignorance. In this age of the world, my dear, a true lady knows how to carry her liquor without losing her poise as well as a man does. However, that is a small matter. How about your rudeness in monopolizing the host of the evening and then in running away without a word?"

"Aunt Eloise, I did not even know the name of the young man who came into the library where I was sitting quietly alone, until he introduced himself to me. I did nothing to make him come, or stay, and when he asked if he could get anything for me I asked him if it were possible for me to get a taxi to take me home without disturbing the rest. I told him I was very tired and had a bad headache, which was quite true. Then he offered to take me in his car, and called his aunt, and made my apologies so that she was very kind about it. I am sorry if you feel that I mortified you, but I am sure if you knew the facts you would see that I did nothing out of the way."

"Oh, of course if you are going to take that saintly attitude there is very little I can do for you," said Aunt Eloise. "It is bad enough to be rude and ignorant, but to add egotism and self-satisfaction to the list makes you simply impossible."

Sherrill shut her lips tight and remained indignantly silent.

"However, I haven't any more time to spare in arguing with you. I can see it is useless. You are blindly set in your own way as I feared you would be," went on the aunt complacently, "I called you in this morning to advise you of our program for the rest of the day. I have arranged with

Professor Fronzaley to give you a dancing lesson at two o'clock down in the music room. Please be prompt for he charges frightfully for every minute's delay. Then I'm giving a tea at four-thirty to a friend of mine and her daughter who are going abroad next week, and I shall expect you to be at that, in the receiving line. You can wear the Paquin. There will be none of the same people you saw last night so it's all right. Carol will explain to you what to do in the receiving line. I don't suppose you ever had to be in one before. And then in the evening we have tickets for the symphony orchestra. Carol and I have another engagement, but your uncle thought you might like to go with him. We may be there later, but he always goes so frightfully early and it bores me to extinction to sit through all that long program. So you'll have to be ready at eight. The same dress will do of course. Then on Sunday—well, we can see about that later perhaps."

Sherrill took a deep breath and sent up a swift prayer before she answered.

"That will be very pleasant, Aunt Eloise," she said simply, "all except the dancing lesson. You'll have to excuse me from that. I'm sorry I didn't make it plain to you last night. I do not dance from principle, you know, not just from ignorance, and I do not care to learn. I hope it won't make you any trouble."

"Principle! Really!" said her aunt contemptuously. "Well, my dear, I shall have to tell you once more as I've told you before, that I am the judge in this case. I suppose that's some more of your peculiar mother's fanticism, but let it be thoroughly understood, once for all, that while you are here there is to be no setting of yourself up to be better than other people. Every girl in good society must dance of course, because that's what they do everywhere you have to go. Also, I'll have a teacher in to make it possible for you to play a good game of bridge. You may have to take a hand now and then when there aren't enough players, and you should be able to play well so you won't bore the rest. I shall expect you to go down for your dancing lesson at two, remember."

Sherrill stood looking steadily at her aunt, and when she spoke her voice was quiet in spite of the rage that filled her soul.

"I'm sorry to displease you, Aunt Eloise," she said, "but I can't do what you've asked. If you feel this way about things it would be better for me to pack right up and go home, and not make you any more trouble, for you're asking something I can't and won't do."

"Mercy!" said the aunt contemptuously, "are you also stubborn? Well, don't be childish and get off that old threat of taking your doll dishes and going home. We'll waive the whole thing till you have a talk with your uncle. I fancy he'll be able to bring you to your senses. Now go! I'm sick to death of the whole subject."

Sherrill went to her room struggling to keep back the angry tears and resolving that she would pack at once and leave before anything more could possibly happen.

When she reached her room she locked the door and dropped upon her knees to pray, the tears raining fast down her face. Beaten! She was beaten right at the start. There could be no peace in this household unless she sacrified principles that were deep laid in her life, and had all of them real reasons for their being. Oh, why had she come? Were Mother and Keith and Aunt Harriet all wrong in their decision that this trip was a duty? Had she been mistaken in thinking that it was God's leading? And if it was must she go back like a whipped kitten with her ears back and own herself unable to be in the world and yet not be of it, and keep sweet and happy through all the testings?

An hour later she went down to lunch with a quiet serenity she would not have believed possible. Somehow on her knees she had been made to understand that she must not run away, not yet anyway. She was going to give New York a real chance to show her why she had come.

The luncheon hour was notable for the arrival of a big florist's box for Sherrill. Carol looked at her cousin in angry amazement as the maid brought the box around to Sherrill's seat and asked if she should open it.

"There!" said Carol triumphantly, "now, I hope you see, Eloise! She certainly must have done some funny business to get flowers from Barney the first day off!"

But Sherrill had been examining the card the maid brought, and looked up with a pleasant smile.

"Don't worry," she said with a twinkle of mischief in her eyes, "they're only from one of the boys at home," and she laid a card down on the table where her cousin could read it.

"Alan MacFarlan," said Carol insolently, "who is *he?*"

"Oh, just a boy I've known all my life. We've been schoolmates."

The maid had opened the box now and the flowers were brought to view. Great masses of exquisite forget-me-nots, and feathery fine baby's breath.

"Great Cats!" said Carol astonished. "He must have plenty of dough. They're out of season! I didn't know you could get them anywhere."

"You can get anything, my child, for money," said her mother eyeing the name on the box.

"Forget-me-nots!" said Carol thoughtfully. "H'm! *Love stuff!* You *would* be that way. Mid-Victorian!"

"You might put them on my tea table this afternoon," suggested Aunt Eloise languidly. "Since they're out of season it's a pity to waste them upstairs."

"Why, yes!" said Sherrill pleasantly, "I should like to. I'll just take a few upstairs for that cunning little vase on my dressing table and you can use the rest any way you like."

"Is he rich?" asked Carol impertinently.

"Oh, not especially," said Sherrill amusedly.

"Is he good looking?"

"That depends on what your standard is," said Sherrill. "I always felt he was all right."

"Are you engaged to him?" Carol always went to the point without hesitation.

"Oh, no," said Sherrill still smiling. This would be one thing she couldn't tell Alan about in the letter she meant to write him that afternoon. But she could tell Mother—or no—perhaps not. You never could tell. Mother might read it to Aunt Harriet and Aunt Harriet would just think it would be fun to tell Alan—no, she mustn't. Meantime her thoughts helped to keep her face smiling and not a bit ruffled at the catechism she was enduring.

"You certainly are queer!" vouchsafed her cousin smothering her cocoa with whipped cream.

Sherrill politely refrained from giving her opinion of her cousin. As soon as lunch was over she took her handful of blue-eyed flowers and went upstairs to her room leaving the expensive out-of-season masses to the general public. But when she saw them again in an expensive crystal bowl on the tea table she smiled tenderly at them as if she felt they understood. They were perhaps doing more for her on the tea table than they could have done on her corsage or in her room, and the blessed thing about that was that Alan would understand when she told him about it. Alan always understood.

The tea was not so bad, Sherrill thought. There really were some very nice people there, a few of them. She had a lovely talk with a sweet white-haired old lady who wore one or two magnificent diamonds, and some exquisite old lace in the folds of her plain black velvet gown.

Sherrill wore her great grandmother's rose taffeta, and looked charming.

"That's not a Paquin, is it?" asked Carol coldly as she came down early.

"Oh, no, it's a Washburn," answered Sherrill brightly.

"A Washburn? I never heard of him. Is he somebody new?"

Sherrill laughed.

"Very new," she said, "I made it myself, Carol, out of Great Grandmother's nine-breadth gown of long ago. But I copied it after a dear little model made by Lanvin."

Carol stared.

"I don't believe it!" she said rudely.

"If you don't believe it get me some silk and I'll make one like it for you."

"Are you a dressmaker, then? Where did you ever learn?"

"Making doll clothes when I was a kid," said Sherrill. "I'm not a dressmaker, of course, but I often make my own clothes."

An influx of guests at that moment broke in upon the conversation, but Sherrill caught her cousin's eyes upon her gown several times that afternoon, and once she overheard her telling another girl:

"It's a Lanvin," she said boastingly. "My cousin gets all her clothes abroad."

What an extraordinary world this was into which she had come to abide for a time. She had a feeling that it was going to be a very brief time however. Her heart was longing deeply for home.

She wore the white velvet to the symphony concert. It seemed to belong with beautiful harmonies, and besides she was going out with her uncle and she wanted to look her best. Her uncle was the only one of the family whom she felt had the least in common with her. Also she still had her doubts about staying very long in New York and she wanted to wear it at least once.

Carol and her mother were not in sight when she came down to go with her uncle, so she felt no critical eye upon her; but later in the evening, during the last lovely number on the program they rustled in and made quite a disturbance getting settled. Almost at once Sherrill was made to feel the glances that were turned toward her, and did she fancy it, or was her aunt actually more pleased with her after studying the lines of that lovely white velvet?

Sunday started out very well. Sherrill came down dressed for church but finding nobody in the family usually got up before noon she went off by herself to find a service, and happened, or was guided to a place where a world-noted speaker gave a burning message of truth. She came back refreshed, with her heart throbbing with eagerness to witness for such a Lord as hers, and her mind made up to bear the unpleasantness of the way, if only she might be used somehow, somewhere.

But the rest of the day was anything but satisfactory. Carol turned on the radio and filled the rooms with jazz. Groups of gay callers dropped in, and giddy young people who stared at Sherrill, danced a little and finally went off on a joy ride, Sherrill pleasantly but firmly declining to participate.

The remaining company presently resolved itself into tables of bridge. At this point Sherrill was planning to steal away to her room, but to her dismay Barney Fennimore arrived to call upon her, and she was forced to remain.

He was there when Carol and her friends returned, and Sherrill felt embarrassed and unhappy, knowing Carol's cold gaze and set lips boded no pleasant to-morrow. But Barney was oblivious of jealousy, and pursued the even tenor of his way, chasing this new admiration.

The evening was no better. More people came. More dancing and cards. More jazz music. A young man with long hair and a languid air arrived with a violin under his arm and played for them some of his new compositions. Sherrill did not like any of them. They sounded to her trained ear like a desecration. She had not thought before that music could express anything but the highest and best emotions, but this seemed coarse, and evil, like the worst secret thoughts of wicked spirits creeping stealthily out in the open. All sense of the Sabbath day was gone. Sherrill had a hurt in her heart for lack of it.

Sherrill really loved the Sabbath, and she was glad indeed when she could reasonably get away to quietness and her

Bible. Fervently she hoped that she might see her way clear
to get away before another such day came round again. How
could one live so close to this world and not be of it?

And then Barney sent her a great box of orchids the next
day which did not make things any better between Carol and
herself. Carol resented every bit of attention Sherrill had.

Sherrill wrote a long letter home the next morning describ-
ing in detail the beautiful home of her uncle, the appearance
of her aunt and cousin, the furnishing of her room, the city of
New York in general, and not telling any of the things the
family wanted to know. But Grandma keenly read between
the lines.

"She's not telling everything!" she declared after the letter
was read. "She's not having a very good time. You needn't be
surprised if you see her back pretty soon. She's true blue, that
girl is."

Now that she was gone, and the die was cast, Grandma
trusted Sherrill utterly. She also trusted God.

"Oh, I hope not," said Keith with a disturbed glance, "I'd
like her to get all the benefit of this visit. It will scarcely be
likely she'll get another such a chance at luxury and beauty
and culture. It's the chance of a lifetime in a way."

"Benefit, if any!" soliloquized Grandmother who sometimes
caught a slang phrase from the young people and used it with
true intelligence.

"Well, I'm glad she had the right dresses," sighed Sherrill's
mother, "I suppose that's worldly pride, but I just couldn't
stand seeing my dear girl patronized."

"Well, there's one thing, Mary," said Harriet Masters who
was listening to the letter, "nobody but an inferior would
attempt to patronize that girl."

Harriet Masters had a letter from Sherrill, too, telling
gleefully of how her clothes had been received, and thanking
her over again for having made it possible for her to appear
at ease among these creatures of fashion who judged people
only by their clothes.

Alan came in while they were talking to see Keith about an
order he had got for him, and the letter had to be read all
over again. Alan had a letter of his own, but he felt shy about
sharing it, so he didn't mention it. Perhaps later he might tell
Keith, but just now he wanted the joy of it all to himself.

Alan was hard at work. With Judge Whiteley's help he was
getting things into good shape. Judge Whiteley had been
wonderful, fixing up that note, getting the mortgage paid off,

and offering some sound advice. He also offered to be right hand advisor during Mr. MacFarlan's illness, and suggested that Alan run in every evening for a few minutes and tell any perplexities and problems of the day.

Alan had not been slow to follow this suggestion and the result was not only a warm friendship formed between the older wise man and the boy, but the avoidance of a number of serious mistakes that Alan in his ignorance would very likely have made.

In addition to his other duties he had undertaken to follow up Sherrill's work with the Flats people, and had finally won enough friends for his cause to organize a Bible study class over there which met once a week with a teacher from the city. Some of the young people from church went over too and served lemonade and cake afterwards. So the work grew, and Alan wrote down all the doings for Sherrill's approval and suggestion.

Besides that, Alan had to write to Bob Lincoln.

Three letters had come from Bob, filled with the wonders of the way and with shy questions about the Bible, which in addition to the reading prescribed by the study class, he had started to read through from the beginning.

So three weeks passed, and Rockland was beginning to feel the vacancy left by Sherrill Washburn's absence, and incidentally what a power Alan MacFarlan had become. Even the other business men were beginning now to call him MacFarlan, instead of Mac, or Al as it had been, and Mother MacFarlan looked up one day from the coffee she was pouring and was suddenly struck with the idea that her boy was growing up, and that he looked and acted like a man, and she sighed even while she rejoiced over him.

Alan's father was decidedly better. He was even well enough now to have a few minutes' conference with his son every day, and to approve and commend the various things that had been done.

"I guess I had to get sick so you would put things on their feet for me," he said in his slow pleasant way one day. "I guess I had to find out what a fine son I have. It was the chance of my lifetime, son!"

Alan looked up startled, and then smiled to think how often that phrase had been in his mind of late. He had thought that about the desert trip, and Bob had said it was *his* chance, and Sherry's family thought her going to New York was the chance of her lifetime! He sighed at that thought—

Oh, what if it should prove to be a chance that would take her away from him forever!—Who was that poor fish that had brought her home from that villainous party, anyhow? Wasn't there anything besides sending forget-me-nots that he could do?

"Say it with Flowers" flaunted an advertisement in the weekly local, as he turned the empty pages over, so he went out and said it with Parma violets, and then, sauntering home, he passed her house and saw the old stone barn set way back in the lot next door, a big elm etched against the evening sky above one end, and a group of spruce trees down in one corner near the street. That was an idea! Why hadn't he thought of that before? Sherrill wanted to build that over into a house! Well, why not someday? He would see if Henderson would give him an option on it? He could pay a sizeable deposit on it if he used his old car for another year instead of turning it in, and that would give him something to think about and plan for anyway, while Sherrill was gone. So Alan went to see Henderson.

And the days went busily on.

CHAPTER XVIII

Sherrill had had a heart-to-heart talk with her uncle on the way down to the symphony concert, and he must have said something very decided to the rest of the family afterwards; at least no more was said about either dancing or bridge lessons, and when there came an invitation to a dance or any other function which Sherrill felt would be out of her sphere she was allowed to stay at home.

It may be that this state of things was helped on somewhat by the fact that Carol was fiercely jealous of her cousin, and was just as well pleased to have her stay at home, rather than have her winning personality and her lovely clothes to compete with.

It cut Carol sorely that Sherrill seemed to have landed the catch of the season right at the start, for Barney Fennimore continued to drop in every day or two, and ask for Sherrill. Carol always acted just as if he was calling on herself personally, and did her best to claim the center of the stage, but she knew in her heart that it was her cousin he came to see and she was furious about it.

A climax was reached one Friday afternoon when Carol and her mother had been away nearly all day attending various shopping and social functions, and arrived home just in time to see Barney Fennimore take his departure, a more than usually serious look upon his face. Uncle Weston had been away all the week on a business trip and Sherrill had not had an especially easy time.

"I think it's time that something was done about this!" stormed Carol stamping her expensively shod foot. "Eloise, are you going to sit and see my cousin take away my men friends right from under my nose?"

"Really, Sherrill," said Aunt Eloise, giving her niece a withering glance, "I think for a saint, and a novice, that you are doing very well. I scarcely anticipated when I invited you here that you would be so ambitious as to set your cap for the most inaccessible man in town. I think you scarcely can realize his position, and his wealth and family. He wouldn't *marry* you, you know. He's only playing! Young men like that do play around with a girl without any thought of getting settled in life. He doubtless thinks perhaps that you have money just because you have managed somehow to get some clever clothes, but when he came to find out, he would have some excuse—"

The danger signals flamed out on Sherrill's fair cheeks, and a brilliant flash came into her eyes. She swung around toward her aunt and opened fire in the midst of her sentence:

"Stop!" she cried. "You've no right to talk to me in that way! I have never asked that young man to come and see me, nor urged him to stay, nor encouraged him in any way. And I have no desire whatever to marry him; or anybody else at present, anyway. And if I had I should not have come away from home to find somebody. I will not stand being spoken to in that way! I think you are—*disgusting!* Oh!"

Her voice was trembling with tears. She could not trust herself another instant. Pressing her fingers to her eyes to stay the torrent that threatened she fled from the room.

"Oh, so the little saint has become a spitfire!" pursued the clear icy tones of her aunt as she hurried down the hall.

Locked into her room Sherrill fell upon her knees beside the bed and sobbed her heart out. She had failed, failed, miserably and abjectly. She had lost all chance of being a witness in that house. She had let her tongue get away with her pride, and abased herself so low by answering back that she felt the case was hopeless. She could never undo what she had just done. No woman, especially Aunt Eloise, would ever forgive being called disgusting! Oh, why had she cared so much after all? The nasty little things they had said had just been the enemy's way of trying her. And she had fallen!

Over and over came the words about her Savior in His hour of trial: "And He answered them not a word." Oh, if she only could have done that! Have remembered that it was not flesh and blood she was striving against, but the rulers of the darkness of this world. If she had only remembered the resurrection power that was hers to claim in any time of temptation, over the weakness of the flesh.

Well, but now, having done this she must go and apologize. That of course was the obvious thing for a lady, much more a Christian, to do.

So after praying for strength she arose, bathed her eyes, and went back to her aunt's door, tapping gently for admittance.

There was an irritable permission to enter and Sherrill opened the door and came to the point at once:

"Aunt Eloise, I'm sorry I lost my temper and spoke to you as I did. I don't suppose you realized how very angry it would make me to have you say what you did, but I was very wrong to let my tongue—"

The elder woman interrupted her pettishly:

"Is this supposed to be an apology you are making? Because if it is you may spare your breath and my time. I never listen to apologies. People never make apologies except to show how much better they think they are than anybody else. Actions speak louder than words. Just let the matter rest. I have my opinion and you have yours!"

Sherrill looked at her aunt blankly for a moment and then with a quiver of her lip turned and went back to her room. This was the end, surely. One could not live with a woman who would not even allow an acknowledgment of wrong done. She was impossible!

Sherrill knelt down again and prayed softly,

"Oh, God, my Father, please let me go home now. I can't stand this any longer."

Then she got up and began to pack.

It gave her swift pleasure to be folding her pretty garments into her trunk. She had prevailed upon the maid to leave her trunk in the ample closet and not send it to the trunk room, so now she did not have to make public what she was doing. She felt that she must make this final, and get all ready before she told anybody she was going, even get her trunk off if possible.

She worked rapidly, carefully, with a clearness of thought that brought results, and soon the closet was empty and the trunk about ready to close. Then she went downstairs to reconnoitre.

Maida came from the dining room to get the mail from the post box and Sherrill asked her if she knew whether the chauffeur was going down town that afternoon again. She wanted him to do an errand for her.

"He's just taken the Madam to that tea, but he'll be back soon. He has to take Miss Carol's suit case to her at the dressmaker's, and perhaps he can do your errand then. I'll leave word with the cook to tell him and he'll let you know when he comes. I have to pack now for Madam and Miss Carol. They are going to that week-end house party on Long Island. They go for dinner. You're not to go, Madam said?"

The words were a statement but the tone was a question.

"No," said Sherrill brightly, "I've changed my plans, and—I'm going home. I find I have to."

She passed on into her room, her head up.

The house party! She had forgotten it! It had been a mooted question, and she had wanted to get out of it, but the hostess was the sweet old white-haired woman in black velvet and old lace whom she had met at her first tea in New York. The invitation had been especially pressing, so that her aunt had been insistent. But now it seemed she was going without her. She drew a breath of relief. Just so easily had the way been made plain for her to go home. They would all be out of the way and she might write a note of farewell and take the midnight train. But she must work quickly.

Taking advantage of the temporary absence of everybody Sherrill went to the telephone booth and called up the Pennsylvania Station to find out about trains. Then, to burn the bridges behind her she sent a telegram to her brother. "Taking midnight train from New York. Homesick for you all. Sherrill."

They would wonder, and be a little worried, but not much, and they would not have long to worry. Anyway, they would get used to the idea of her return before she had to explain it. It was humiliating to be a failure of course, but she ought not to have come at all. That was very plain. She had prayed and prayed to be shown the way and why she was here, and nothing had come but more trouble. Now it was good to be going home.

Swiftly she put the last things in her trunk, made sure that everything was left out that she would need on her journey, packed her little overnight bag, and was ready when the chauffeur tapped at her door.

"I'm having to leave to-night, Morton," she said pleasantly, slipping a bill into his hand. "I'm wondering if you could find it convenient to just look after checking my trunk. Here's my ticket, and it's the midnight train South. Can you get me a reservation on the sleeper too?"

Sherrill knew the tip was generous even for New York, but she wanted service and had done it intentionally. The man melted and was gracious accordingly. In another hour Sherrill received her tickets and checks and saw her trunk depart to the station. She drew a long breath of relief and began to feel thrilled at the thought of being at home in the morning. Home! Dear home! She would never leave it again. It was all the chance in life she wanted.

There was just one more thing to be done before she left New York, and that was to return a couple of books that she had taken out of the Public Library on her uncle's card which he had put at her disposal. Nobody else in the family ever read books, and she did not wish to trouble anybody to return them.

So she put on her hat and coat and started.

The bus at the corner would take her downtown in the neighborhood of the library. It was good not to have anyone there to question her actions. Her aunt would probably not return from the tea before half past five, and she could be back in her room by that time. Then if her aunt wished to speak with her she would send for her. She did not wish to go away like a coward, but on the other hand there was no use trying to explain anything to Aunt Eloise. She was just impossible.

So Sherrill climbed happily into the bus with a sense of new freedom she had not had since she came to New York, and suddenly remembered that Christmas was almost at hand, and she must get something for each of the dear ones at home to take back with her. Christmas at home! A great wave of joy went over her. And she knew just what she meant to get.

She had thought it all out for each one. She had saved a nice little nest egg from the money Keith had given her for clothes for just that purpose. She went over the items now in her mind and decided to stop at the library first and leave her book and not have to carry it about the stores with her. It was late of course, and she must hurry. She glanced at her watch. Four o'clock! Perhaps she better go to the shops first.

Shopping is more expeditious when one knows before hand just what one wants, and Sherrill had spent some happy moments several times during the past three weeks looking at and pricing her gifts. She went straight to the spot and got through with it in short order, and then wended her way through the late afternoon traffic.

But suddenly out of the crowd of Fifth avenue there loomed up the tall attractive form of Barney Fennimore, and though Sherrill tried to drop her eyes and not be seen, he greeted her joyously.

"Do you know, I was just going back to see you," said he. "I felt I had come away too soon."

"Oh," said Sherrill in a small worried voice, "I was just on my way to the library. You see—I find—I have to go home!"

"Go home!" echoed the young man with a blackness in his voice. "But I don't want you to go home."

Sherrill laughed, there was something so genuine and friendly in his tone.

"You haven't got bad news, have you?" he asked sympathetically.

"Oh, no," she said joyously, "it's all good."

"When are you going?" he asked, frowning.

"To-night!" There was a ring of triumph in her voice.

"To-night!" he said it in honest dismay. "And just as I was getting to know that there was such a girl as you! Well, then, you and I've got to get busy. May I go with you? And why all these bundles. Where is your car?"

"Oh, I'm on my feet, and those are just gifts for the folks. I'm on my way to return a book to the library."

"Good! That's a much better place than the house with your ever present relatives getting in the way. You haven't answered the most important part of my question yet, whether I may go with you, but I'm going anyway so it's all right. I have to have a heart-to-heart talk with you."

There was nothing for Sherrill to do but give him a

welcoming smile, although she had momentary visions of the Washburn car driving by, with Carol or Aunt Eloise looking out watching her.

But she was presently within the sheltering walls of the stately library, and what did it matter anyway? She was going home. No words of malice that any Aunt Eloise could write would ever turn the dear hearts of the home folks against her, and she would not have to bear contempt any more. Why not be happy?

When she had returned the book Barney led her to one of the small reading rooms that happened to be deserted, and put her in a chair, sitting down close enough to talk in low tones, and yet be able to watch her face.

Sherrill was dressed in her knitted silk sports frock, and the gay bands of colored border on the brown of it gave her a vivid setting, as she threw back her fur coat, pulled down the little close brown hat, and listened.

"Now, when can I come to see you?" demanded the amazing youth.

A vivid color flashed into Sherrill's cheek but she tried to keep her voice steady and gay as she replied:

"Oh, are you coming to see me? Why, that will be nice. I'm sure my family and all my friends would enjoy knowing you, but it's a long trip to make a visit."

"Not when the girl is you. You see I'm going to be very plain with you. I've fallen for you mighty hard. I think you and I could hit it off pretty well. I don't see why we should waste any time, if you're agreeable. I know we haven't been acquainted long but what's that if we know what we want? I was just coming back to hunt you up and ask you if you'd marry me. I like to get things settled after I once make up my mind."

Sherrill had turned very white and her ungloved hand flew up to her throat and caught the string of pearls she was wearing as if they were a life line.

"Oh, don't, please! You *mustn't!*" she said earnestly.

The joy in his face faded suddenly into perplexity and then into blankness.

"But why not? Why shouldn't I ask you? I love you with all my heart, and I'm sure there's nothing wrong in telling you so. I hoped you'd care for me too."

"I'm sorry," faltered Sherrill in consternation, "I never thought of such a thing. You were only—a pleasant— stranger. I like you, of course, and you've been awfully kind—but you mustn't—you really mustn't!" Nevertheless she would not have been human not to feel a throb of triumph when she remembered her aunt's words.

"But why?" demanded Barney again, "are you engaged to someone else?"

"Oh, no! Not engaged!" said Sherrill drawing a long breath, and trying to be her natural self, but she still hung on to the pearls.

Barney eyed her intently.

"Not engaged!" he said speculatively, "but—there *is* somebody! Somebody else?"

Sherrill's eyes said yes, but her lips only trembled into a wan little smile.

She pressed her fingers flutteringly along the beads, and Barney's eyes followed them hungrily. Such pretty, characterful fingers.

"Then there is somebody—" he said again slowly, watching her, "and—*he* gave you *those pearls!* Am I right?"

Sherrill started, and the pink, telltale color flooded her face happily with a kind of joyous glow.

"Who is he?" asked the disappointed Barney. "Is he rich? Is he good looking? Would I stand any chance of cutting him out if I tried?"

"You wouldn't try," said Sherrill firmly, "you're too fine for that!"

"The dickens I am!" said the youth under his breath.

"And you couldn't if you did," she finished softly.

"Really?" he said and studied her face. "Is it that far?"

"It isn't far at all," said Sherrill. "We've never talked about such things. We've just been comrades always since we were little,—No, he's not rich, nor he doesn't resemble a movie star, but he's rather wonderful! At least I think so. Of course you're wonderful too, in quite another way—but—*he* belongs to my world—"

"And I *don't,* you think," finished the young man sadly. "But listen here. I'd decided to go into this thing and try to please you. Wouldn't you like to take me and reform me and make something real out of me?"

"I couldn't do that," said Sherrill earnestly, "only the Lord Jesus could do that, and if you really wanted to take Him into your life you wouldn't let it depend on whether I was around or not. You would take Him anyway above all the world. And it wouldn't be genuine if you just did it to please me."

"So!" said Barney Fennimore, suddenly realizing that here

at last was something in his pampered life that he couldn't have and money couldn't buy. Then suddenly he drew out from his pocket a little white box, and took from it a blue velvet case.

"I want to show you what I bought for you to-day," he said. "At least I can *show* it to you."

He sprung open the case and there gleamed forth the most gorgeous diamond that Sherrill had ever looked upon, set in a hoop of emeralds.

"Oh!" she said tenderly, sadly, as if she had looked upon the death of something sweet and tender.

He watched her a moment eagerly, his hungry look appearing again, and then a sternness seemed to settle about his gay features.

"And you won't wear it?" he asked sadly.

"I couldn't," she said.

He snapped the case shut and stuffed it in his pocket out of sight.

"You're real!" he said, "You're the dearest thing that ever happened." and suddenly he put his big, firm, well-kept hand down over her small one and gave her a quick close clasp like a long farewell. "If I had a girl like you I might amount to something."

"You will," said Sherrill quickly. "I hope you'll give your splendid self to Christ, and he'll find the right girl for you—some day. Keep the ring till you find her, and tell her I'm glad for her when she gets it!"

He looked at her tenderly, with his heart in his eyes for a moment more, and then he took his hand away from hers with a gesture of finality.

"I will," he promised, "and I won't forget all you've tried to teach me. Perhaps I'll potter around and find out what it all means after all some day. I wouldn't expect to get into quite the same heaven with you, of course, but I'd like to be where I could see you sometimes. Say, would you mind if I run down sometime later and just see if you're still wearing those pearls?"

"Oh, no," said Sherrill with tears in her voice. "Oh, no! I'll be glad to see you—and to introduce you—to my friends—but I think—I'm sure, I'll be—still wearing them."

"You sweet child!" said the young man with a sigh, and arising helped her on with her coat. The incident was ended.

It was quite dark when they got out into the street, and Sherrill began to be afraid she would not get home before her aunt arrived, and so would have to encounter her in the hall. She did not want to see her unless she sent for her.

Barney called a taxi, took her to the door, and bade her good-by gravely. They did not talk much on the way. But his handclasp at the parting was heartening and reassuring.

She was relieved when she got into the house to find that her aunt had not returned, but she had scarcely reached her room before she heard the querulous voices of her aunt and cousin hurrying up the stairs. She waited quietly in her room expecting a summons but presently she heard the sound of their going away again, Morton carrying out bags and suit cases, and Maida hurrying along with wraps. They were going without saying a word to her! Had Maida told her mistress that her trunk had gone to the station? Well, whatever they knew she was being punished. She was being left behind like a naughty child with no apology. But, it didn't matter now. It made it all the easier for her. Of course if her uncle had been at home things couldn't have happened in just this way, but she would write him a nice note and leave it where he would see it, perhaps in his dressing room. She would say she felt she must go, and thank him for his kindness, and never let him suspect how she had been treated in his house.

She sat down at the desk and began to write, but suddenly she thought she heard slow steps coming up the stairs, hesitating steps, coming up a little way and then stopping as if to rest. It couldn't be her aunt had returned! It couldn't be the butler for she had heard him go back to the kitchen. She tiptoed over to the door and opened it a crack to look down the hall, and then she saw her uncle coming up the stairs with such a strange look on his face that it frightened her. His face was white like a sheet and his eyes were like dark coals burning. He stared around but did not seem to see anything. He clutched the hand rail and reeled and tottered. Could he be drunk? Oh no, he had a more ethereal look, like one suddenly stricken with some terrible illness.

As she stood there he shuffled his way slowly to his dressing room door, and opened it. He almost fell as he went in, and he left the door open behind him.

"Uncle Weston!" she called, and stared after him in alarm, "Uncle Weston! Has something happened? Are you sick?"

CHAPTER XIX

She hurried to his door and saw him lying across his big leather couch as if he had fallen. He must have hit his head against the wall.

"Uncle Weston," she called again, "you are sick!"

"Yes—" he mumbled, "sick! sick! That's it! Couldn't think what it was."

"Oh, shall I get someone? Do you want me to send for Aunt Eloise?"

The man on the couch laughed a strange weird cackle.

"Oh, by all means, send for Eloise! She'd be of so much use—"

"Uncle, you need a doctor!" said Sherrill frightened.

"Yes! Doctor. That's it. Get a doctor."

Sherrill turned and fled down the hall to call one of the servants, but to her amazement no one answered the bells. Even the butler had disappeared. The master and mistress were out, and they had gone out also, every one of them. Or if they had not gone out at least they did not care to hear a call to service. Frantically she rushed to the telephone. What should she do? She had no knowledge of the family physician, his name or number. But it was evident that there was great immediate need.

She called the operator.

"Get me a doctor quick, please. The nearest one to this number. This is an emergency call, a very sick man and I'm a stranger in the city!" She gave the street and number and hanging up rushed back to her uncle. He was moaning now and tossing as if in pain, moving his head from side to side. She went to him and laid her hand upon his hot head, but he only moaned and shrank away from her. Then she heard the telephone ring and ran to answer it, praying that help might come quickly from somewhere.

Her hand was trembling as she took down the receiver.

"This is Dr. Grant around the corner. Did you give an emergency call?"

"Yes," said Sherrill's shaky voice. "My uncle, Mr. Washburn, has come home very sick and there is no one in the house but myself. The servants have all gone out, and I am a

162

stranger here. Won't you come at once? I think he is terribly ill and I don't know what to do."

The doctor asked one or two quick questions, and then said, "I'll come!"

Half an hour later Sherrill stood anxiously in the hall with the doctor.

"He's a very sick man," he said. "He's evidently been sick for several days, and he's got a bad case of smallpox. Where are the family?"

"Gone to a house party on Long Island."

"That's good," said the doctor, "they wouldn't be much help. How long have you been near him? Well, I'm afraid you're in for a quarantine, but we'll try to keep you from getting the disease. You better get out of the house as quickly as possible if you have any place to go. You'll have to wash your hands with this antiseptic soap and you better put those clothes you have on out in the sun to-morrow. There really isn't as much danger of contagion to-night as there will be a little later in the game. You better get out at once."

"But I can't leave my uncle alone," said Sherrill aghast!

"Well, if you don't go now you won't be allowed to go, you know. I'd send him to the hospital but I'm afraid it might be fatal. The weather has changed the last two hours and it's bitter cold and sleeting. I wouldn't dare risk moving him now. Besides, it would take time to arrange to get him in anywhere. Not all hospitals will take a case like this. I can't think where he picked it up. We haven't had a case around New York that I know of for some time, at least nothing as bad as this. You say he's been away? Well, you better get in touch with your aunt and find out what she wants done. She'll probably want to come right home and nurse him, but of course that wouldn't be wise. However, she has the right to say. Of course I'll phone to the hospital and try to get an experienced nurse at once."

Sherrill searched through her aunt's desk and after great difficulty found the invitation which gave a clue to how to call her, and at last succeeded in getting Eloise Washburn on the wire.

"This is Sherrill," she began, and the querulous voice broke in:

"Well, what do you want? I should say you had made trouble enough for one day without interrupting me at a dinner. Don't you know—"

But Sherrill broke in:

"Uncle Weston has come home and he's very sick!"

There was a silence at the other end for an instant and then an impatient voice said:

"Well, I can't do anything about it now. What's the matter with him? What do you suppose I can do at this distance? Tell him to call the doctor."

"I have called a doctor," said Sherrill, "the one around the corner. Uncle Weston is delirious. I couldn't ask him who to call."

"How tiresome! Well, what does the doctor say is the matter?" demanded the aunt.

"He says it's a very bad case of smallpox!"

"What nonsense!" said the wife sharply. "I don't believe it. There's no smallpox around. However, you'd better be on the safe side and have him sent to the hospital. Any hospital the doctor suggests will be all right."

"The doctor says he is too sick to be moved. It might be fatal."

"For pity's sake! I never heard of such a thing! They always take people to the hospital for everything. I have always heard it was the only safe way. Well, I'm sure I don't know what to do. I am not there. You'll have to do what you can. I suppose they can get a nurse. Of course Carol and I can't come back now if it's really that. But probably they'll find out it's a mistake by morning. Weston always does get awfully sick and thinks he's going to die if he just scratches his fingers. You better call Dr. Grainger. He's our doctor. He'll know what to do. I'll call up in the morning and find out what you've done. Meanwhile don't, for pity's sake, let the contagion get through the house. Tell the servants to close up the rooms downstairs, and keep everyone out. This certainly is tiresome! I can't think how it happened. Smallpox! The idea. How horrid! It seems somehow so plebeian. Weston ought to have been ashamed to come home with a thing like that."

In great disgust Sherrill hung up the reciver, and turned away, her heart sick with weariness and fear. Her dear home to which she had been going! And now she could not go! Her trunk was gone already! She had an instant of satisfaction that her beautiful things were at least out of contagion and would not have to go through fumigation. Oh, why hadn't she left a few hours earlier?

And then she turned from the thought as contemptible.

Who then would have cared for her uncle? Who would have given the alarm to the family and sent for a doctor?

Like a flash she suddenly knew why she had been sent to New York. This then was the opportunity, the "chance of a lifetime," they had talked about. Well, if it was the chance that God had planned for her then He had something for her to do here for Him, and she must not murmur.

With new resignation she walked upstairs and talked with the doctor. Then she went to her room and took off her pretty dress, hanging it on a hanger in the open window. She took off her shoes and put on her Pullman slippers, donned the little close Pullman cap Grandmother had made to wear in the sleeper, and after an instant's hesitation put on the china silk kimono she had in her overnight bag. It was slippery and would wash, and was better than a heavy dress.

Then she slipped down to the kitchen and hunted out a maid's apron and was fixed for service. Coming back she presented herself at the door of the sick room.

"Now! What shall I do? I can obey orders," she said with a brave look.

The doctor was not a high and mighty specialist. He was just a plain grave man with a genius for healing, and his hard way to make in the world. He had done his best at the telephone to get in touch with Dr. Grainger the great favorite of the wealthy, but was told that Dr. Grainger was up in Canada shooting things for his health and would not return for a month. Whereupon he turned his attention to getting a nurse, two nurses if possible, but it appeared there was suddenly a dearth of nurses for contagious diseases. There wouldn't be one free until sometime the next day, possibly not until toward evening.

"You're just a child!" said the doctor turning in despair from the telephone. "I can't leave you here even to go out and look for someone."

"Tell me what to do," said the child bravely, giving him a wan smile, "and don't waste time worrying about me."

So at last the doctor left her for a time to go out and try to get a nurse. He suggested that probably the servants would return some time that night, and that she should warn them to come up the back stairs, and observe certain precautions used in quarantine.

"You're a brave girl," he said, unbending from his brusque manner. "Aren't you afraid?"

"No," said Sherrill. "It will be all right. It must be what I was sent here for."

He went away wondering what she meant, and determined to relieve her duty as soon as possible.

It became apparent that the servants would not return that night. They had evidently gone away for the weekend also. So Sherrill sat alone in the great house filled with many strange noises that step abroad in silence of the midnight. She listened to her uncle's moaning, and his muttered words, and became filled with a great longing for him that he might know the Lord and have peace and rest in his heart; and while she sat there waiting, giving the medicine as the doctor had directed, applying all the means ordered, she was praying.

Once in the night she realized that she had not eaten anything in a long time, so washing her hands very carefully in antiseptics she went downstairs and found something to eat. And then she suddenly remembered her telegram to Keith. She must send another. They would be alarmed if she did not arrive in the morning. So she called up Western Union and sent another message.

"Unavoidably delayed. Don't worry. Will wire later. Please get trunk, check no 1021365 started on midnight train."

The doctor called up in the night to ask how things were going and report he had not found a nurse yet, but was on track of one. The night wore on, the longest night of Sherrill Washburn's life, and morning dawned at last, slowly creeping in, grayly, at the windows, throwing long ghastly shadows on the sick man's face.

The doctor came presently and took her place beside the patient ordering her to lie down, and blessed sleep enveloped her for a time. But she was too young and too anxious to sleep long, and came back again on the dot of an hour. And there began the slow monotony of another day.

Sherrill knew her family would have been vaguely alarmed by her nonappearance and more so by her telegram, and later after a talk with the doctor she decided to tell the truth, at least a part of the truth, and so she evolved another message:

"Uncle Weston has the smallpox. He is very sick. Am under quarantine. Cannot get away at present. Doctor is watching out for me, and says you need not be alarmed. Don't worry, I'm all right only disappointed, but I guess this is why I had to come.

Can't write at present, but will telegraph any change. Pray for Uncle Weston. Lovingly, Sherrill."

Two hours later the telephone began to ring and Long Distance took a part in proceedings. Keith called up from the store, guardedly to know the whole truth and not to worry the rest. Sherrill laughed for sheer relief to hear his dear voice. Grandmother called up while her daughter was down doing the day's marketing, and told Sherrill she might tell her everything and she would keep it to herself. Sherrill laughed again and told Grandmother all the funny things she could think of, but gave no hint that she was the head nurse still.

Mother called up almost at once from the grocery so Grandmother wouldn't hear her, and said precious things as mothers can, and gave good cheer she didn't feel herself, and made Sherrill promise she would take every care for herself, and run no risks. Made her promise to wire at once or phone if she felt the least bit sick, and all the other things that mothers make you promise at times of great distress.

Then Alan called up, dear Alan, and made her laugh and cry, and got to know the truth, the whole truth and nothing but the truth about the case.

"Well, I knew you would. It's like you, Kid. Well, I'll pray! Oh sure. I been doing it. And I won't let on. But if you don't get a real nurse before to-morrow night *I'm coming*, see? I may not be experienced but I can take orders, and I'm not going to have you get sick. It's all right, Kid, I can get somebody to take my place in the store. Or something. But if you don't get somebody else right away *I'm coming*."

Somehow the day went easier after that, and by night the nurse had arrived, a capable experienced elderly woman who had had the smallpox, and bore its marks in her face. But she was motherly and knew her business and sent Sherrill to bed at once.

However, before she went Sherrill called Alan and told him the news.

Monday morning the servants arrived, stealthily, as if they had not been gone, but when they saw the sign upon the door, and when they heard the news Sherrill had to tell them, calling it down the back stairs, they vanished like the morning dew upon the mountain. They stole fearsomely up the back stairs, it is true, and claimed their worldly goods, throwing them out the area window and gathering them up below, but they left en masse, and completely, without so much as a word of apology or offer of help to the frail girl who stood at the top of the stairs and watched them depart.

Then Sherrill set to work in earnest, and began to lay out a daily routine, for now she had a house to run, and meals to prepare.

She prayed much in those days, as the sick man lay between life and death, hour after hour; besought God to save him, and to bring him back to life if possible. Then after long days of waiting he began to get a little better and at last the doctor told her that he would.

Telegrams were common things in those days, flying back and forth between New York and home. Alan extravagantly used Long Distance almost every night. It was a great comfort to Sherrill in her exile to talk with him a few minutes before she slept. Christmas came and the telephone was her only celebration—except the flowers that Alan sent, and a box of good things to eat from Mother, and a check from Keith. But there came a day when Uncle Weston was so much better that he wanted Sherrill to read to him.

She sat behind an antiseptic curtain which the nurse had established as soon as she was installed, and read snatches of things to him, little bits out of books, occasionally something bright or unexciting from the newspaper, but finally she ventured to read a story from the Bible, then a psalm, to him every night, and he grew to seem to like it. At such times she began to see what chance had been given her to reach this dear member of her father's family with the word of God.

Then one notable day her uncle began to talk with her about the scripture she had been reading, and she had an opportunity to make it all plain to him about the way of salvation.

He lay a long time thinking after she had ceased to talk, and at last he said:

"Little girl, you've been very wonderful to your old uncle. You've stuck by and saved my life. I shall never be able to repay you—"

"I don't want pay, dear Uncle Weston," she said eagerly.

"No, I know you don't," said the uncle, "that's the best of all. Little girl, you've made me see what Jesus Christ is. I never believed much before in the Bible or religion, but now I have seen Him in a human life, and if it's anything to you, I want you to know that you brought me to a place where I know that I need Jesus, your Jesus, and I am going to serve Him the rest of my days."

Wasn't that reason enough for Sherrill to rejoice? Hadn't she seen at last why she had to go to New York and go through all the hard things. Oh, God was great!

At last Uncle Weston was well enough to walk about his room, and to read to himself, and to take a hand in the planning of life again. The weeks had been long but they were over and finished.

A day came when the doctor signed her release, gave her a clean bill of health, took the quarantine sign off the door, and sent Sherrill home.

Joyously with a full heart, she gathered up her letters,—there was not much left of her own but letters, a few plain garments they had sent her through the mail, and a few dried rosebuds from the multitudes Alan had sent her almost daily,—and started home.

Aunt Eloise and Carol were wintering in Florida, and Aunt Eloise called up on Long Distance, sweetly, almost every day to know how things were going. She was negotiating plans whereby they could sell the Riverside house and live abroad for a time, as soon as the husband and father was well enough to leave. Aunt Eloise said she would never be able to enter that pestilential house again. Smallpox was so devastating to a complexion, and really Carol was growing up and needed foreign advantages.

"You will pray for your old uncle, little girl?" said Weston Washburn with a tired patient look upon his face. "You know it won't be easy for an old worldling like me to keep steady under fire. Pray that I may not fail. Pray for my little girl, too, Sherrill. I wish she were like you. Then pray for my wife. I know she's been hard on you, child, but pray for her. She needs it. And don't forget your old uncle needs you. Good-by, little nurse. My little precious missionary!"

And with these words ringing in her ears Sherrill went home. Back to the dear home town, and the dear home folks. Back to new opportunities, and new understandings, back from the chance of her lifetime.

The first evening Sherrill spent at home Alan came to dinner, and after the family had been gathered listening to her many stories of her visit, often gently softened to hide some of the hardest places, by and by they all stole out into the other room on one excuse and another and left Alan and Sherrill alone.

"There isn't any such thing as the chance of a lifetime, Alan," Sherrill said, lifting her eyes with a shining look, "every opportunity is the great chance, and the only thing is to find out where God is leading."

"You're right," said the young man with an answering look. "I've been learning that all winter. If through nothing else, Bob's letters would have been enough. You ought to see how he's changed and grown. He loves the Bible. He simply eats it up! And now that he's got there he's beginning to take a deep interest in hunting out things that prove the Bible stories. I declare I never saw anything like it. But you must read his letters."

"Yes," said Sherrill. "I heard a little bit about it this afternoon from Lancey Kennedy. Do you know, he's been writing to her? I didn't know they were friends, did you? But she came over this afternoon a few minutes and told me about it. She said he had been telling her how he found Christ, and he had said he wished she would give herself to Him too. So she had come to me to find out what to do. It was pitiful almost, she was so eager. She's a lovely girl, and she was ready to kneel down with me and surrender herself. Why, Alan, it choked me all up so I could hardly pray with her, it was so wonderful! And I was thinking, Alan, do you know if you had gone to Egypt, maybe none of these things would have happened. Maybe Bob would have gone to the dogs, and Lancey would never have wanted to find the Lord Jesus. So it was really the chance of a lifetime that you were offered in that telegram, don't you see?"

"I sure do!" answered Alan with a ringing voice. "The biggest chance I could have asked. And there are other things too, not as important, but still worth while, connected with Dad's business, things I'll tell you later. But there's something else, Sherrill—" Alan got up and came and sat beside her on the couch.

"Sherry—" he began shyly, and then reached out a masterful hand and took hers in a close grasp. "Sherry! I asked your mother and Keith if I might tell you this right away, and they said I might. Sherry, I love you, you know—I've always loved you—for the matter of that, but this is different—!"

Sherrill looked up half frightened, but he hurried on.

"Sherry, you didn't pull off any of those grand marriages or engagements your aunt suggested, did you—not yet?" He waited breathlessly for her answer, and Sherrill sparkled at him mischievously.

"Not yet!" she laughed.

"Well, then, Sherry, may we—do you—can I—?" He

plunged his free hand into his pocket and brought out something bright, and thrust it forward. It was a ring with a big pearl in a quaint sweet setting.

"Will you wear this for me, Sherry? I wouldn't have dared ask so soon, but I saw you still wore my pearls, and I hoped. Will you, Sherry? Sherry, I love you so! I've missed you so!"

Sherrill surrendered her hand to the ring, and he drew her close to him and set his lips reverently upon hers.

"Oh, Sherry, my darling!"

"You know we're only kids yet!" gurgled Sherrill from the folds of his nice rough coat. "You said so yourself only three months ago."

"Yes, that's the glad part of it!" rang the boy's voice joyously, "Please God, there'll be more time ahead for us together. But, Sherry, dear, it's not half so bad as it sounds. Dad has sold a lot of land he thought was worthless, and he insists on my having the whole proceeds. He says it's my bonus for staying home from Egypt and pulling the business out of a hole while he was sick. Yes, he found out about it. Judge Whiteley told on me. Well, it's a slick little sum, and Sherry, I—we can start as soon as you say. Dad's made me a partner. What do you think! That is, we'll wait till your mother feels we've had a long enough engagement of course—"

"Oh, Alan!" said Sherrill, "I didn't know there could be anything so sweet—! And God had this waiting for me all the time while I thought I was having a hard time! That and what he let me do in reading to my uncle! Oh, I must tell you about that too. There is so much to tell."

"Yes, but I've another one yet, Sherry. I bought the old barn, and if you still think you'd like to build it over into a house why you can begin on your plans to-morrow. Dad says he can fix a way to finance it, and he's willing. Then I wouldn't have to take you far away from your family, and it wouldn't be so hard for them all. I had a chance to buy the lot cheap, and I thought it was the chance of a lifetime,—that is, if you like it, Darling."

Sherrill lifted shining eyes.

"How good God's way is, when you just trust everything to Him, isn't it, Alan? Oh, I'm happy, happy, happy! All my dearest dreams are coming true!"

Mary Washburn stole near to the door to offer some late refreshment in the way of cake and lemonade, but she changed her mind and concluded she would leave her tray on the dining room table. The children did not seem to need any other refreshment than the presence of one another. It was a moment that would never quite come to them again, this first time of understanding between them. So she smiled and slipped away murmuring:

"And we thought that going to New York was the chance of a lifetime for her, and here God had her joy all planned close by, for her and for us all! The chance of a lifetime! There is no such thing as chance!"